F
MAY   Maybury, Anne

          Green Fire

GREEN FIRE

GREEN FIRE

Anne Maybury

Thorndike Press • Thorndike, Maine

Library of Congress Cataloging in Publication Data:

Maybury, Anne.
  Green fire.

  Reprint. Originally published: New York, N.Y.:
Ace Books, c1963.
    Large print ed.
    1. Large type books. I. Title.
[PR6063.A885G7 1982]   823'.914   81-23195
ISBN 0-89621-339-0   AACR2

Large Print edition available through arrangement with
Harold Ober Assoc., Inc.

Cover design by Miriam Recio.

GREEN FIRE

I

I had thought I would never see Max Forrest again. Now I knew that at the end of my journey it was inevitable that we should meet.

I was on my way to Hong Kong to spend two months with my brother, Gerry, who had a Government appointment there.

When I had opened my handbag at London Airport, I found that I still had his last letter to me. I remembered opening it at the breakfast table only a few days ago, reading with such pleasure the last-minute reminders about inoculations and travellers' cheques, his request that I should bring out my father's old binoculars if my stepmother did not want them.

So far, the letter had only served to accentuate the anticipation of a lovely journey.

And then I read the postscript:

By the way, Max has turned up in Hong

Kong. His paper wants him to cover this part of the world and so he is making his headquarters here.

Gerry would have no idea the impact those words had upon me.... So closely had I been able to guard my secret that I could actually manage to smile across the breakfast table at my stepmother and say:

"What do you think? Max is in Hong Kong!"

From my window-seat on the plane, I looked down on the rosy clouds drifting across the gentian-blue sky. Damascus, Bahrein, Bombay were far over the horizon. Singapore was just behind us. I could still remember the odd metallic "gulp" the plane had given at the last take-off. In such a little time now I would arrive in Hong Kong. I eased my feet out of my shoes and closed the brightly-jacketed book on my lap. We had been delayed in Bombay and now there was fog over Hong Kong.

I had never flown before and everything was new, strange, exciting. Yet, at moments on the flight when I was off-guard, memory surfaced and everywhere I looked it was Max's face I saw. I would switch my gaze, but the face was still there, superimposed on clouds, on landscape, on strangers' faces. . . . Max's brilliant, light-grey eyes; Max's lean, eagle profile; his smile, slow to come and yet oddly sweet; his lean controlled body; his low voice. . . .

To force him out of my thoughts now, I glanced about me purposefully.

The man in the next seat to mine had left the plane at Bahrein. I had been sorry to see him go because he had talked to me and had been interesting and kind. Across the aisle sat two men who had not stopped arguing since they joined the plane at Damascus. They looked Italian. Behind me, a man and woman laughed continuously as though they were very excited. And just ahead, across the aisle, a girl sat alone.

Like me, she had made the journey from London and occasionally I caught a glimpse of her. She was lovely to look at in an arresting, colourful, defiant kind of way.

She got up once to go to the back of the plane and glanced at me as she passed. We smiled at one another cautiously, as strangers do. When she returned, she paused by my seat.

"This delay is the sort of maddening thing that *would* happen!" Her voice was quick and impatient. She was leaning against the arm of the empty seat by my side. "Just when I can scarcely wait to get to Hong Kong!"

I looked at her with interest.

"Is this your first visit?"

"I'm going to be married out there," she said. "I've never been farther east than Switzerland before."

She put up her hand to her rich, copper-coloured hair and I saw that she wore a gold link bracelet with four little charms hanging from it. I had a link bracelet, too, only mine was the more usual kind with just one large seal that had a Roman emperor's head carved in the white agate.

I thought casually, as she stood there, obviously wanting to talk, how sheep-like we were. Someone started a vogue for something—outsize ear-rings or tinkling bracelets—and we all rushed to buy. . . .

"Do you know Hong Kong?" she asked.

"I've never been East before," I said. "It's thrilling, isn't it?"

She eyed me with interest.

"Are you going out to a job or is this a holiday?"

"Holiday," I told her. "I'm joining my brother for a few weeks."

She crossed her hands on the back of the seat and leaned her chin on them.

10

"I wonder how we're going to like it? Some people have told me I'll love it, that it's gay and glamorous and exciting. Others have said it's noisy and overcrowded and humid."

"My brother thinks it's the most wonderful place in the world," I laughed. "Knowing Gerry and his love for his own comfort, I think living in Hong Kong must be pretty plushy!"

The air hostess was coming along the aisle, telling us to fasten our safety belts. The girl said:

"Here we go!" and her eyes sparkled.

When she had moved to her seat I looked down and saw that little puffs of mist, like gauze, were floating away and there were flat green paddy fields backed by amethyst hills. In the distance was a maze of ships' masts, dark brown sails, and, beyond, mountain peaks.

The plane began to circle Kai Tak Airport.

I could feel my heart beating fast; there was a drumming in my ears. Soon now I would see Gerry.

And Max?

Stop thinking about him! A man in his late twenties, with the whole world for a hunting ground, would have found his girl by now. And anyway, he never loved you. He never pretended

11

to.... It was all on your side.... Just the odd kiss after a dance; an arm slid round me at a party, no more affectionately than a brother's! Chocolates; flowers on my birthday; at Christmas....

Max had lived in the house next door since he was fifteen. I had been nearly eleven at the time. Whenever he came home from school for the holidays, we three had been together. I grew up in the shadow of Gerry's hero-worship for the slim, quiet adolescent two years his senior. In spite of his slight build, Max was strong. He was a fine rugger player and he swam as though he had been born in the water. He was fearless and when the three of us went for camp holidays together in France or Austria, we would follow where Max led. Sometimes, since, I had wondered why we hadn't broken our necks climbing or been killed riding tricky horses in the wild Massif of Central France.

When Max was twenty-five, an uncle died and left him a legacy of two thousand pounds. He threw up his Fleet Street job and travelled, writing articles about any part of the world in which he found himself. I saw his name at intervals in his old newspaper.

Gerry told me that Max had the makings of a fine journalist, but that he had said he wanted experience of the world before he settled down in one place.

I was nearly twenty when he went away. He had kissed me good-bye, cautioning lightly:

"Be a good girl!"

"I happen to be a woman!" I had reminded him haughtily, "earning my own living."

He had touched my cheek.

"You're so very young, Francie!" His voice had been gentle and he had smiled that particularly sweet smile of his.

I never saw him again.

I stirred restlessly in my seat and felt in my handbag for my compact and lipstick.

The face that looked back at me from the tiny mirror was not in the least beautiful. My mouth was too large, my chin too square. My stepmother, who always chose the kindest things to say, had once told me my eyes were the colour of her favourite sherry—deep gold. My hair was very fair and I wore it short with the ends swirling in all ways.

I looked best in colours and I wore now a dark red suit of uncrushable linen. There was a topaz phoenix, which had belonged to my mother, pinned to my lapel.

As I drew lipstick across my mouth, I could see the scar at the side of my cheek. One day, I had been told, it would disappear altogether.

I touched it and as I did so the aquamarine ring on the third finger of my left hand glittered.

The scar and the ring!

I knew when Max left England that I had to remake my life. I told myself at the time that it would not be hard, I had a stepmother who encouraged Gerry and me to invite our friends home. She often helped to organise our parties and then went off with her own friends, leaving us to enjoy ours in our own way. So, I met men; I danced and was kissed. But at that moment when I should have felt that the sun and the moon and the stars were mine, something inside me would whisper— *"But this is not Max...."* And the magic would be still-born.

Then, only three months ago—almost three years after Max had left England—I met Lucien Blake. He was a young actor, tremendously charming, temperamental, with a lean, poet's face. Someone had once said that he should play Iago in *Othello*. He had just finished a long run in *Cat's Eye* and was hoping for the lead in a play by one of London's newest playwrights.

Lucien magicked me simply by giving me no time to stop and think. He whisked me into a life that was entirely new and exciting.

The people I now met had well-known names, employed publicity agents and lived at concert pitch. I felt at first like Cinderella, not quite certain if the glass slipper really fitted.

Then, ten days after I met Lucien, he told me he loved me and that I must marry him.

I shall never forget that night in his flat, high up over a London lying white under a cloak of snow with the traffic muffled and the stars like spangles; never forget that Beethoven's "Pastorale Symphony" was playing softly and there was one scarlet balloon, a relic of Christmas, still hanging over a Chagall picture.

To be loved, to be wanted after all those blank years. . . .

I could not understand what made Lucien love me. I had no interesting career. I had trained as a nurse, but had injured my back and was no longer strong enough to lift patients. Then I learned shorthand and typing and became a secretary. I was in my first job, working for a television company, when Lucien and I met.

Once, in a moment of confidence, wanting to be completely known and understood, I told Lucien about Max.

Lucien's long fingers had curved round my cheek. His eyes had narrowed with laughter.

"A poor little one-sided schoolgirl crush! We all have first loves, darling! But we give them away, like old toys. Don't tell me you still think you love him a bit, because you don't."

And warmed by the fact that I was loved, I mattered, I said: "No, I no longer love Max."

Common sense told me that this was true. It had been just part of my adolescence—something so precious to the secret part of me that I had been loath to let it go. Now I had grown up . . . Lucien belonged to my adulthood. . . .

And then one evening, the Cinderella dream broke.

Lucien did not own a car. He hated driving. So I had taken ours to fetch him from the theatre. We were to go to a late party together given by a famous theatre critic who was one of Lucien's greatest admirers.

When I arrived at the theatre Lucien came rushing out, slid into the car and was about to kiss me when he stopped. The gaiety went out of his face; he stared at me unbelievingly.

"You can't go to a party looking like that! What do you think you are, a beatnik?"

I had on a sweater and skirt and an ancient leather coat. My hair was unkempt and I didn't care.

I explained that I had a headache and my

throat hurt. There was a 'flu epidemic and I knew I had caught it. I would drive him to the party and then go to bed.

"But you can't!" Lucien had said. "I'm sorry you feel ill, but you really must come with me. Take an aspirin or something—"

I replied coldly that I had no intention of taking anything until I went to bed—and that would be very soon.

"But you can't do this to me!" Lucien protested as though it were a major catastrophe.

I knew what was in his mind.

Lucien's romance with me had been worked on by his publicity agent. We had been photographed together.... "The Young Inseparables" one newspaper had called us. And if I didn't turn up, Lucien said, someone would be bound to start a rumour that we had quarrelled. It wouldn't do his reputation any good to be thought of as a man who flits from girl to girl. The argument was idiotic but I was feeling ill and for once Lucien's refusal ever to be thwarted in what he wanted angered me. We argued.

It was then that a tiny girl, who should have been in bed hours ago, rushed off the pavement and right into the way of the car. I swerved and braked. The car skidded, avoided the child and crashed into a lamp-post.

17

I knew nothing more until I was in hospital. I had got off lightly with a concussion and a cut cheek. Lucien had a broken arm, two broken ribs and a badly lacerated face.

As soon as I was able, I went to see him in hospital. Directly I entered the room he began his attack. He blamed me for the accident; for the fact that he had lost his chance to star in the new play; for the damage to his face. I tried to reason with him, but I couldn't. I went in dismay to see the doctor attending him. Shock, he told me, had strange effects upon people. Lucien was very highly-strung and the accident had tipped him over the razor's edge to a break-down. He would need psychiatric treatment.

And after that would he be all right? I asked. Perfectly. And I was not to let myself be so upset. Everyone knew that the accident was not my fault. I had done what I did to save a child's life. Lucien's unreasonable blame was a feature of shock. Given time he would recover complete rationality.

I asked about the scars on his face. I was told that they weren't deep. They would heal and leave scarcely a mark. If Mr. Blake would give the doctors time, and have patience. . . . But patience was something I knew Lucien did not possess.

The psychiatrist told me, however, that it would be advisable for me not to see Lucien at all for the next few weeks.

"Perhaps it would be better if I broke off the engagement," I said.

That, I was told, was something I must not do.

"But I upset him so!"

"On the surface, where the shock is, yes. But deep down, he needs you. Lucien Blake is an actor of brilliance. Sometimes such great talent goes with a tendency to instability. Oh, nothing serious, of course!" he had added hastily. "But you are strong, Miss Mannering, you can help him so much when he is better. At the moment, however, it is for the doctors to help him."

Then he had given me advice. He suggested that I should go away, *right* away, for a couple of months. Lucien would be told that I, too, had been shocked after the crash and I had gone away for my health. Then, when I returned, the doctor promised me that Lucien would be cured.

"Except," I said, "that he will not forgive me!"

"That is not the pattern such shocks take after expert treatment," the doctor had looked at me as though my words had questioned his skill.

It was my stepmother who had suggested that I go to stay with Gerry in Hong Kong. When I had protested that I could not possibly raise the fare, she made a characteristic comment:

"I've always felt that the money your father left is yours and Gerry's as well as mine. So don't be proud, Francie! Now, let's start right away making plans."

Sitting there in the plane in those last few minutes of my journey, I remembered my stepmother's dark, dancing eyes glancing at the pages of a geographic magazine she had found which ran an article on Hong Kong. She might have been going herself, she was so thrilled about it all! There were times when I suspected that she did not like Lucien. But she never passed any comment and I did not ask her. Lucien gave me a love to which I was able to respond. He was the only person who could make me forget Max. . . .

I put my compact and lipstick away.

Outside the plane, the earth seemed to be rising to meet us. I saw the runway, the airport buildings. This, then, was Kai Tak. I felt an uprush of excitement.

Nothing is slower than officialdom when you are in a hurry! There was noise and confusion around me and the heat beat on me making my skin feel as though it were being pricked with needles. Chinese and European faces moved in a kaleidoscope before me; I was ushered to the coach which was to take us to the Peninsula Hotel where Gerry would be waiting for me. From the window-seat I gazed fascinated at the bustling, crowded, vital street life outside. In a seat nearer the front, the girl I had spoken to in the plane also sat alone. I guessed that she, too, would be met at the Peninsula Hotel.

It was not a very long drive. We circled a roundabout, drove down a long street and at last swept into the forecourt of the hotel.

Gerry was standing outside waiting for me.

He seemed, I thought studying his face while the coach drew to a stop, to be extremely well. A great deal of sea-bathing had bronzed his skin so that his eyes looked light gold. His crisp hair was bleached. He was middle-height and strongly-built and I thought he looked infinitely more rested than when I had last seen him on leave in London. Irene, his wife, had been with him then, plaintive and pretty and hyper-critical. The thing I remembered most vividly about her was the way she had always been on the watch lest someone, my stepmother, a friend or myself, would be getting more attention from Gerry than she.

Five months ago Irene had left him. She hated Hong Kong, she said, and if Gerry loved her he would go back to England and find himself a job worthy of him. The last thing my brother wanted was to go back to London or to find a job that was too demanding. He had a little money of his own and he was for the easy life. I knew Irene and her type. By her possessiveness and her jealousies, she had killed his love for her. And I knew, too, that if there were a divorce, it would be a long time before Gerry tied himself up again.

I made my way along the coach, climbed down and walked slap into my brother.

"Fran!"

The old familiar name for me warmed my heart.

"You look wonderful!" I said.

He seemed pleased: "Being a bachelor suits me, I guess!"

"Still no Irene?"

"No Irene!" he grinned back at me. "Just a Chinese house, a wonderful house-boy and a laundry amah. That's the set-up."

He turned and looked at my luggage.

"I'll arrange for this to be taken to the ferry." He gave instructions to a Chinese porter and then took my arm. "Come on. We

22

won't waste time here. I hope you didn't have lunch on the plane. I told you not to."

"It looked delicious," I said nostalgically, "but I just had a drink. I think the hostess thought I was ill or in love, or something—"

"Well, you are, aren't you? How's Lucien?"

"It'll take a long time," I said cautiously and Gerry knew my tone well enough to take the hint.

"Star Ferry is only just over here," he said, "and in no time at all when we land on the island you'll be home and you shall have a slap-up lunch."

The mists had cleared and the sky was brilliant. I drew a breath of air and seemed to smell spices and dust and jasmine. Or perhaps it was my overstimulated imagination and all there was to smell was petrol and heat and my own Mitsouko scent. . . .

At the ferry I turned my head and saw the girl who had travelled with me on the plane. She was standing alone, gazing about her, turning her head quickly, expectantly. Yet, I thought, most of the flame I had noticed about her on the plane had gone.

"Come on, Fran!" Gerry urged.

I said, hanging back:

"That girl standing alone. I talked to her on the plane. She was to meet her fiancé here—"

He followed my glance.

"Your plane was late so if he'd been coming, he'd be here by now."

"But he wouldn't just leave her."

"Perhaps they quarrelled on the way over—by remote control, I mean!" He grinned at me.

But as I saw her, jostled by crowds, standing there, so alone, so uncertain perhaps as to the wisdom of trusting her luggage to Chinese coolies, I thought: "Suppose it had been me!"

"We can't just leave her," I said. "She obviously doesn't know the drill. I think she's wondering what to do about her luggage."

"She'll pick it up on the island," Gerry said easily. Then he shrugged his shoulders. "Oh, all right, I'll be Sir Galahad!" With all the ease and friendliness in the world, he walked across to where the girl stood:

"My sister says she talked to you on the plane. Are you waiting for someone?"

She managed a bleak smile.

"I was expecting my fiancé to meet me. But he's not here."

"The plane was delayed because of fog so I don't think it will be much use waiting. He'd have been here now if he was coming. I think you'd better join us on the ferry."

"It's kind of you—" she began.

"Are those your suitcases?"

She looked down at them, smart, navy-blue, and brand new.

"Yes. They wanted to take them from me at the hotel, but I didn't know—"

"The porters put them on the ferry and you collect them at the other end," Gerry explained.

She had her trousseau in there, I thought. Lovely, carefully chosen clothes and she was terrified of losing them.

"Where are you staying?" I asked.

"At the Gloucester. Just for a few days—"

"That's right in the city," Gerry said, "and on our way. So we'll take you. If your fiancé comes along later, he's bound to conclude that as he arrived late, you've gone on. You know what has possibly happened, don't you? Some official could have given him the wrong time of arrival."

Which, I thought, was unlikely. But I saw how eagerly she accepted the explanation.

Gerry arranged for her luggage to be taken on the ferry. Then we went aboard and sat on wooden seats. I lifted my face gratefully to the sea breeze.

This was China, a place which had drawn my brother more strongly than any ambition. These were the people he loved and wrote home so glowingly about; the courteous, generous Chinese. . . .

I loved every moment of that journey to the Island although I was aware of the girl by my side, tense and silent and probably, I thought, angry with good reason.

When we arrived, the boat eased its way to the pier and the sampans moored nearby swung and rocked on the churned water. We landed and collected our luggage which was taken to Gerry's car, parked in a warehouse yard.

"The place belongs to one of my Chinese friends," Gerry explained. "He exports jade and silk to Europe and he lets me leave my car here whenever I'm this way."

The crowds, the noise, were bewildering and exciting. The steamy heat made my sleeveless cotton blouse and linen skirt feel like a damp swim-suit.

"It's not usually as hot as this at this time of year," Gerry told me. "It must be putting on the pressure for you, Fran!"

I said I was going to love it. I glanced about me as we began the hazardous journey to Gerry's house. I caught glimpses of stepped streets and tattered stalls, of banners painted with Chinese signs, of pedals and cycles and bamboo baskets laden. Then we turned into the city centre and the buildings were splendid and modern and the traffic a maze of rich "hong's" cars, taxis and a few rickshaws.

The girl by my side had been very silent all the way. I turned to smile at her.

"Don't be too upset," I said gently. "I'm sure Gerry was right and a mistake was made in the time of our scheduled arrival at the airport."

"Yes, of course," she said. "Eric will probably be waiting for me."

We had arrived in one of the main streets. Gerry was slowing the car down.

"I'm afraid we won't be able to see you into the hotel. If you stop in these streets, traffic piles up and all Hong Kong is put out of action."

"You've been very kind and thank you so much!" She was easing her big coat over her arm, picking up her handbag, the charm bracelet gleamed in the sunlight.

Gerry had got out and was supervising the removal of her luggage. I leaned out of the car and called to her:

"By the way, my name is Francie Mannering."

"I'm Marcie Gallard."

"I hope you have a lovely wedding," I said, "and heaps of good luck."

"Thanks. At any rate the setting will be

quite something!" She looked about her as she spoke.

Gerry, who had found a boy to take her luggage, said:

"You'll both probably run into each other sooner or later. Hong Kong is that sort of place! Good-bye, Miss Gallard. You're all right now, aren't you?"

"Quite all right! I'm sure Eric will be waiting for me inside. And I think I'm too excited to be mad at him!" she shot us a laughing look and turned towards the hotel.

"She *is* lovely!" I said thoughtfully. The dark green skirt of her dress swirled a little as she walked. Her copper hair had the sheen you see on a bird's feathers.

"Don't talk to me about lovely women!" Gerry was saying shortly. "I married one!"

"But you're happy now?" I asked anxiously as we drove on.

"Sure I am! I've got an easy job, plenty of leisure, lots of friends and a charming house. You wait till you see it!"

We left the main streets and in no time at all drew in close to a high, blank wall in a narrow street.

"Here we are!" he turned off the engine and sat back and watched my face.

II

From all the houses, washing hung out to dry on littered wooden balconies. A coolie, balancing a bamboo pole weighed down with watermelons, passed so closely that he almost scraped the side of the car. Colour rioted. Everything, it seemed, was yellow or vermilion, coral or purple or blue.

I said a little helplessly:

"Which house is yours, Gerry? And does *your* washing hang out over the street to dry?"

He laughed.

"I live behind this wall. Come on, get yourself out of the car."

I climbed out and stood in the street. Beyond the rims of my sun-glasses, I could see the brilliance of the late morning light. The humid heat caused by the closeness of the tall, tattered buildings, hit me across the face. From the shops, the banners with their painted signs hung motionless. Overhead, the sky was powder-blue.

Gerry took my suitcases from the boot of the car. Then he reached across me and lifted the latch of the heavy wooden door in the high wall.

"In you go!" he said.

I took a few steps through the door and stood quite still staring about me. Nothing was more surprising in the huddled, narrow street than to find this charming garden. Azaleas and irises flowered in raised brick beds between old flagstones. There was a large bronze bell half-way down the path and a beautiful little model of a Tang horse with flying mane stood at the foot of a peach tree. Near the house was another tree which Gerry told me was a casuarina, although how it managed to grow there was a mystery to him.

The house, he explained, was Chinese-style, but, unlike most of them, it had two stories instead of one. It had graceful wing roofs and a veranda ran round three sides of the building. Tall glass doors led on to it.

In the courtyard towards which we walked, chairs were set out round a low, tiled octagonal plinth. In the centre grew the tiniest tree I had ever seen. It was in shape and substance a pine, and was perfectly formed.

But it was barely two feet high.

I went towards it.

"It's a Bonzai," Gerry said. "They take years to train and grow."

I put out my free hand and touched it, half expecting it to feel artificial. But it was fresh and vibrant with life. On the green-tiled surround, stood a box of cigarettes, a lighter and a Hong Kong newspaper.

"Come on inside," Gerry said. "I can't hold these suitcases much longer. I think you must have packed gold nuggets in them!"

"Those binoculars of father's," I reminded him, "weigh a ton!"

As I spoke, a man came round the side of the house. He was small and olive-skinned and his hair gleamed blue-black. He wore a snowy white Chinese coat and trousers and his bright, slanting eyes smiled at me. He was small-boned and his features were delicate.

"This," Gerry said to me, "is my invaluable house-boy, Yee Sze." He laid a hand on my arm. "This is my sister, Miss Mannering."

The little man's smile was wide, his teeth were very white.

"You welcome here, missie. You like it?"

Gerry answered for me.

"I think my sister is overwhelmed at the

moment. I've never known the airport so crowded!"

Yee Sze took my big cream coat from me and picked up my suitcases. "You rest. You feel happy here."

I said:

"I know I'm going to be very happy here, Yee Sze."

Gerry led me up the veranda steps into a large, cool room.

I stood looking about me.

On the wall were a few very old scroll paintings; the carpets were delicate apricot and green; the furniture dark carved wood. On the settee and easy-chairs were cushions of yellow silk and from an ebony pedestal, a beautiful porcelain statuette which I recognised as Kwan Yin—the Goddess of Compassion—looked across the room.

On a rosewood table there were some books, a camera, a couple of little black fans such as the Chinese use, and Gerry's brief-case.

"It's a lovely room," I said warmly. "Now I understand why you are so happy out here!"

I knew that when Irene had left him, he had given up his flat in one of the blocks on the Peak, and had rented this house from a Cantonese family who had gone to live in Kowloon near their silk factory.

I followed Gerry up the stairs to a room that looked out over the garden to the sea.

There was a rosewood dressing-table, a chest, a very English looking bureau and an enormous divan bed with mosquito netting draped over it. The floor was highly polished and bare except for a few small Tientsin rugs like the one Gerry had sent home to my step-mother.

The colour-scheme of the room was an unusual blue with touches of lacquer-red.

"I'll leave you now," Gerry said. "Come down when you're ready. There's no hurry."

When the door had closed, I went to the window and pushed the shutters back. Spread out before me beyond the city was the sea. Fishing junks, with their bats wing sails, were like brown butterflies pinned to the water. Far in the distance I could see the dim outline of the mountains of Red China.

Behind me an electric fan whirred softly. As I turned, I saw at least two dozen yellow roses in a green lustre jar. There was a little card propped up against it.

"Welcome to Hong Kong.
                                    Max."

Flowers, just as he had so often sent me in

the past. . . . Flowers from Max with his kind wishes. . . .

In my delight and excitement, Max had been forgotten.

I crossed to the bed and sat shakenly down. White dragons were embroidered, rearing and clawing, on the thick Wedgewood-blue silk. I stroked the raised pattern of one of them and knew that, with his gift of flowers, Max had come right back into my life.

If only he had not been out here, then this journey east, so uncharged with old memories, might have exorcised his ghost! . . . Or if a child had not run out into the road on a dark night, Lucien and I might have been married by now. And life with him, full and passionate as it would have been, would have been sufficient exorcism. . . .

I lay down with my cheek against a rearing white silk dragon, and closed my eyes.

I felt my throat constricting and the beginnings of resentment, even of self-pity, rose in me. Lucien's psychiatrist had called me strong. Strong! I who could not even fight against an old love that had never done me any good!

III

Quickly, I swung myself off the bed. This was crazy!

I was here in Hong Kong and I was going to enjoy every full, lovely moment.

I checked my watch by the little clock set on jade feet which stood on the bureau. Then I went to my overnight case and got out my sponge bag. When I had slipped on the white house-coat which had been one of my luxury purchases before I left England, I remembered what I had heard about the water shortage that was always prevalent on this island.

I called down to Gerry and asked about a bath.

"Go right ahead!" he told me. "You'll find the bathroom next to your room."

When I had bathed, I put on a brown and white dress and slid my feet into low-heeled bronze sandals.

I had brought my gold bracelet out to Hong

Kong with me and I took it from my zippered jewel-case and put it on. It did not have the flippant little jangle of Marcia Gallard's with her four charms but I was fond of it.

Lunch was set out on the veranda and Gerry was waiting.

I said, as I sat down:

"There are some flowers in my room. From Max."

"You can thank him this evening," Gerry said easily. "He's coming to dinner."

I traced the raised pattern on a turquoise dish full of tiny seeds and remained silent.

"He often comes round," Gerry added, "and I've been grateful these past few months for his company."

I bent forward and looked into the little bowl.

"What are these?"

"Melon seeds." Gerry took one, cracked it edgewise between his teeth, peeled back the shell and ate the kernel. "That's how you do it."

Lunch was a cold meal and delicious. I tasted fruits I had never seen before, I drank thin green tea out of handleless cups. And I was careful not to mention Max's name again.

When the meal was over, Gerry explained that there was a rush of rather important work which he had to return to the office and finish.

"But I can take off to show you your way around. Or would you rather rest?"

"I haven't come here for that!" I said scornfully.

"You'll learn!" he grinned at me.

I fetched my sun-glasses and joined Gerry in the living-room. He was studying an unframed watercolour painting and I peered across his arm.

"It's of this street! Gerry, it's lovely!"

He handed it to me. It was bold and strong and the colours sprang vividly from the paper.

"I was talked into commissioning an artist to paint the house and the garden," he said. "When I argued that I didn't want pictures of something that was all round me, I was told that when I was old and rheumy-eyed and back in London, I could sit and gaze at them and remember my glad days!"

I tried to read the signature.

"Harriet Craig," Gerry said.

I darted a laughing, suspicious look at him.

"I'm beginning to understand!"

"You aren't at all!" he said, swiftly on the defensive. "Wait till you see her! In fact, the whole thing's a waste of money—and believe me, she doesn't go in for undercharging for her work!"

"I shall be interested to meet her."

"You will!" he said. "She'll be round this afternoon—she says it's the best time to get the feel of the full blaze of colour."

"Does she live by her painting?"

Gerry shook his head.

"I believe she was born and brought up in India of British parents and she has money of her own. She came to Hong Kong quite recently and someone at my club introduced us. Now that I've commissioned the two paintings, I'm not so certain I like her coming at all odd hours to sit herself in my garden! I only hope she works quickly."

We were walking together to the terrace and, as Gerry had foretold, there was a woman setting up her easel and stool under the peach tree.

"Does she just walk in and out of your garden like that?"

"The divine privilege of an artist!" he said drily. "She does!"

I paused in the shadow of the veranda for a moment and watched her. She was tall and very thin and she walked as though she would break in the middle. She wore a speckled black and white dress and low white shoes. On her head was a huge yellowish straw hat. From a distance, she was one of the most unprepossessing women I have ever met.

"You'd better come and be introduced," Gerry said, "because for a week or two she'll be around quite a bit!"

We went down the veranda steps and across the garden. Near where she sat, the bronze flanks of the beautiful little Tang horse caught the sunlight; the peach tree gave deep shade and from somewhere came a scent I could not identify. I lifted my head and sniffed delightedly.

Gerry laughed.

"Sandalwood joss sticks," he said. "You'll have to get used to them. Yee Sze burns them in the kitchen."

He paused, his hand on my arm, pretending to show me a raised, bricked-up bed of lilies in heavy bud.

"Down here, things bloom much earlier than on the Peak—if, that is, they bloom at all with all the difficulties of right soil." He moved a little nearer me. "By the way, it's best not to get too friendly with Miss Craig. I may be maligning her, but I feel it wiser to have a purely professional arrangement with her."

I agreed mechanically. Such caution was not like my brother, however. He was both gregarious and hospitable. I gathered from that little aside that, although he admired her as an artist, he did not much care for the idea of her as a friend.

Seen close to, Harriet Craig must have been over fifty. She had black greying hair and large dark eyes with heavy white lids. It was a strange face and when Gerry introduced us, her smile was slow, conjecturing and without warmth.

I glanced at the stretched paper on her easel and saw that the house with its graceful wing roofs was taking shape.

"It's beautiful, isn't it?" I said conversationally.

"Beautiful," she agreed. "But a little large, don't you think, except for a family?" Her eyes watched Gerry. "I'm sure you'll love having your sister here. It must be lonely for you!"

"Don't you believe it!" His tone was airy and faintly annoyed. "No man's lonely with a job he likes, plenty of friends and a boy who cooks all his favourite dishes. Don't waste pity on me, Miss Craig! Though it's nice having Fran." He took my arm. "Come and have your lightning tour of the city centre. I haven't much time!"

I walked enchanted through the crowded streets, gazing at people, at shops, at the glittering super-abundance of everything. I registered the names of streets—Pedder, Des Voeux, Queen's Arcade. We passed the Gloucester Hotel and I looked up at the wide façade.

"That's where Marcia Gallard is staying. I wonder if I should ring her later, just to see if she'll be all right?"

Gerry guided me through a group of sightseeing Europeans; I nearly fell over a little mongrel dog following a small Chinese girl.

"I should leave well alone," he said. "You're strangers, after all, and that girl didn't look to me to be the helpless type and her boy-friend must have shown up by now. Now," he went on, "*you* take *me* home—just to see if you know the way."

Without any difficulty I walked us both back to Tai-yuan Street. Harriet Craig was sitting absorbed in front of her easel. We smiled at one another.

Later, when Gerry had left for Government House, I lay on the bed for a while, drowsing. But the noises beyond the garden made me restless. I needed action.

I had seen, as we had walked earlier through Queen's Arcade, two little celadon lion-dogs in a half-shop there and I wanted to buy them for my stepmother. I had a wad of Hong Kong dollars in my wallet and they were there to be spent. I knew I was merely finding an excuse to go out again.

When I went into the kitchen to tell Yee Sze that I would not be away long, there was a middle-aged Chinese woman with him. He introduced her politely as the laundry amah, Lau Fai. She was plain and tending to fat but she bowed to me with a smiling dignity.

As I went down the garden, Harriet Craig called to me.

"Out again, Miss Mannering? You'll get tired! It's only diehards like me, born and bred in the East, who have energy and to spare in this climate!"

I laughed and said I would see how far my own energy stretched and maybe I would be brought home in an ambulance.

I felt her watching me as I passed her and pushed open the nail-studded gate. There was something uncomfortable about those odd, white-lidded eyes.

Finding my way to Queen's Arcade was not difficult. I went into the shop and bought the two little pale-green guardian lion-dogs for my stepmother. But the second walk of the after-noon had tired me after my long journey and I decided to go straight back home and ask Yee Sze for some tea.

I was nearing Tai-yuan Street, weaving my way past coolie carriers laden with melons and oranges, amused at some children playing hop-scotch, the tiniest tumbling solemnly at my feet, when suddenly a girl streaked through the narrow street.

She moved so fast, with a wild, terrified urgency, that heads turned and eyes stared at her. I felt the brush of her arm against mine as she passed. I, too, stopped and stared at her.

Some yards from me she pulled up, as though impelled by a violent brake.

For a moment she stood there, unaware of the stares; poised, hesitating. Then, turning her head, she looked at me. And I saw that it was Marcia Gallard.

At the same moment that I recognised her, she began to walk back quickly until she was level with me. She was breathing hard and every line of that slender, streamlined body was taut as a pulled wire.

"Miss Mannering . . ."

"Hallo," I said. "What's the matter?"

Her words came jerkily.

"What is that sound?"

The question was so completely unexpected that I looked at her in astonishment.

Then I listened.

From somewhere behind me I heard the thin twitter of singing crickets. Street pedlars, Gerry told me earlier, sold them in tiny cages and the poor Chinese made pets of them.

"Just a street pedlar with his singing crickets," I said.

"I heard them before when—" she broke off sharply. Her eyes flashed at me and away.

"When what?"

"It's an odd little sound, isn't it? Like ... like tiny starlings in Trafalgar Square." She tried to speak naturally but I saw the panic still in her eyes.

"Look," I said and touched her arm, "won't you tell me what scared you?"

"It was nothing, really!" she managed a small travesty of a smile. "I'll be quite all right in a minute or two. I wonder"—she eyed me uncertainly—"if I might walk a little way with you? Just down the street?"

"Of course. In fact," I said on impulse, "come back and have some tea with me. I'll be all on my own."

"Thank you. I would like that so much."

I cast a sideways look at her as she walked by my side. She was holding her head stiffly as though she did not dare look over her shoulder, and her breathing was still a little laboured.

We turned into Tai-yuan Street and it was quieter here.

"Was your fiancé waiting for you at the hotel?"

She hesitated for a moment.

"No."

"But I don't understand."

"Nor do I!" she said bleakly.

"But surely there was a message. Something..."

"There was nothing! Miss Mannering," she broke out, her voice trembling, "it's as though I don't even exist! As though no one here has ever...heard...of me...."

"There's been some mistake," I said to comfort her, "that's all! By the way, what happened just now to make you so scared?"

Again she did not answer immediately and I said, jumping to an obvious conclusion in this teeming eastern city:

"Did someone try to snatch your handbag?"

"Handbag?" her head turned and she stared at me. Then her face brightened. "Yes. Yes, that's what happened! Someone, back there in that street with all those stalls, tried to steal my handbag."

I had my head turned, watching her as she spoke.

My immediate reaction was that she had

seized on this guess of mine almost too eagerly. Her face had cleared with too much relief at my words. Also, from the impression I had already formed of her she did not appear the kind of girl to lose her head over a bag-snatching incident that had obviously failed. Anyway, her handbag was a neat cream envelope which she carried in her hand. Like that, it would not have been easy to snatch. Under her arm she, too, carried a parcel.

"The crowds are bewildering, aren't they?" I said conversationally.

"They are, rather!"

By the time we had reached Gerry's house she had still not told me what had really scared her.

"Here we are," I said and stopped.

She drew back. Her hand rested against the heavy wood and I saw at close range the link bracelet and the little golden charms. One was a miniature ship, one a flower with garnet petals, and one a bird. But I remembered counting four! Then I saw a tiny gold ring swinging emptily from one of the links as though the charm that had hung there had dropped off. She saw my gaze and quickly lowered her hand.

I closed the gate behind us and Marcia stood quite still.

"What a lovely house!"

"My brother is so fond of it that he's having a painting done of it, to look at in his old age." I laughed. "Come and meet Miss Craig."

I introduced them and left them for a moment while I went to tell Yee Sze to bring tea. When I returned, Marcia was saying cautiously:

"Yes, they're—friends of mine—" She turned to me with a faint relief as though Harriet Craig had been asking her questions she did not want to answer.

"Come and sit down," I said to Marcia. "You must be very hot and very tired! I am."

We sat in two rattan chairs in the courtyard shade and I offered Marcia a cigarette.

"I don't really smoke—" she began. But she took one and as I lit it, I saw that her hand shook.

"Tell me what's happened since we left you," I said.

"Nothing. Just nothing! I waited for Eric and then I telephoned. There was no reply. I kept trying. Then this afternoon I couldn't bear it any longer. I knew I had to go along to Kam Ho Street where Eric has his book shop. I asked a porter where it was and..." she brushed a hand over her lovely copper-coloured hair. "Well, that's all I can tell you."

47

Yee Sze was by my side. On a lacquer tray was a little painted tea-pot and delicate porcelain cups. I looked across at Harriet, wondering whether to ask her to join us, but she had already packed up her things. Before I could call her over, she had walked to the gate in her long, bent stride.

As I poured out the thin, scented tea, I said: "So you went to the shop and saw Eric? And then . . .?"

"It isn't easy to find one's way about in this city, is it? All those odd little side streets, narrow and stepped—"

"You mean you lost your way?"

She looked down at the parcel lying near her handbag:

"Eric asked me to bring two books out with me. They're rare editions I had to collect from a dealer for him." She paused and took her teacup and saucer from me. "I was on my way when that—that incident happened."

Once more her eyes did not quite meet mine. I felt that she had gone a roundabout way to tell me that she hadn't reached the shop! I considered her. In the pale green nylon shirt-waister and the white court shoes, she looked touchingly defenceless and beautiful. Yet there was something suspect in her story.

"You are quite sure"—I leaned forward—"that someone tried to steal your handbag? It wasn't something else that frightened you?"

She did not move a muscle.

"Having one's handbag snatched is scaring enough, isn't it . . .?" She broke off and turned her head quickly at a sound way down the garden.

I looked too.

Max Forrest was coming along the path between the brilliant clusters of flowers.

I felt my heart-beats leap and throb in my throat. I took a long drink of tea to prove to myself that I could still swallow. Then I smiled brightly, formally, saying with just the right amount of wonder in my voice:

"Why—*Max!*"

He hadn't changed in the least during the three years I had not seen him. Still slim, still with that quiet, disciplined walk; those steady, brilliant eyes.

"Why—Max!" I said again, a little less breathy. "After all these years!"

He put out his hands to me. I wished mine could have felt cooler and steadier to his touch.

"You haven't changed a bit, Francie," Max appraised me. "Only you're doing your hair differently."

"I'm over three years older than when you last saw me!" I reminded him and turned and introduced Marcia. "We travelled on the same plane from England," I explained. "You'll have some tea, won't you?"

"Thank you," he pulled up a chair and sat down.

As I went towards the kitchen to ask Yee Sze for another cup and saucer, I heard Max asking Marcia about the flight. When I returned, he was giving her laughingly, the names of places in which to spend her honeymoon. Bangkok... Mandalay....

I realised that Marcia had not answered my last question to her. She had merely made a generalisation that had meant exactly nothing.... But I had to let it pass for the moment.

My hands were busy with the tea things. I said gaily:

"You should be studying South-East Asian politics, not sitting in a garden having tea!"

Max laughed, refused a cake and said:

"I knew Gerry wouldn't be free until later, so I thought I'd look in to see if you would like a drive out to see something of Hong Kong. Have you been around at all yet?"

I explained that Gerry had shown me my way to the main streets. Then I told him what had happened to Marcia, that she had expected to meet her fiancé but he had not yet shown up. I told about meeting her in the street just now, and about her bag. Max had always been a good listener. When I had finished he said:

"That was a horrible experience on your first day here! But with so many thousands of refugees pouring from Red China, I'm afraid the bad arrive as well as the good!"

Marcia raised her eyes; her gaze flicked warily at me and I was again certain that there had been no handbag episode.

I asked Max if he knew Kam Ho Street.

"I seem to remember Gerry once pointing it out to me. I think he said the name meant 'Beautiful Peach.'" He laughed and said the Chinese would make poetry out of a rubbish dump.

"Marcia's fiancé has a bookshop there," I explained. "I thought perhaps, after tea, we might give her a lift on our way to wherever we're going."

"Of course," Max said readily. "I want to go to the post office first, anyway."

For a moment I thought Marcia was going to refuse his offer. A guardedness clouded her eyes.

"Thank you, but I can find my way perfectly well. I wouldn't dream of putting you to any bother!"

"It's no bother. The car is outside," Max said easily. "I don't know if I can get right up the street. It may be stepped – but I can take you to the corner."

A faint smile that could have been relief touched her face. I supposed she did not want us around when she and Eric met.

We stayed for another ten minutes in the shady courtyard, touching on old times, pulling ourselves back to the present when we realised that Marcia could not share our memories. I watched Max's strong, sunburned hands; I looked across the little rattan table and met his eyes. His mouth, I thought, was a little more grave than I remembered it.

I said suddenly:

"Oh Max, thank you for the roses. They're lovely!"

"I seem to remember you always liked yellow flowers best," his eyes danced. "Or have you changed your colour tastes as you've changed your hair style?"

I said "No"; handed the little cake-dish across to Marcia and wished with all my heart that I could say to myself: "I've changed underneath. I no longer love you, Max!...I'm free of you..."

One day, I would be!

IV

Driving down the street was like a terrifying game of human ninepins. Coolies, trousered women and children with rice-bowls moved miraculously out of the way of the car's dark blue nose.

My arm brushed Max's occasionally. My gaze was continually drawn to his quiet, light hands on the wheel. On my other side, I could sense Marcia's tension. I doubted if it were a case of nerves because she had not seen Eric for so long. I had formed a strong impression, already, of Marcia's type. She would go walking on wings towards someone she loved.

Yet here she was, muscles tense—so tense, indeed, that her arm, crushed against mine, was like a piece of unyielding steel.

Presently we came to Des Voeux Road and when we were nearly at the end of it, Max peered at a turning. It was Kam Ho Street.

"It would be quicker if you got out and

walked to the bookshop," he suggested. "I'm going to the post office and you can pick me up there, Francie, O.K.? You know how to get there? It's just across this road and down Pedder Street. I always park my car when I'm in this part of the city in Mr. Tong Hui's yard. He has an umbrella factory there. You'll find the entrance down a passage by the side of a spice and grocery shop called Hwang's. All right?"

I nodded. But before I could speak, Marcia said swiftly, rather loudly:

"You've been so kind! I can't let you bother any more. I'll be quite all right now. And thank you, I—"

"Nothing is going to stop me delivering you safely to the door of the shop," I told her firmly. "And it's no bother!"

As I edged her out of the car, she protested again.

"Come along!" I chivvied her. "Hey!" Then I steadied her as she nearly collided with a woman carrying a baby in a sling across her back. I turned and waved at Max.

Kam Ho Street was considerably less tattered than most Hong Kong side streets.

Marcia walked by my side with that free, graceful movement I had noticed before. But she didn't look, as I did, left and right of the street, searching for No. 43. She just walked straight on as though she were going somewhere else and the place had no significance for her.

We were passing a shop that had shutters across the inside of the window. The door was closed and padlocked and a coolie, wearing a gold wrist-watch, leaned up against the wall, watching us.

I glanced up at the number over the door; I read the name painted in green letters on a dirty white ground across and down. They were in English and Chinese. The English letters said:

Farson. Bookseller.
And the number of the shop was 43.

I had gripped Marcia's arm without realising it, forcing her to stop.

"You said your fiancé's surname was Farson, didn't you? Well look, the shop is all closed up!" I said unnecessarily.

Her face in the brilliant late-afternoon light was drained of colour. She dragged her arm out of my grip. Her lips moved, but it was some moments before she made a sound.

"Eric ... must have ... gone away! He told me he sometimes does. I ... I'd better go back to the hotel ... and wait...."

"Does he live over the shop?"

"I don't know—"

"But you must know where you write to him!" I said sharply. And then a thought occurred to me. "There's just a chance that he has only closed the shop to customers. He could easily be somewhere upstairs." I jerked my head towards the blank windows. "Let's see if there's a back entrance into the place."

"Please, I'd rather leave it now." There was a ragged pleading in her voice. "I'll telephone him again from the Gloucester."

She was dragging at my hand and there were little beads of sweat on her forehead.

"You surely haven't come thousands of miles to give up now, just because a shop door is locked!" I said, determined to get to the bottom of her fear. "Old places sometimes have an alley running along the back of them, at least they do in England! Come on, let's see."

"I . . . I can't!"

I looked at her with mounting suspicion.

"What are you afraid of?"

"Nothing!" she flashed back.

"Marcia," I said again. "What are you afraid of? Tell me. . . ."

Then I saw the defiance go out of her eyes. Quite suddenly it was as though she could not fight me any more.

"All right," she said. "Let's go and see if the shop has a back entrance."

I almost ran her down the short block. Her heels made a metallic sound on the pavement. The flat slippers I wore made no sound at all.

There was, as I had hoped, a narrow alley at the back of the row of shops. Unlike the tenement blocks I had already seen whose alleyways swarmed with children, this one was deserted. Inside the doors, as we passed, we saw the passage piled with crates and cardboard boxes.

On our left was a high wall. As we walked along, searching for the back of No. 43, a door opened in the wall and a girl came out.

An open door, a lighted window, were always a magnet. We turned our heads and had a brief glimpse of a lovely garden, far more ornate and lavish then Gerry's. There were riots of flowers, little trees artistically clipped and tiny, brilliant birds darting among the branches, their crimson feathers and jade breasts catching the sunlight. They must be rare, I thought, and confined to this garden. I suppose they had their wings clipped.

The girl who came through the door was Eurasian and very beautiful. She had raven hair and a pale honey skin and she wore a black and gold *cheongsam,* those enchanting slit-up-the-side dresses the Chinese girls wear so beautifully.

As we squeezed past one another in the narrow alley, her friendly eyes lingered on my face. I caught a waft of expensive French perfume; I saw the glint of scarlet lacquered nails as she put out her hand to close the heavy door.

Then I forgot her and turned my attention to the back of No. 43 Kam Ho Street.

"At least," I said as we came level with it, "it hasn't got the uncared-for look about it that the others have. The passage inside is actually free of storage stuff—" I leaned forward and peered through the pane of glass.

It was dark in that passage. I put up my hands and shaded my eyes from the reflection of a tree, topping the wall behind me.

"There's something on the floor inside—" I began.

And then I stopped.

I shut my eyes, opened them and forced myself to look again, dreading what I would see. My heart hammered and I was hot and cold at the same time; I was vaguely aware of Marcia leaning against the wall by my side, making no attempt to look over my shoulder into that passage.

It flashed through my mind that she knew

already what I was looking at.

On the floor, just inside the door, lay a man. His face was toward us and his arms were flung out.

And I knew he was dead. . . .

My knees were shaking. I wiped a damp hand across my forehead and turned to Marcia.

"Why . . . don't you . . . want to take a . . . look inside?" My voice cracked a little.

She didn't answer.

I leaned against the door, still shaken. My eyes did not leave her face.

"You know, don't you, what you'd see? Marcia—is that man your fiancé?"

"No. Oh, *no!*"

I had known that before I asked. Marcia's reaction was fear, not grief. . . .

And suddenly shock made me angry. I turned on her.

"Nobody tried to snatch your handbag, did they?" I demanded, my voice too loud. "It was what you saw in that passage that frightened you, that made you run in a panic—"

She was flattened against the wall at the side of the door and there was a beaten look in her eyes. The handbag and the parcel were held tightly against her as her arms were clasped across her breast. There were damp strands of hair on her forehead.

"I lost my head," she spoke in a monotone. "I—I'd never seen a dead man before—"

"But why didn't you go to the police?"

"It—it didn't occur to me!" she said with simple honesty. "I lost my head and just ran blindly. Then I saw you—"

"Marcia, we'll have to report it at once."

"We could just go away," she suggested, watching me. "After all, the man is dead. We can't do him any good. So, if we just said nothing and let someone else find him—"

"But we can't!" My voice was brisk to hide the sick feeling in my stomach. "Tell me honestly, are you quite certain he was dead when you saw him before?"

She nodded.

"You...couldn't mistake...that look, could you?"

No, I thought, you couldn't mistake that look!

Suddenly, I realised that we were standing outside a door where a dead man lay. We were almost in the very presence of death.

"Let's get away," I said shakily. "Talk somewhere else...."

It was as though she were rooted against that wall.

"I'm sorry—involving you, I mean...I

shouldn't have stopped you in the street . . . it's too . . . horrible!"

The small breathless outburst of words was so sincere that it shook me out of my resentment at her lie to me. This girl was alone in Hong Kong. She had come here to meet the man she was going to marry and had met, instead, a dead stranger. . . .

"Here," I said as I saw the parcel of books slipping from her arms as though she hadn't the strength to hold them. "Let me take those."

As she gave them to me, a corner of the parcel caught in her bracelet. She dragged it off with a jerky, agitated movement and opening her handbag, dropped the bracelet in.

"We'll go and find Max," I said. "He'll know what to do."

We half-ran, half-walked and neither of us made any more attempt at talking. We turned off Pedder Street and I saw at last, with relief, the long nose of Max's car sticking out of Mr. Tong's courtyard.

"We'll sit inside and wait." I threw the car door open.

Sitting by my side, looking ahead of her through the windscreen, Marcia was as still as a statue.

Someone sidled up to the car and a skinny,

yellow-brown hand thrust a bundle of fire-wood in at the open window.

"Sometime velly cold. Firewood, Missie?" asked a sing-song voice.

I shook my head and the bundle disappeared.

Suddenly Marcia began to shake with silent laughter.

"Firewood! On a day like this!"

"He probably thought we live where Gerry says most British live, on the Peak. And one day it'll be winter and I believe the mists make it cold up there at night. . . . *Marcia!*" I turned quickly to her.

The laughter was pure hysteria. She just sat staring ahead of her and trembling and crying. I reached round and gave her a sharp shake and she jerked her head back as though I had slapped her.

"That doesn't help!" I said sharply.

"I'm sorry." Her voice quietened; her body fell into relaxed lines. She brushed her hand across her eyes. My heart went out to her.

"It's all right," I said more gently. "I understand! All this must have been a terrible shock for you. Only, you've got to keep calm. Nobody ever achieved anything in a flummox." Impulsively I touched her hand. "Don't worry, Marcia. You aren't alone any longer!"

"But you don't know me!" her voice was bleak and without hope. "You can't risk helping someone who's a stranger—"

"It seems I won't be able to help myself! I've become involved whether I like it or not. You forget, I saw that dead man, too." I gave a little inward shudder. Behind the glitter and the glamour, I had suddenly come upon the menace that was also Hong Kong. . . .

It was hot in the car. For all the advertiser's assurances about the linen of the dress I was wearing being crease-proof, the tan-and-white striped pleats over my knees looked tired. I glanced at myself in the rear mirror. Like Marcia I had feathers of hair clinging damply to my forehead; my nose shone.

I took off my sun-glasses and closed my eyes and tried to think.

Marcia was alone in Hong Kong. What were we going to do about her? We could not just report what we had seen to the police and then leave her. Suppose Eric Farson never showed up! She might not even have her fare back to England. And even if she had, someone had to make certain she was all right until a passage could be found for her on a home flight.

I opened my eyes, put my sun-glasses on again and saw Max coming toward us. Immediately I felt as though a responsibility had been removed from me. Max would cope.... For a flashing moment I forgot the dead man as I met Max's silver-grey eyes and saw them smile at me.

He looked surprised to see Marcia and before he could urge me to move over so that he could get in behind the wheel, I was out of the car and standing on the pavement.

"Something terrible has happened!" My voice rushed at him. "We found the shop and it was shuttered. We went round the back and..."

"And that was closed, too?"

"I don't know." I took a grip on myself. "Max, there's a dead man lying just inside the door!"

He looked at me for a long moment.

"Did you go inside?" he asked sharply.

"No, I — I didn't even try the handle to see if the door was unlocked," I said in slow wonder at the obvious thing I had left undone. "I just looked through the glass panel and saw him."

"Then how can you be sure he was dead?"

"There was...absolutely...no doubt," I said sickly.

Max glanced quickly from me to Marcia. Then he got into the car, nudged me gently over to give himself room and sat behind the wheel.

"Are we going to the police?" I asked.

"I want to see what you saw with my own eyes first."

"It . . . was . . . horrible!"

For a moment his hand rested on mine lightly, reassuringly. Then he started the car.

"Let's go and see, shall we?"

We finished the short drive in silence and parked the Sunbeam at the entrance to the alley behind Kam Ho Street. The door in the high wall on our left where the little birds fluttered was closed.

When we reached the back of the bookshop, Max stepped up to the panel and peered through. Then he shaded his eyes, as I had done, and changed his angle. I felt Marcia draw near me.

Max tried the door-handle but it would not give. The place was locked up.

"Well?" I demanded as he turned to me.

"It's as well I came to see for myself before we went to the police," he said. "You both let your imaginations run riot. There's no one lying dead in there. There's just a bundle of clothes."

I stared at him for a moment, without

moving or speaking. By my side, Marcia gave a little gasp.

Then I pushed past Max, went to the window. At first, because of the reflection of the tree behind me and the light, I could see nothing. Then, I saw for myself.

A man's coat and trousers were draped across the floor with such uncanny realism that, at first glance, one might have thought the body of a man was inside. Only there was no face and no feet....

Slowly I turned.

"You . . . look . . . too!" I whispered to Marcia.

She moved reluctantly forward, took my place at the glass panel and peered through. I watched her. As she turned to us again, there was a kind of wild relief on her face. She avoided me and looked at Max.

"You're right! We must have made a mistake," she said breathlessly.

"You could easily have done so. It's dark in there and it could have been a trick of light and shade made by the tree behind us," Max said.

"I *saw* a man lying there!" I said with sharp emphasis. "His skin was pale like a European's. And I saw his feet." I swung round on Marcia. "You did, too!"

Again she avoided my direct gaze and looked down at the hard cracked earth of the alley.

"I *thought* I saw someone there. But I can't have done! This proves it—"

"It proves nothing!" I tried to force her to meet my eyes. Because of shock and fright and now this seeming anti-climax, my voice sounded high and angry. "You want to ignore the whole thing, don't you? You're only too anxious to believe what Max said. *Why?* Why, when you were in such a panic before?" Then my voice softened. "Or perhaps I understand! Is it because you're afraid your fiancé killed the man?"

"*No!*" She almost shouted. Then she added with desperate triumph: "Besides, there *is* no dead man, is there?"

"Because someone was watching and came and removed him before we could call the police." I raised my head as I spoke, and looked along the rows of blank windows above us.

No one was there, of course. But I was quite certain we had not come unobserved before. Someone *had* watched us from a window, or from the deeper shadows of that empty shop. . . .

"There's no point in hanging around here," Max said practically. "Come on, let's go."

"Where to?"

"For a run in the car."

"As though nothing had happened?" I murmured. "But Max, we *can't!*"

He pretended he had not heard.

"Miss Gallard, will you come with us? We'll only go a short way. Perhaps, together, we can think of a way to find out what has happened to your fiancé."

"Are you *really* going to do nothing about this?" I stood in his way.

He looked down at me.

"That's right, Francie. I'm doing absolutely nothing! And after a day spent down here in this humidity, I need a breath of clear air and so do both of you." He spoke kindly but with a firmness that rejected refusal. I could scarcely believe that he was merely taking the easy way out of a horrible situation. But there was nothing I could do; no argument I could use because Max had not seen a dead man. . . .

We sat Marcia between us.

For the first ten minutes we drove in silence while he concentrated on getting us out of the traffic congestion. Then we began to climb up the Peak, past the houses clinging wildly to the steep slopes. We passed gardens with their palms and frangipani trees and camellias. Victorian houses and modern blocks of flats stood among the rich, tropical vegetation.

When he could relax a little at the wheel, Max turned his attention to Marcia.

"Your fiancé gave you no indication that he was closing his shop?"

"None. In fact," she touched the brown paper parcel on her knee, "he asked me to collect these two books from a dealer and bring them out to him. So he can't have been planning to go away, can he?"

"What are the books?"

"I don't know. I haven't opened the parcel, but I believe they are two first editions and rather valuable."

"Didn't you think it strange that he wasn't at the airport to meet you?"

"I knew his job took him all over the island and into Kowloon. He once told me in a letter that there are a number of rich Chinese who fled from the Revolution and who are putting their money into collections. He had an assistant in the shop whom he could leave in charge."

"But he would surely have timed any business visit he had to make so that it did not coincide with your arrival!"

"We don't even know if there's a bookshop business any longer, Max." I turned towards the strong, sun-tanned profile, leaning a little forward across Marcia. "The shutters were up and the place might have been cleared of stock."

"That's right!" she agreed eagerly. "Perhaps the building was condemned and he had to move quite suddenly."

"Kam Ho Street wasn't derelict," Max said soberly. "The thing for us to do is to go to the authorities—"

"*No!*" she cut in violently. "I won't do that yet! I must wait a few days. I *know* there's an easy explanation! Eric won't have just vanished."

"If he had been taken ill and gone to hospital," I said, "then his assistant would carry on at the shop. So that's not the explanation. Max"—an idea occurred to me—"perhaps this is where Gerry could help us. After all, he's at Government House and Eric is an Englishman."

"I can't think he'll know anything about an empty shop," Max said. "But I suppose one of us could find out what's happened. Englishmen don't vanish."

"You don't think he's gone to Red China—?"

"He would never do that!" Marcia said quickly.

I had a sudden idea.

"Come round and have dinner with us tonight," I invited. "Max is coming and Gerry would love it. He's a very gregarious person. Between us all we might be able to help."

"Thank you," she said after a moment's hesitation, "I'd like to."

We were reaching the top of the Peak. Max stopped the car and we got out. The crisper, cooler air met us and we took deep grateful breaths of it.

Far below, beyond the streets, we could see the waterfront with its network of sampans and junks and toiling humanity. A ferry trailed a V of silver foam over the sea. Away in the distance we saw the dim turquoise outline of the Nine Peaks of Kowloon—China's Nine Dragons....

Max offered us cigarettes. I took one. Marcia refused. When he had lit them, Max asked:

"Has your fiancé any relatives in Hong Kong, Miss Gallard?"

Marcia shook her head. Her eyes gazed over the sea.

"Then has he mentioned any particular friends?"

"No. He used to live in Shanghai. His father was a British businessman there. Eric left there just before the Revolution and made his home here; but he never talked of anyone special."

"You say you've brought some books out with you from England?"

"Yes," she answered readily. "I've often collected books for him, ordered by some client, and sent them out. This time, he suggested that as I was coming out to Hong Kong, I should bring them with me."

"And you're staying at the Gloucester?"

"For the time being. Though I'll have to find somewhere less expensive."

"I might be able to help," Max said. "Providing, that is," he added, "you intend to stay here."

"I must, mustn't I?" she said simply. "I've come out to make my home here. I've got to wait now until Eric contacts me."

I repressed the strong impulse to amend: "*If* he ever does!" Marcia had had quite enough shock for one day. And as she had said, there could still be some simple explanation for what had happened.

My commonsense immediately jeered at me. Simple? When a dead man had vanished from a shop passage?

We sat in a little semi-circle on the grass verge. I looked around me in wonder at the strange and lovely mountain slope. Frangipani, oleander and azalea . . . birds I had never seen before, yellow-faced and green-backed. . . . A black-crested bulbul flew between myself and the sun. In a way I had when I was puzzled, I had pushed my sun-glasses up on to my forehead and was squinting at a dazzling world. Max reached over and gently lowered the fly-away frames on to my nose.

"It may be ten degrees cooler up here, Fran, but the sun's fierce. You know that glare gives you a headache!"

So he remembered that, too, from the past! . . .

I said, without removing my gaze from the distant sea:

"Max, why do people disappear?"

"We have no proof yet that anyone has! It could be as we've said, that Miss Gallard's fiancé was called away and his assistant may have left, changed jobs. In that case, he had no alternative but to shut up the shop."

"Knowing that Marcia was coming out and without leaving a message of explanation or arranging for someone to meet her when she arrived? Oh no! Max, no!" Then I turned to her. "I'm sorry if we seem to be discussing you as though you weren't here! We just want to find a way to help you."

Her lips curved into a smile.

"I should be grateful to you!"

But was she? Or did she already regret that

wild impulse that had urged her to speak to me in the street this afternoon? I studied her face. Nothing changed my first impression of her. This girl had courage and defiance. I had instinctively liked her but I wasn't certain yet if I trusted her. . . .

In the grass at my elbow I saw a tiny orchid. My hand went out to it and then withdrew. If I picked it, it would die quickly in the humid heat. I left it to its shady hollow.

The loveliness and the peace up there was something I did not want to share with a third person. Max and I, I thought . . . just Max and I. . . . I lifted my head and saw that he was looking across at Marcia.

So swift was my reaction to his intense, absorbed gaze that I could not check it. I had never in my life seen him look at a girl that way. . . . And it struck me like a pain that came from nowhere I could place. A poet had once written about "the soul's pain." Perhaps that was it.

I, too, turned and looked at Marcia. She was unaware of our gaze. She was looking at the crowded city below us and I guessed she was thinking of Eric.

"I wonder," Max's voice broke the strange, poignant silence, "if Miss Gallard would like the Aberdeen Hall Hotel? It's small, but the food is good. . . ."

Before he had even finished speaking, I had leapt to my feet.

"Let's try it." I spoke with such urgency as though my life depended upon it. "We're wasting time up here!"

I brushed my dress. Then, too eager to be gone from this lovely mountain place, I walked in front of the other two to the car.

When I had pulled open the off-side door, Marcia was at my side.

"It isn't true, you know, that Eric had walked out on me!"

"Then," I said as I climbed into the car after her, "have you any idea, the smallest, most seemingly unimportant, why Eric hasn't shown up?"

"But of course I haven't!" she said in astonishment. "If I had, Francie, I'd tell you."

I could say nothing. I did not know her well enough either to believe or disbelieve her.

Max closed our door and went round and settled himself behind the wheel.

When we reached the Aberdeen Hall Hotel, Max went inside to inquire about a room vacancy.

"Does your friend, Max, live in Hong Kong?" Marcia asked.

I explained about his job. She listened, her

eyes on the door of the hotel.

"Is he married?"

She could have waited to find out in a less brash way, I thought.

"No, he isn't!" I told her coldly.

She turned and flashed at me.

"I suppose it's because I'm here alone, in a strange place, that I want to *know* about the people I meet! To establish connection with one or two; know who they are and what they do. You understand, don't you?"

I said of course I did and smiled at her. I was rapidly learning how she could disarm.

Max was coming back. There were no vacancies at the Aberdeen, he told us, but they had suggested we try the Spencer, just one block down. When we drove there we found that hotel also full up.

In the car again, Max said:

"I'll take a bet with you that we'll have the greatest difficulty in finding a moderately priced hotel. Suppose I drop you at the Gloucester, Miss Gallard, and then slip into the office and see if I can find a list of possible hotels?"

I said, careful to sound kind:

"Let Max do that for you. Then I'll get Gerry to pick you up at about a quarter to seven and bring you along to us for dinner."

She had put on sun-glasses so that I could not see her eyes, but her full, deeply curved mouth was smiling for the first time.

"Thank you. That would be lovely! But I seem to be putting everyone to a lot of trouble."

"Your parents wouldn't thank us for leaving you high and dry in a strange country," Max said.

There was a small pause.

"I have no parents," she told him matter-of-factly. "They died when I was very small. I spent my time, until I got a job, living in a sort of boarding school, holidays and all. It wasn't too bad."

I fixed my eyes on a distant advertising banner covered with Chinese characters written in gold. Since I had met Marcia on the plane, I had three times acted on impulse. I had persuaded Gerry to give her a lift to her hotel. I had asked her back to tea and now I was inviting her to dinner. Long ago, when I was eight years old, my grandmother had been impatient with me.

The memory of what she had said, her pale eyes exasperated, came back to me now.

"One of these days, Fran, your impulsiveness will be the death of you...."

V

The car was drawing up outside the Gloucester.

We stopped only long enough to let Marcia get out, and remind her of the time Gerry would fetch her. Then we drove on.

I waited until we were out of the worst of the traffic.

"I know it sounds incredible but, Max, there *was* a dead man in that passage!"

"I know you think so." I heard the undertone of laughter in his voice.

"But you've got to believe—"

"Only my own eyes, Francie, I'm sorry. But you know that newspaper men are sceptics anyway!" He flashed a look at me. "Has it occurred to you that this man might have been hurt—fallen down the stairs or knocked out in a brawl? That he had just passed out? When you'd gone, he probably came to and made off."

"Leaving his clothes on the floor?" I asked sarcastically. "Even in Hong Kong, a man wouldn't be allowed to walk the streets without his trousers!"

Max chuckled.

"They may not have been his! And anyway . . ."

"Max, we have no right to ignore a crime!"

"If there was a crime! Francie, have you ever come face to face with death before?"

"Not until to-day," I said. "It was horrible, and—and it could have been . . . murder!"

"Suppose, then, you really did see a dead man . . ." he laid a light, detaining hand over mine as I prepared to protest that it was no supposition. "All right, he *was* dead! That means someone else found him before I got there. And took him away. How do you know he had not died of a heart attack or a fall? Neither you nor Marcia went in to make certain—"

I saw Max's point. Someone had been there after us. And how could we now prove a murder without a body? Yet there had been violence on the man's face. That was what haunted me, darkening my first brilliant impressions of Hong Kong.

When we reached the house, Max got out of the car and said he was going next door to buy cigarettes. I went on ahead.

There was a man leaning against our wall selling cheap black fans. His beard was shaved like the heads of Buddhist monks and he wore a greyish-blue Chinese gown, high in the neck.

As I paused to unlatch the gate, he turned his head and gave me a strange, long look as though he wanted to memorise my face.

"Missie English? I know London." His voice was soft, his smile nostalgic. "I live long time Bayswater."

I looked at him with interest and he came a step nearer.

"Missie buy fan?" The hand that held the black fan almost touched mine.

"No, thank you." I turned quickly away. But in that brief meeting I had registered that there was something odd about him. Then, as I went through the gate I realised what it was. He wore Chinese clothes, his skin was palest saffron, he addressed me as "Missie." But his features were European.

The stare he had given me still lingered as I went through the garden; the smile, like that of friendly recognition, made me shudder. I must get used to beggars!

Gerry was perched on the veranda rail watching me. I climbed the steps.

"I've been for a run with Max," I said, "and

he has come back with me. That's all right, isn't it?"

"We had open house for him in England, and the same applies here. He was coming to dinner anyway, I told you. Where is he?"

"Buying cigarettes."

Gerry slid to his feet and stretched his arms with a luxurious slowness. "Irene was the only one who didn't welcome him. But then Max never fell for her pseudo-enigmatic black eyes!"

"Gerry," I said, "I've seen Marcia again. Eric Farson didn't turn up at her hotel."

Gerry lifted his eyebrows.

"It seems your beautiful girl-friend either wasn't wanted out here or has walked into trouble! Have you been out together?"

I shook my head.

"Not in the way you mean. We haven't been enjoying ourselves. In fact, it's been a horrible afternoon!"

"For Pete's sake, you haven't given yourself much chance to like the place, have you?"

"It has nothing to do with Hong Kong! Gerry, this afternoon I ... we ... Marcia and I ... saw a dead man."

He said matter-of-factly:

"People get run over in London, Paris or New York. You can't blame Hong Kong if some careless ass walks in front of a 'hong's' car!"

Beyond the edge of my sun-glasses, I saw Max coming up the veranda steps from the blinding sunlight into the cool shade under the leaded roof. Without looking directly at him, I said:

"I'm just telling Gerry about this afternoon."

I began slowly, explaining how I had gone to Queen's Arcade to buy the two celadon lion-dogs.

He interrupted me, grinning:

"I might have known it wouldn't be long before you began to spend money. Women shouldn't be let loose in Hong Kong—they go berserk!"

I drew an impatient breath.

"Gerry, *listen!* That's not important!" I bent my head, keeping my eyes on my shoes, noting vaguely that the lovely newness of the bronze kid was greyed by dust.

Like that, avoiding Gerry's mock-patient face and Max's quiet eyes, I told my brother every detail I could remember about our two visits to the Kam Ho Street shop.

When I had finished, Gerry turned to Max:

"And all you saw when you got there was a heap of men's clothes?"

"Yes."

"You think that's all the girls saw?"

Max walked to the edge of the veranda and stood looking out over the blaze of azaleas.

"I don't know," he said honestly. "I want to think that, yes. And yet Francie isn't the sort of person to imagine things."

"No," I said urgently, "I'm not! Gerry, there *was* a dead man there and Marcia knew it, too! Only when Max suggested we could have made a mistake, she jumped at the idea."

Gerry frowned at nothing in particular.

"We don't know anything about this girl. Do you trust her?"

"She didn't tell me the truth when we first met. She wanted me to think, then, that she was in a panic because her bag had been snatched. She only came out with the truth when she couldn't help herself. She didn't want me to go with her to Kam Ho Street but as I did, and saw what she had seen earlier, she told me the truth. At least, I suppose she did."

"She could still know more than she had admitted about the affair," Gerry said. "Between the time you and I dropped her at the Gloucester and you met her in the street, all kinds of things could have happened!"

"I know," I agreed unhappily. "And yet—"

"Let's have a drink on it." Gerry went to the

corner of the veranda and called Yee Sze.

He came at once, walking silently. Gerry asked for drinks and ice. When the boy had gone back into the house, I said:

"I hope you don't mind, but I've invited her to dinner to-night. It was a kind of impulse. I don't know, now I think about it, that it was altogether wise, but it seemed mean to leave her to eat alone in a huge hotel where she knows no one."

Gerry grinned at me.

"Well, whatever else she may be, at least she's easy on the eye! I haven't dared have glamour around the house while I was living here alone in case Irene set her watchdogs on to me! It'll be nice to have some feminine society for the evening!"

Yee Sze returned with the tray of drinks, and Gerry asked me what I would have. I chose a long cool drink with lime in it. Handing me the glass, Gerry said:

"You know Hong Kong is, as usual, crowded. This girl will never get a room at a small hotel at a moment's notice. Suppose we ask her to stay here? There's plenty of room."

I saw Max turn his head sharply and look at Gerry.

"But we don't know her!" I protested.

"She looks nice enough to me! And she's

damned pretty! You like her, and it'll be company for you while I'm out. Besides, I don't suppose it'll be for long. This man Farson must turn up some time!"

A red light flashed in my mind. Beyond an urge to agree with Gerry that I liked her and it would be fun to have her here, a signal warned me that this girl was dangerous. My commonsense immediately mocked me. *Just because you've seen a dead man, don't start looking for trouble everywhere! How could Marcia Gallard be dangerous? And to whom? Gerry, Max?* . . . I kicked the low scrollwork of the veranda with the tip of my shoe.

"Yes," I said defeated. "Let's ask her. Why not?"

"Anyway," Gerry said, "if this man Farson doesn't turn up in a few days then, like it or not, she'll have to go to the police. Maybe he's a criminal and the police have caught up with him!"

"You don't think it's risky, having her here?"

"Why? She's innocent enough!"

I hoped he was right. I saw Max look at Gerry as though he were about to say something. The sunlight and shadow slanted across his face, sharpening the angles.

"I'll check up with the news editor about

Farson. Maybe he can find out something," he said, abstractedly.

But that was not what he had been going to say. He knew Gerry so well! He knew that, like me, he was impulsive....

"Go and ring Marcia," Gerry said to me.

I went into the living-room and looked up the telephone number of the Gloucester.

When the page had tracked her down, and I spoke to her, her gratitude made me glad that we had asked her. I had a feeling that not so long before I had called, she had been crying. Her voice sounded forcedly bright.

When I had rung off and called to Gerry that she would love to come, I went up to my room, washed and changed into a full skirted dress of apricot silk nylon.

Down below I could hear the men talking and then Yee Sze's voice. I suppose Gerry was telling him that we would be having a guest to stay.

I wandered to the window, fixing a thin necklace of plain gold.

Far away, the sea was like blue glass and the sampans and junks as small as child's toys. The tall new blocks of office and flats stood up stiff as oblongs of white sugar. I felt the humid heat beat about me, draining me of energy so that all I wanted to do was lie down and not to think . . . not to think at all! . . .

Later, when I was ready, I went down and met Gerry in the hall.

"I've told Yee Sze to get a spare room ready. I thought Marcia could have the one on this floor, next to the living-room. Come and I'll show it to you."

He went down the hall and pushed the door open. Yee Sze was setting out towels and soap.

"You want flowers for missie's room, *Taipan?*" his teeth gleamed. "I get blue vase."

"He thinks of everything," Gerry remarked as the boy went to fetch the vase. "You'd better cut some flowers or he'll be hurt."

Because the room was yellow and grey, I asked if I might cut just two or three flame-coloured azaleas.

Gerry said I could take what I liked, but to cut them from the backs of the bushes so that the effect of the garden would not be spoilt.

After I had arranged them, I went back to the living-room. I found Gerry leafing through the telephone directory. Eric Farson's name was there, he told me, lifting the receiver and calling the number. I wandered to the veranda door, listening. There was no answer. Gerry flashed the operator and asked if there had been any change in the number or the address listed for a Mr. Eric Farson, Bookseller of

87

Kam Ho Street. I gathered he was told that there had been none.

I stood between the french doors for a moment watching Max on the veranda. From this angle I could not see his face, but he was very still in his chair. I had noticed in the past that he never fidgeted; he moved with a disciplined energy which was probably the reason why he seldom seemed tired.

Gerry said from behind me:

"I'm off now to fetch Marcia," and went past me down the steps, whistling softly. Gerry loved company and I guessed he was looking forward to having us both in the house after being alone so long. I guessed, too, that it would be a relief to have people around him and know that there would be no scenes and sulks and jealous temperaments.... I was thankful that Irene had left him before she had completely destroyed his happiness.

I went to the table on the veranda and mixed myself a gin and lime, and dropped ice in it. I reached out with my foot and drew a chair forward.

Max watched me.

Something had been nagging at the back of my mind ever since I had arrived back at the house. I looked down into my glass, clinking the ice softly.

"You were very quick getting cigarettes after our drive!" I said to him. "When you came through the door did you see a man leaning up against the wall selling fans?"

"No. As a matter of fact, the street seemed fairly empty," Max said and sat down by my side. "Though there must have been a pedlar round because I remember hearing the sound of singing crickets."

VI

For a while our conversation was of ourselves, touching on memories. But I was curious about his life since we had last met and began to ask him questions. He told me readily enough about some of the places he had seen—Damascus and Petra and Lambaréné. I had been sitting curled up in my chair while he talked, staring ahead of me at the tattered glamour of the housetops beyond the wall.

Max talked so vividly, as though those had been the days when he had really been happiest, that I found myself turning in my chair to watch him. And, in these first really quiet moments we had had together, sitting in Gerry's Chinese garden, I saw Max at last without the blinkers of adolescence.

I understood what it would be like to be married to such a man. He would never be quite possessed. However much he loved a woman, there would be times when he had to get away to places where he could be alone. The woman who loved him would have to be prepared to live for weeks without him. If she tried to be possessive, tried to mould him, she would lose him. . . . Max would never catch the eight-fifteen every morning to an office in the city.

I thought in despair and love.

I would understand! I would be happy knowing that however long he was away, he would always come back to me!

But he did not love me, so my understanding was a wasted thing. . . .

And then another thought came to me, poignantly, too late to be rectified. *Perhaps in the old days, he had even grown a little tired of our hero-worship — Gerry's and mine. . . .*

Desperately I sought to change this trail of associations for something less painful. When there was a lull in the conversation, I reached on the table for a shagreen box, took a cigarette I did not really want and let Max light it for me.

Two small rings of smoke hung on the still air.

"Max, why do we so often not do the obvious?"

He turned to me laughing:

"What's the reason for that question?"

"This afternoon," I said, "at the shop in Kam Ho Street. Why didn't I try the door to see if it was unlocked?"

"I think it better that you didn't!"

"If I had," I persisted, "I would have been able to prove to myself that the first time I went there I saw a man and not just a heap of clothes!"

"Perhaps when Marcia went there before you, she did just that!" Max said.

"But surely she'd have said—"

"It's the things people leave out of their stories, Francie, that often have most importance!"

"You mean she might have gone in and made certain he was dead?" I asked.

"She might even have met her fiancé there—this man, Farson. She might have found him with the dead man and that's why she panicked."

"In that case she wouldn't have let me go back with her to the shop, surely!"

Max gave me a long, thoughtful look.

"You've no idea how many people involved in a crime are impelled to go back! The thing they dread and never wish to see again is like a gigantic magnet."

I played with the pleats of my skirt. Max had infinitely more knowledge of the twists and turns of minds caught up in sudden drama, than I. After all, he was Fleet Street trained; he put facts before illusions. But I still fought on Marcia's side.

"She wouldn't have run out on him if he had been in a terrible spot like that! At a guess, I'd say she was very courageous."

"Farson could have sent her away. Or run for safety himself and left her alone, so that she had to escape too."

"Max," I sat up straight in my chair. "Do you think that's what happened?"

"I don't know. I didn't see a dead man, remember! But, in any odd, unexpected situation, there are any number of possibilities."

I sat staring ahead of me at the burnished light over the distant line of sea. Max rose and stood at the veranda rail, his back to me.

"You think that Marcia could still not have told me the truth?" I asked.

"She could be afraid to," he replied gently. "We are strangers to her, remember!"

I got up out of my chair and went to Max's side, leaning my arms on the rail. I stared at the casuarina tree and at the flaming petals of the azaleas.

Max said without turning his head:

"Gerry tells me you're engaged."

It was odd that we had been sitting talking

so long and neither of us had mentioned it until now. As though it belonged to another part of me, another life that Max would never enter.

"That's a charming ring," he said. "It's an aquamarine, isn't it?"

I said, "Yes." Then: "Did Gerry also tell you about the car crash and Lucien's illness?" I looked up at Max's profile, etched against the gilded sky.

"He did, and I'm sorry, Francie. It was a bad break for both of you!"

"The doctors say Lucien will be fine in a month or two," I told him brightly. "And by that time I'll be home."

My gaze was on Max's hands. They rested quietly on the rail and the golden drink in his glass was steady. He was showing not the slightest emotion at either our nearness or our conversation. Well, he had never done so before, I told myself realistically, so why should he now?

I sought to get away from the subject of Lucien and myself.

"When we went down the alley at the back of Kam Ho Street, a girl came out of a door and I saw the most lovely garden. Do you know who lives there?"

Max thought a moment.

"That'll be Mr. Lam Tat Chee's house. He's one of the rich 'hongs' of Hong Kong, although I think he has more or less retired from business now. He lives in the house with just his granddaughter and his servants among a mint of treasures."

"If that was his granddaughter I saw come through the door," I said, "she looks Eurasian."

"She is. The old man's two sons married English girls, much to his disapproval. Nobody seems to know where the family is—some say they went to America, some say they are still somewhere in China. But this girl, Tiffany Lam, escaped from Peking at the beginning of the trouble. She had a cousin who, I believe, escaped with her. But I think he went down to Bangkok."

I turned my head as I heard the gate clang. Gerry had been quick. He was coming up the path carrying two suitcases. Marcia walked a little in front of him. She had changed her dress and wore palest grey silk. Her skirt flared at the bottom like tulip petals.

"She is very beautiful," Max said from my side.

We had a kind of gala dinner in my honour. We began with shark's fin soup—"best quality" as Yee Sze insisted, which meant that the base of the dish was chicken. We had fried quails with bamboo shoots and Dragons' Tongues, which I discovered was deep-frozen Dover Sole. We finished an hour and much conversation later, with little blue lustre bowls filled with melon seeds and dates. This time I showed Marcia how to crack the seeds.

We had carefully avoided mention of the Kam Ho Street shop although all four of us knew that sooner or later we would have to discuss it.

Grouped in chairs on the veranda we smoked and drank tea. The great moon had risen and the Peak wore a diadem of little lights.

I felt that the subject of the bookshop was now ready to spring into the conversation and I did not want it to. I wanted to hold on to these pleasant, relaxed moments. Creamy moths with fairly veined wings, fluttered round the light over the veranda door and somewhere in the distance I heard the eerie wail of Chinese music.

I broke the silence saying to Gerry:

"Would you like to see the little celadon lion-dogs I bought to-day?"

"Nothing is going to stop you showing them to me, anyway," he said from the shadowy depths of his chair.

As I went through the hall I heard the telephone bell ring. I was nearest to where it was tucked in an alcove below a shelf on which stood a cloisonné stork.

I picked up the receiver almost at once. It could be for Gerry, or it could be Eric calling Marcia. . . .

I looked over my shoulder. Gerry had not come to see who it was and I guessed he left the answering of the telephone to Yee Sze, who had not heard that single ring.

"Hallo?"

"Miss Mannering?"

"Speaking," I answered in surprise.

The voice was a man's and it spoke softly.

"We have never met, Miss Mannering, but I know you. In fact, what I know will no doubt upset you."

"I don't understand. What news have you? Is it about—?" I had been going to say "Lucien?" But the voice interrupted me.

"That's better! It's useless to dissemble, isn't it? And we'd better be careful what we say. Even whispers can sometimes be overheard!"

"What have you to tell me?" I knew suddenly that whatever the man had to say, it was not about Lucien. "Who are you?"

"My name would mean nothing to you!"

The pause was almost theatrically timed. "Miss Mannering, I was at a certain shop this afternoon. A man was killed there."

My fingers tightened round the telephone receiver.

"I don't know what you're talking about. Please—"

"Don't hang up on me," the voice quickened, rasped a little in anger. "If you do, I shall find other, less pleasant ways of contacting you. Women who wear gee-gaws should be careful to keep away from crime! I have a piece of evidence—a pretty but nasty little piece! A fancy gold medallion. Did you wear it on a chain round your neck? Or on that bracelet of yours? *Now* do you know what I'm talking about?"

Instinctively I looked down at the bracelet I wore. The little emperor's head still hung from it.

"You are making a mistake," I said, my voice too loud, "I have not lost a medallion. None of this . . . has anything to do . . . with me . . . and . . ."

"Don't be a silly girl!" The voice softened to a macabre fatherliness. "You don't want to be in more trouble than you are already, now do you? I found this medallion of yours caught up in the coat of a dead man."

I held my breath. Somewhere in the guest room of Gerry's house, Marcia had the bracelet with the little empty ring. . . .

"You're talking to the wrong person," I almost shouted. "But I shan't call the . . . the one you . . . really want. . . ."

"You can't, Miss Mannering, because I don't make mistakes. *You* are the one I want! And I know what you brought with you."

"Brought . . . with . . . me?"

"From England," the voice grew impatient again.

"I came with three suitcases," I said angrily. "And this is ridiculous! I won't listen. . . ."

"Hanging up on me won't do you any good," said that odd, soft voice. "You'd better hear me out!"

"I'll call. . . ."

"You'll call no one! And it's useless to pretend that I'm speaking to the wrong person. You've been watched ever since you arrived here. I know . . ."

"But you've got everything wrong!" I cried. "I'm telling you the truth! I don't know what you're talking about. I'm not the girl. . . ."

"Are you trying to tell me that I should be speaking to the friend you have staying with you? Well don't, Miss Mannering! It's such an obvious ruse! She is not the one we're interested in. . . ."

"If you'll only let me . . ."

"Don't waste time in protests," his voice was sharp-edged again. "You have something, and I want it. I want the green fire you brought to Hong Kong with you. Do you hear me? The green fire. . . ."

"I'm calling my brother," I said, "perhaps you'd like to speak to him." I turned my head in the direction of the veranda. "Gerry!" I called. *Gerry!* But the big living-room absorbed my voice.

"Your brother is in Government service," I heard the man say. "It would be very unwise to involve him! I'm sure he doesn't know, does he?"

"No," I said. "But he will! And so will the police."

"It would be foolish to go to them." The voice was quite untroubled. "The price would be too high—for you, I mean! Someone would get hurt, just as an example of what happens to those who try to cheat! Someone quite near to you—"

"Who *are* you?" My voice was faint. "What is your name?"

I heard him laugh. "That is unimportant! But if you want a tag, you can call me—Sam Kang Pun Ye."

"Well, Mr. Sam Kang Pun Ye," my voice was ragged, "you can threaten as much as you like, but I shall tell my brother. He'll know what to do!" I was trembling so that I could scarcely hold the receiver.

"*I'll* tell you what to do if you want to be allowed to forget this ever happened!" The man's voice had sharpened again. "You will bring the green fire to No. 43 Kam Ho Street at ten o'clock on Wednesday night. That gives you forty-eight hours in which to decide that I am not joking! If you fail me, I warn you, someone near to you will get hurt!"

"You think I can be threatened—?"

"I think you would very unwise to underestimate my intelligence, Miss Mannering," he said. "So, *don't go near the police!*"

The line went dead. I sat with the receiver in my shaking hand. I could not hear a sound from the veranda, nor from the kitchen quarters. I might have been quite alone in a Chinese house with the echo of a threat in my ears. I did not see the silken scrolls on the wall nor the graceful blue cloisonné stork. I was thinking again of a tiny gold ring hanging emptily from Marcia's charm bracelet. . . .

Somehow or other, the man on the telephone had us mixed up—Marcia and me. . . .

I rose from the chair into which I had sunk

and found my legs weak as though I had been a long time ill. I put out my hand as though I were blind, felt my way along the wall and into the living-room. From there, I could see them all on the veranda talking together. The sight of them gave me courage and brought me back to sane reasoning. None of this had anything to do with me. It was terrifying, but it was not my problem. All I had to do was to pass on the man's macabre message to Marcia.

Gerry and Max would, I was certain, advise her to go to the police. But my optimism was short-lived. My heart plummeted. And if they did, someone would get hurt.... One of us— Gerry, Max, myself.... Whatever happened, they must *not* go to the police—not until we could identify the man who called himself Sam Kang Pun Ye.

I managed to walk across the living-room floor.

Gerry turned his head and saw me.

"Put something on the gramophone, Fran. Something light and gay. You'll find an album of French songs there somewhere—"

I took no notice. I went and stood by the veranda rail and said over my shoulder:

"Didn't you hear the telephone bell?"

"No—did you answer it? Who called?"

I leaned back for support against the rail,

my fingers touched the still-warm metal.

"A man," I said, "trying to blackmail me."

No one spoke. I think they thought it was some sort of rather silly joke.

And then I told them as nearly as I could what the man had said.

Gerry reacted at once.

"There's no wasting time! We're going to the police."

"No," I said. "Wait! He wasn't talking for talking's sake. He meant what he said. If we make one step in the direction of the police...." I broke off and turned sharply to Marcia. "That call was meant for you, wasn't it?"

She jerked her head back a little as a flying insect crossed her face. But she did not speak.

"I don't know how he mixed us up, or whether it's deliberate. But you were the one he should have spoken to." I heard the hardness of my voice. "What is it you are supposed to have brought illegally into Hong Kong?"

She stared at me as though I were hypnotising her.

"I am as completely in the dark as you are!"

"*Are* you, Marcia? Don't you know what this thing called 'green fire' is?"

"Of course I don't!" She was holding her hands very tightly clasped in her lap, her eyes met mine in a queer, glazed way as though she were stunned.

"I doubt if we can trace the call," Max said, "but we can try." He rose and went into the living-room.

"By the way," I said, "the man's name is Sam Kang Pun Ye."

Gerry stared at me, got to his feet and said:

"He's having some sort of joke with you, Fran! Those four words are Chinese for 'midnight'!"

So that was why he laughed when he told me! I pushed myself away from the veranda rail and heard, vaguely, Gerry saying that he was damned if he was going to let some unknown crook threaten us. He was going to the police.

I went toward the living-room.

"No, Gerry!" I said, "don't do that! Not just yet. He wasn't joking when he said that if we did, someone—one of us—would get hurt! We can't—we daren't—do anything impulsive!" Then I said, "Marcia!" and waited for her.

She rose from her chair like a stunned but obedient child and joined me. Max was on the telephone.

"We'll go to your room," I said. "I want to talk to you."

She knew, as well as I, that the call from

Sam Kang Pun Ye had been meant for her. She must be very frightened, too. That was why I wanted her to myself. Out there, if we questioned her, she would feel she was facing a kind of tribunal. She and I must talk first, quietly.

I switched on the light in her room and faced her.

"What was that call about?"

"I've told you! I know no more than you. Why should you think I do? Why...why... me?"

"Because," I said, "you were in Eric's shop earlier, weren't you? You went into that passage and...touched the dead man."

"I don't know what you're trying to make me say," her hand went to her throat as though she were finding it difficult to speak. "But I wasn't there when the man was killed. I *wasn't!*"

"Then how did something of yours—a small gold medallion—come to be found on the body?"

"I don't know!" She raised her eyes and met mine with an honesty I could have sworn was real.

I regarded her for a moment or two. She was a stranger and a proved liar. Yet that direct gaze disarmed me. Besides, I knew I could get nothing out of her by anger. She would just clam up.

"Marcia, listen!" my voice softened. "I don't believe you had anything to do with killing a man any more than I did. But that telephone call *was* meant for you. I don't know how that man got us mixed up, but sooner or later they'll find out their mistake, and then it'll be you—"

"You talk about something called 'green fire.' I've told you, I don't know ... I don't *know!* ..."

She sank down into a chair and put her fingers up to her temples as though they throbbed. From the kitchen I could hear the music from Radio Hong Kong.

"I can't think straight any longer!" she said in a voice muffled by the palms of her hands. "I don't know what to say...."

"The truth," I told her steadily, "is the best!"

She stared up at me. She looked white and defeated. I could see from her face that this time I was going to hear the truth.

"I did go to the shop earlier. You know that! But I didn't tell you that the back door was open that time and I saw the man lying there. I didn't know he was dead. I thought ... for one terrible moment ... that it was Eric. I tried to turn him over to see if he had just fainted. I . . . managed to move him. But it wasn't Eric. And — and the man was really dead. My bracelet got caught up in one of the buttons of the man's coat. I panicked and pulled. Then I thought I heard a sound so I turned and ran." She paused. With her eyes closed, she said, "You know the rest."

"And you couldn't have told me all this when you first came here?"

"I didn't know you. I thought you — you might have disbelieved me and handed me over to the police."

"What did you have to be afraid of if you were innocent?"

"I touched the man and I realised later that when I dragged my bracelet free from that button, the medallion must have been torn off. Besides, I'm sure . . . I'm *quite* sure . . . there was someone watching. I heard a sound from the stairs. . . ."

"If someone had really watched," I retorted, "they wouldn't have mistaken me for you! Why did they? Why me. . . ?"

"Or me?" she cried.

"Isn't it obvious? You'd better face it, Marcia! Somehow or other Eric features in all this. And come to that, how do you know it wasn't your fiancé who killed that man? After all, it was his shop. If anyone was there, the odds are it was he."

"Eric would never kill a man!"

"But he *has* disappeared, hasn't he? And that's the act of a guilty man!"

"There's only one thing to do," she said quietly.

"If you mean go to the police . . ."

"No! *I* must keep the appointment with the blackmailer, not you!"

"But what good can that do? You say you don't know what it is he wants, so what's the use of you going any more than I?"

"Because, as you say, they have mixed us up. Whatever else I can do, I must straighten that out!"

"This is something we'll have to talk out with Gerry and Max," I said.

"Oh no, it isn't!" her voice was strong as though she had made her decision and there was no more to be said. "I shall go to the Kam Ho Street shop on Wednesday night and explain."

"Just like that!" I snapped my fingers. "And what will you do about the 'green fire'?"

"I shall tell them I don't know what they're talking about. Even a blackmailer can't make me give up what I haven't got, so he'll have to believe me."

"That shows how little you know about the criminal world you're obviously dealing with!" I said bitterly. "They have a good reason for believing I am the one they want. You aren't going to convince them otherwise."

"But, of course, if I say I know Eric...."

"That would be no argument against my knowing him, too!" I said sceptically. I moved restlessly about the room.

"This threat of theirs was obviously only to terrify me into handing over what they think I have. They'll give me every opportunity because that's what they really want—this thing called 'green fire.' It must be highly valuable! Then, when they've lost all hope that I intend to hand it over to them, they'll act as they've threatened. Someone will get hurt, just to show what could happen to me if I don't hand over—"

"I keep thinking, Francie, that none of this is really happening!" There was genuine distress on her face. "People don't go around killing, threatening the innocent."

"Oh, but they do!" I said. "If you and I had a chance to read the police archives we'd see that crime, like goodness, is everywhere."

Marcia was at the door, she had opened it and was swinging it slowly.

"The man we saw dead—whoever he was—

will be buried immediately. So how could they possibly prove that anyone had anything to do with him?"

"If you really think that, then you're under-estimating crooks' intelligence!" I told her. "Someone who has killed once, can kill again, and your medallion could be twisted round the button of *his* coat! And you may be sure it would be at a time when you had no alibi. . . ." A small shiver checked me. I had been speaking as though I were an onlooker. But I wasn't . . . *I* was the one who was threatened. . . .

"Francie, I'm so sorry, so dreadfully sorry to have involved you!"

I heard Gerry's voice from the hall, calling us.

"What are you two doing?"

"Just talking."

Marcia leaned against the door.

"Francie, would you mind if I went to bed? I know it's early, but I'm so tired."

"Of course, you can go to bed when you like." Secretly I was relieved. The three of us could talk more easily without her.

I glanced round the room.

"Have you everything you want?"

The bed was turned down and the mosquito net in place. There was a thermos of boiled water on the bedside table and the little oval-faced clock on the dressing-chest pointed to the right time. Yee Sze overlooked nothing.

As I turned to go out of the room, Marcia touched my arm.

"I think I'm really going to bed to be alone to think!"

"You'd do better to get some sleep," I said, studying her white, exhausted face. "I don't know whether cats or dogs prowl here," I said, "but I should keep the veranda door closed if I were you. There is a ventilator at the top which is open. That'll give you plenty of air—"

"—And no intruders!"

"Oh, Gerry doesn't seem to worry over-much about locking doors..." I began. Then I stopped. That had been before the telephone call had invaded the easy peace of the house....

I kept my sober thoughts to myself, said "Good night" to Marcia and left her.

I found Max and Gerry still on the veranda, sitting in the luminous, milk-white moonlight. There was a bottle of brandy and glasses on the table between them.

"That call," said Max, "can't be traced."

"But it's obvious who it was meant for," Gerry said. "Where's Marcia?"

"She has gone to bed."

Gerry glowered!

"Why did you let her go? She should be here to answer some questions."

I said:

"Perhaps I can answer them. I've been talking to her."

"Or perhaps the best people to do that," Gerry snapped, "are the police!"

"If you go to them," I protested, "something more terrible may happen. . . ."

"Rubbish!"

"Let Francie speak," Max put in quietly.

"I know," I said, "that the man wasn't talking wildly. If we make one step towards the police, someone . . . will get . . . hurt . . . just to . . . to warn us. . . ."

I sat down in the chair. Max pulled up for me, swung my feet on the rest, put my hands behind my head and peered up at the vibrating stars. Like that, seemingly relaxed but taut right inside myself, I told them about my conversation with Marcia.

"So she went in and touched the man and someone saw her . . ." Gerry began.

"No," I said, "or they wouldn't have made the mistake in thinking that I was the one who had been there. But someone heard her. . . ."

"But why accuse you?"

"That's what puzzles me. Gerry, it can't be just a careless mistake...there must be some real reason why I've been deliberately victimised instead of Marcia."

"I think," Max said quietly, "that we must first establish that the 'green fire' is something of great value that has been smuggled into Hong Kong."

"And either Marcia knows what this stuff 'green fire' is," Gerry said, "and can't—or won't—tell us. Or, quite innocently, she has led you into a criminal set-up. Green fire! Ye gods! But I should be used to the flowery phrase by now after living here for three years!"

"Marcia is determined to go to Kam Ho Street on Wednesday," I said.

"Why?"

I thought Gerry was being deliberately obtuse.

"To explain. To clear me."

"That's something in her favour," he conceded. "But she can't possibly go alone!"

"You really think there's danger—" My voice trailed off. With one dead man and a threat to harm us, I did not need to ask that question. And nobody answered me.

I looked sharply from one to the other of the two men.

"*Does* Marcia know what they're talking about?"

"If I'm any judge of character," Max said, "I think she's as bewildered as the rest of us."

"So do I," Gerry agreed, "but that doesn't stop me wishing I'd never set eyes on her at the ferry!"

"Eric Farson is the man to find—" I said. "We must trace him—"

For a moment no one spoke. Then Max gave me a searching look.

"I think we'll leave talking for to-night. Fran looks pretty tired! To-morrow we might get a different perspective—"

A moth came to rest on the table. It was palest green and nearly transparent. I watched it rise again and flutter away on hesitant, uncertain wings as though it did not know where it was going.

Max was saying good night to us. He was standing quite close to me and I reached up and touched his hand. He must have been faintly surprised because in the old days we had never shaken hands on parting; we had come and gone easily, with a family casualness. But Max held my fingers for a moment.

"We'll sort this out, somehow, Fran. And I'll contact you to-morrow." He turned to Gerry. "Maybe, in the meantime, I can

114

find out something about Farson."

"You wouldn't like to take Marcia Gallard back to the Gloucester, would you?" Gerry called after him, "and out of our hair?"

Max paused on the steps.

"I'll find her a hotel if you'd rather she left."

I looked from one to the other. How could we send her away now that she was securely here, with her things unpacked? I was convinced that she knew no more than I did about this thing with the fancy name; "green fire" meant nothing more to her than it did to me.

"No, let her stay! It'ud be pretty mean to punish the innocent! If we can't get to the bottom of this between us, then it's a good thing we're not in the police force!"

Max still hesitated.

"I don't think Marcia will do any good by going to Kam Ho Street. She will try to prove that she is Farson's girl; that she touched the dead man. But without Farson himself to corroborate what she says, her story could be suspect. . . ."

"Thought up by us to confuse the issue," Gerry said, "and so serving no purpose. All right, then, she mustn't go. We'll just wait for the next move."

"And perhaps there won't be one. Perhaps

nothing will happen!" I heard the false brightness of my voice.

"There'll be one, I'm afraid!" Max said, "but we'll cope with it when it happens. In the meantime we do nothing."

I watched him go, longing for him to stay.... Later, in my room, I stood for a few minutes in the darkness and looked out of the window.

The sea lay invisible; the sky was a vivid living thing of indigo blue with quivering stars and a riding moon. The waterfront lights glared mint-green and candy-pink down where the coolies, the sailors and the street-women walked.

Later, I lay for some time listening to the playing of thin Chinese music. I pictured Marcia in the room downstairs, wondering if she were asleep. Or was she lying awake on her first Chinese night?

Green fire. I puzzled over it, fascination mingling with fear. Green fire.... How the Chinese loved the elegant phrase! Dragons and phoenix... "Midnight" which meant "three beat half night"!... "Sun, Moon and Star Street".... "Land of Jumping Dragons"....

It occurred to me that had it been an Englishman who had telephoned me, he would have used the practical down-to-earth name for the precious thing I was supposed to have brought with me.

I did not think I would sleep. For the first time in my life, I had come face to face with menace. I closed my eyes and tried to tell myself that I was in no danger. I was not really involved. . . . If you were innocent, you had nothing to fear. But one man, the most dangerous of all, did not believe I was innocent. . . .

Gradually my thinking became muddled; my body felt heavy. I turned on my side, and, while the night outside was still filled with sound, I fell into a dreamless sleep.

VII

I had arranged to have Marcia's breakfast sent to her in bed.

Gerry had never been communicative first thing in the morning. He always used to say it was probably a hangover from some dream he couldn't remember. But I wanted to talk to him before he left for the office and I did not want Marcia there.

"If you get a chance, will you make some inquiries about Eric Farson?" I asked.

"Max had already rung me," he said. "He made inquiries last night. The shop is still in Farson's name; his rent is paid up. Someone in the newspaper offices bought a book there only two days ago."

"So he vanished quite suddenly," I said. "In fact almost at the time Marcia arrived in Hong Kong."

"It looks like it," he took his second coffee-cup from me. "You know, Fran, these things take on a different aspect in the morning! *Of course,* we just leave it. Let the man make another move. Who the devil are we to act tamely on a blackmailer's order when we have no idea what it's all about?"

"You seem to forget that Max talked about such threats as never being made idly!"

"We only have two ways open to us," he said. "Either we go to the police: or we ignore the threat and wait to see what will happen next."

"I think you'll find that Marcia will make alternatives unnecessary," I said drily. "She's determined to go to Kam Ho Street."

"Then Max and I will have to talk some sense into her to-night, won't we, Fran?" Gerry said pleasantly.

Just before he was ready to leave for Government House however, he said:

"It's probably a mad idea, but I suppose no one could have smuggled something into one of your suitcases or Marcia's on the way here without either of you knowing? You lost sight of them, remember, from Peninsular Hotel to the island."

"With someone else to collect it out here?"

"But it would be risky and you'd discover it for yourself when you unpacked! And so would she. Anyway, the whole thing's crazy.

They would run the risk of perhaps having no possibility of collecting it."

"Nobody smuggled anything into my suitcases, I'm certain of that!" I said, "but suppose they managed it with Marcia's. Suppose they had planned to break into her room at the Gloucester and collect it? Only she left there too soon and then somehow or other they got us muddled up. But the next thing that puzzles me . . . and scares me . . . is *why* have they mixed us up, Marcia and me?"

"I've a feeling that as soon as we find Farson, we'll know. He's the key and directly I get my hands on him, I'm handing him over to the police to sort the rest out. The blackmailer won't dare put his threats into use after that!"

When Gerry had gone, in spite of the craziness of the idea, I searched my suitcases, among the odd pair of shoes, the face tissues and odds and ends I had left there. Of course I found nothing. Then I went to Marcia's room.

She was lying in bed wearing a silky pink nylon nightdress with a swathed bodice. Her hair was spread over the pillow and she looked very young, very beautiful. But the violet shadows were still under her eyes. She gave me a half-smile. "It's a lovely morning," I said and went to the french windows.

"I've never slept under a mosquito net before," she announced.

"Nor have I. It's not exactly airy, is it?"

She stretched her arms. She looked so luxurious, so without a care that last night might never have happened.

"It's wonderful having all this comfort after living in a London bed-sitter on your own! You know the sort of place—or do you?"

"I do," I said. "I tried it for a time when I took a job and wanted to be independent. It was a slit of a room with a wash-basin in one corner and a cooker in the other." I joined in her laughter with an effort. "By the way, have you completely unpacked?"

My question surprised her. I think she was afraid I was going to tell her we had changed our minds about her staying.

I told her of my conversation with Gerry over breakfast.

"He thinks his idea crazy. It probably is, but I've looked in my suitcases. Suppose you look in yours?"

She flung back the bedclothes and swung her legs to the floor, feeling for her slippers. Her dressing-gown was of navy silk, tailored and with a fringed sash. She padded to the cupboard and dragged her cases out.

"They haven't got linings, you see," she said and opened them for my inspection. They were empty.

I caught sight of the parcel on the shelf.

"We could have a look at those books, too, while we're about it."

"All right!"

She undid the string, unwrapped the brown paper.

The two books were folded separately in corrugated cardboard. We took them out. One book was a copy of *Jane Eyre* and was heavily bound. The other book was a centenary edition of Goethe's *Faust*. It was bound in vellum. I flicked through the pages of both books. Nothing was cut out to hide some small, smuggled treasure.

"Well, Gerry said his idea was crazy!"

I watched her reparcel the books and put them back on the shelf.

"Go back to bed and laze a bit," I urged her. "It's quite early." I laid two magazines I had found in the living-room by her side. "Sorry you've been troubled!" I said on a laugh and went out and left her.

Gerry had said over breakfast that I was not to go wandering around alone. If I wanted to go out while he was away, I was to go with Marcia or take Yee Sze.

I had not come all this way to be a prisoner and I intended to go out, although I would stay near the crowds. No one could harm me in broad daylight, and if I was supposed to have something of great value, I would not be harmed, anyway.

I wanted to have my hair shampooed—there had not been time before I left England. In the address book lying by the telephone, I found the name of a hairdresser, Rosie Chan. I supposed Irene must have been a client of hers and, if that were so, she would be one of the best hairdressers in Hong Kong. I rang up and made an appointment for eleven o'clock. Then I went back to the veranda taking a Hong Kong newspaper with me.

The morning was soft and humid and as yet not too hot.

I sat there reading the news, aware of the alien street noises from the other side of the wall. The events of last night had faded behind a sense of well-being. I told myself that some gigantic mistake had been made and was now put right. But how it was a mistake and how it had been put right I had no idea. My whole attitude this morning was one of wishful thinking, of unrealistic, ostrich-like rejection of unpleasantness. It was a lovely morning and I wanted to enjoy it, relaxed and at ease.

For about ten minutes I had the garden to myself. Then I heard the gate open and turning, saw Harriet Craig come down the path.

I had no right to resent her. She was doing work for Gerry and, at her place down the garden by the peach tree, she did not obtrude.

At the back of the house, near the kitchen, was a small garden shed. I watched her go to it and fetch her easel and paints; I saw her go into the kitchen for water.

I was ready, on her return, with a casual good morning and a friendly word about the weather or the flowers or something that would show I was not being standoffish. But when I glanced up, I saw that she was standing quite still staring up at the glass doors of the guest room. For a moment I wondered if she were listening to something Marcia was saying to her. Then, without a word, she continued on her way to her easel and stool.

"Good morning, Miss Craig," I called.

Her reply was faint; she scarcely looked up from the business of settling herself with her paraphernalia of paints and rags and brushes.

Marcia came out some while later. I saw that, like me, she wore blue but hers was a deeper shade. She sat down and crossed her ankles and looked at me.

"I won't ask you if you slept well," I said.

"Few people do in strange beds. But you look more rested."

The corners of her mouth lifted wryly.

"Most of the time I seemed to be having a nightmare. I must be the world's greatest long-distance runner! I was being chased by a plane that never quite caught me up!"

"I have to have my hair done this morning," I told her. "Will you stay here, or do you want to go out?"

"There may be a message for me at the Gloucester," she said. "I must go and see."

"Then we can go most of the way together. I've looked up the hairdresser's street on a map and it's near the Gloucester. You can wait for me at the hotel—have some coffee; read the newspapers. I'll fetch you and we'll shop-gaze together."

"Yes," she promised. "I'll do that."

We walked along the crowded streets. Only once, trying to take a short cut through narrower streets did I lose my sense of direction. Immediately I stopped at a laichee stall to ask my way, a little group crowded round us, all with slanting, kindly, interested eyes. A tiny Chinese girl with a solemn face reached up as we turned to retrace our steps and pulled at my skirt. Her mother undid the tight little honey-tinted hand and smiled at me and bowed.

"They have beautiful manners," Marcia said.

When we reached the Gloucester, I left Marcia in the lobby and went down a side street to find Rosie Chan's. Her salon was just off Pedder Street and the pretty assistant who settled me in my chair, told me she was Violet, Rosie's daughter.

When I was comfortable, I was offered a cigarette. My hair was washed with a sweet-smelling pink shampoo and very little water. This was the scarcest commodity in abundant Hong Kong.

I was watching with interest, through the big mirror, the Chinese clients around me fastidiously directing the assistants. Bouffant, sleek or windswept. They were also having manicures and pedicures and they were being far more fussy than socialites in a West End salon in London.

Suddenly I realised that someone was being seated in the bay next to mine. I caught her casual glance in the mirror and immediately recognised her. It was the Eurasian girl I had seen come through the door in the wall at the back of the Kam Ho Street shop.

I doubted if she thought she had ever seen me in her life before. But presently, when an assistant dropped a comb and it fell between the chairs, our eyes met and we smiled.

The Chinese are friendly people and, in spite of all the stories about their inscrutability, they love to talk.

She asked me, while the assistant brushed her long, luxuriant hair, if I had been in Hong Kong long and if I liked it out here. I said I had just arrived. I watched, fascinated, the blue-black sheen of her hair as it rippled through the assistant's hands.

"You live on the Peak?" she asked.

"No. My brother has rented a house in the town. In Tai-yuan Street."

"Ah, that must be Lai Kok's house," she nodded. "I know! He went to Kowloon. And your brother is Mr. Mannering. I have met him."

"I'd forgotten," I laughed. "This is a tight little island where everyone knows everything!"

"My grandfather knows Mr. Mannering better than I. He has lived here all his life, you see. I only came here recently from Peking." She spoke very precisely as though, I thought, she were unused to speaking English.

"Did you come here because of the Revolution?"

She nodded.

"You can call me a refugee. My Second and Third Uncles, and First Sister are still in Red China."

From the formal way she spoke of them, I guessed they were pure Chinese. Perhaps her Aunts, Second and Third and Fourth, still had tiny bound feet. I looked at her with interest. I wondered how they approved of a niece with partly Western blood in her veins...

"You are out here on a holiday?" she eyed me with interest.

I nodded.

"For two months."

We were served with jasmine tea in little painted cups.

As we sipped it, I found myself answering her questions about England. I even mentioned Max's name.

She glanced at me with interest.

"But my grandfather knows him too! He has been to our house more than once to see my grandfather's collection of old Chinese scrolls and jade." She turned to me quickly, her raven's wing of hair sliding out of the assistant's fingers. "Perhaps you would come to tea one day. My grandfather likes to talk to people from the West. He has a very cosmopolitan mind."

I knew that, although the Chinese were

hospitable, they seldom entertained strangers in their homes and I was touched by the invitation. I accepted quickly, in case she should change her mind.

Her name, she told me, was Tiffany Lam and her grandfather was Mr. Lam Tat Chee.

I gave her my telephone number and she said she would ring me.

When my hair was dry I glanced with pleasure at the result.

"You have lovely hair," said Tiffany Lam. "It is so fair like—like yellow silver."

It was a curious description. I accepted the compliment with a smile, bade my charming companion good-bye and walked into the hot streets.

It was not far to the Gloucester.

When I entered the lobby, I could not see Marcia. I wandered through the public rooms and she was nowhere to be found.

Puzzled, I asked the desk clerk if he had seen a young woman in a blue dress.

"She checked in here yesterday from London," I explained, "but left to stay with us."

The clerk shook his head. Too many people came and went for him to notice one solitary girl. Besides, to-day there was a conference of newspaper correspondents in one of the meeting rooms and this crowded the lobbies.

He turned, brisk and efficient, to deal with the man behind me.

I went outside and spoke to the commissionaire.

To my delight, he remembered Marcia. She came out of the hotel some while ago, he told me.

"Alone?" I asked.

"No. There was a man with her."

My heart sank. I felt anger and anxiety. I asked if they had taken a taxi. He said: No, they walked off together.

"Did you happen to notice which way they went? I'm sorry to be asking you so many questions, but this young girl is in my charge." I met his black eyes without flinching at my lie.

All he could tell me was that they had turned left.

I thanked him and began to walk away. At the curb I stopped dead. I frowned at the mass of cars and taxis and rickshaws.

This girl had repaid the help I was trying to give her by walking out without leaving a message for me! She was just a little tramp, after all!

Then, quite suddenly, reason broke through my anger. I faced the fact that Marcia might not have left the hotel by her own wish. Someone could have found her there and forced her to go with them. Someone! Eric? Or the blackmailer who had, despite his mockery at what he had called "a ruse," discovered his mistake in identities?

The commissionaire was by my side. Did I want a taxi? I shook my head. He said:

"I think the gentleman with your friend was an Englishman."

And that was no help, either! Eric was English; the voice on the telephone was English, for all he had used the picturesque Chinese phrase, "green fire." I thanked the commissionaire and began to walk slowly away.

In all Hong Kong, where could someone be taking Marcia? I recalled that the blackmailer had ordered me to meet him at the Kam Ho shop to-morrow night. Suppose, wise now about identities and finding her alone, he had forced her to go there with him, too impatient to wait until to-morrow? Suppose she had gone, with all the bravado in the world, imagining that ignorance made her safe? . . .

With no plan of my own, no idea how I could deal with whatever situation came my way, I found myself in Des Voeux Street and quite lost. A policeman — a bearded, blue-turbanned Sikh — directed me.

The sun was now hot and my dress stuck to me. I began my walk, wiping the palms of my hands against my skirt, feeling my newly-set hair clinging damply to my head. When I reached Kam Ho Street I walked on the far side of the road to the book-shop. Then, opposite No. 43 I stopped and looked across, up at the windows. A coolie carrier jostled me; two sailors gave me long glances as they passed. I must have looked haughty for they did not try to speak to me.

I stayed some minutes, watching the windows opposite. Then my heart gave a small, triumphant leap. Someone moved across the window and I saw a patch of blue. Marcia was wearing just that shade. . . .

In my dash across the road, I saw that the door of the shop was still padlocked. I ran down the street to the corner, turned towards the alley and was jerked to a halt by a man standing in my path.

"Miss Mannering?"

I checked my first instinct to turn and run, and looked him squarely in the face. I knew it ᴨs important to memorise his features, his

My heart thudded against my ribs; I

put up a hand and pushed my hair off my forehead.

"Yes?" I managed to say to the waiting man.

"You know Marcia Gallard, don't you?" His eyes were darting about him as he spoke, his expression tight and alert.

"If you want Marcia—" I began.

"Please give her this for me." He thrust a slip of paper at me.

"Wait a minute!" My voice was too loud. "Was it you who rang me last night?"

"No!" his eyes suddenly blazed with fear or anger, I did not know which.

"I don't believe you! *You* rang me and threatened..."

"You are quite wrong, Miss Mannering," he said.

"Then who are you and why ask me to do your errands for you?" I pretended anger to hide my fear.

"I can't stop to explain. But it's terribly important—" he broke off, jerking his head over his shoulder like a marionette pulled by a string.

"Here, take your note back," I cried. "If you want to contact Marcia, leave a message at the Gloucester Hotel and I'll see she gets it..." My voice trailed off. I was talking to the air.

The man disappeared as completely as

though he had used magic. I stared about me, peering round people, pivoting so quickly that I stumbled against two elderly gowned Chinese. I apoligised and, aware that the man could not be far away, shot into the nearest shop, pulling the curtain aside. A startled Chinese face peered at me over mounds of peanut oil, bean curd and ginger. But the man who had spoken to me was not there.

Somewhere not so far away I heard the pedlar pass by again with his singing crickets. . . .

The whole incident had been so swift, so startling that, save for the piece of paper still in my hand, I might have believed it had not happened. I remained for some moments standing on the pavement.

I was quite certain that the man had spoken the truth when he said he had not telephoned me the previous night. My news shocked him. But he, too, had known my name. . . .

Had he been Oriental or Western? He had worn a grey-blue gown, his head was shaven and his skin olive. But his voice was cultured English and his features aquiline. I knew I had seen him before.

He was the man who had leant up against " wall last night and asked me to buy a black fan. . . .

But who was he? Eric Farson? Or the black-mailer?

I glanced at the piece of paper in my hands. On it was written:

The house of Lily Yun.
Shek Ku Bay.
This afternoon.

I put the paper in my handbag and made my way down the alley towards No. 43. I was so shaken that my knees trembled at every step. From my very first day in Hong Kong, I was being watched. My name, my address was known to two people whom I did not know. I was suspected; threatened.... Like the charms on Marcia's bracelet, I was linked in all innocence, with violent death and disappearance ... and the "green fire." ...

The door of No. 43 was open. There were no clothes strewn over the passage.

I gave a swift glance behind me. No one was in sight. I stepped into that dark, narrow passage. Halfway along it, I stopped cautiously and called out:

"Is anyone up there?"

There was a moment's silence. I waited, aware that the door was just behind me and my escape easy. I had even half-turned toward it when I heard footsteps above me on the bare boards. I looked up, peering into the dimness, uncertain as to what or whom I should see.

"Hallo, Francie," said Max's voice. "What are you doing here?"

Relief released a small spurt of impotent anger.

"Have you permission to walk into private premises? And where's Marcia?"

"I can't toss my answers down the stairs!" Max called lightly. "Come along up."

He stood watching me but I refused to meet his eyes. I was only aware, once more, of how still and quiet he could be.

He drew back as I reached the landing.

"I went to the Gloucester to fetch Marcia," I said. "She was supposed to be waiting for me there! But she's here, isn't she?" I pushed past him and entered the room over the shop.

Marcia was standing by a pile of books. She wheeled round as she heard me enter, hands behind her back. There was a strange look on her face, a kind of suffused excitement. I heard the soft thud of a book as she let it drop from her hidden hands.

"Oh, Francie," she said. "I didn't expect to vou here!"

quite certain you didn't!" I hoped I

sounded as angry as I felt. "You were sup-posed to be waiting for me at the hotel. Yet you walked out without even leaving a mes-sage—"

"I'm sorry!" she said with an almost naïve contriteness. "I was sure I'd be back at the hotel before you came for me. You were very quick!"

"I was!"

"Francie, I *had* to come!" she gave me a small uncertain smile.

"I saw Marcia in the lobby of the Glou-cester," Max explained. "We had an idea that if we came here and looked through Farson's things we might get some clue. We thought we might find letters or a diary. Something, anyway, to clarify the situation. The door, by the way, was unlocked."

I walked across Eric's living-room which smelt of dust, faintly mouldy books and oranges.

"Well?" I said looking round, "it's not exact-ly comfortable, is it?"

The chairs and table were cheap bamboo; the slats of the venetian blinds were dusty. Books were piled everywhere. On the wall, enclosed in glass to preserve it, was a beautiful and ancient silk-embroidered panel. A teapot in its padded wicker basket stood on the table and on a small porcelain dish, half an orange lay rotting. Someone had, at some time recently, burned joss sticks in that room.

"We've searched his papers and found nothing but old bills, orders and a sales ledger," Max explained. "Everything personal seems to have been destroyed. Or maybe he didn't have a private life?" He glanced at Marcia.

Little spots of colour stood out on her cheeks. She was either very excited or dreadfully upset. I wandered casually across the room to the untidy pile of books on the floor by which she had been standing when I came in. I looked down at them. But it was impossible to tell which one she dropped so secretively as I entered. I thought: if she's found a clue, she won't leave it lying here. She'll bring it with her when we leave and she'll tell me. . . .

Max was tossing some papers back on a chipped and worn desk.

"Not a hint of anything! Not a clue anywhere! Yet the man must have had *some* private correspondence! *Some* friends!" His head shot up and his eyes were like chips of steel. He was looking at Marcia: "*Your* letters, for ˉtance!"

ˋ was standing with her hands pressed

down on the top of the fragile bamboo table, looking at him.

Then she said through lips that scarcely seemed to move:

"I have no idea what Eric did with my letters."

Max looked about him with a faint disgust at the dirt and disorder.

"There's nothing here. Nor in the bedroom. And I'll make a bet that if I turn the shop upside down, I'll find nothing there, either! Your fiancé, Miss Gallard, planned to disappear. You realise that, don't you? He wasn't dragged away by his hair, kidnapped, shanghaied or anything else!" His voice was hard. "And he made a very thorough job of leaving no clue as to his activities... save for the obvious one of his shop... lying around. I gather we all agree, now, that he must have had other activities? Smuggling, for instance!"

"How do you know that?" Marcia began indignantly. "How can you pass judgment...?"

Max's dark eyebrows shot up.

"With a dead man on his premises? Failure to contact you? A telephone threat? It adds up to something pretty peculiar!"

Marcia's lids dropped over her eyes, her long lashes lay softly on her cheek.

"If you're right, I—I don't know what to

do...what to say. Oh, Max!" The eyes opened, turning full and darkly blue upon him.

"It's a pity," Max continued in a voice that was both gentle and ruthless, "that you won't search your memory, Marcia. Because, whether you know it or not, I believe you have a clue to all this!"

She did not take her eyes from his face.

"Do you think I haven't puzzled it all out for myself?" she demanded. "Tried to think and think—"

"Have you?" The tone was softer. "Yes, I suppose you must have. I'm sorry if I sounded as though I were attacking you!" Max was looking at her with that strange intense gaze I had noticed once before on the Peak. And again I was afraid of it.

I said, a little too loudly:

"We'd better get out of here. We happen to be trespassing!"

"With a purpose!" Max said.

A retort flashed in my mind. It was unjust, I knew, but before I could help myself, I had spoken the words aloud.

"This could be a wonderful scoop for your newspaper, Max!"

He did not flicker an eyelid. Quietly, without anger, he said:

"Pompous as it may seem, I'm doing this for a principle. I hate fakes and frauds!"

It was so completely the last word of the argument that there was only one thing to do. I took Marcia's arm.

"We're going home," I said as firmly as though I were talking to a child. "You can stay if you like, Max."

I felt, as we went down the stairs and out into the narrow slit of an alley, that she resented being dragged away.

At the same time, I knew that I had been guilty of the kind of dictatorial behavior I so resented in others. In moments of stress, I thought, we never quite knew how we would react. Stress? Just because Max had looked at Marcia in a way I had always wanted him to look at me? I, who at school and among my friends, had always been the quiet one, the gentle one. . . .

We were nearing the street when Marcia spoke. Her voice was ragged and distressed.

"I can't believe that Eric lived there! He loved beautiful things so much!"

"Perhaps that is just his business place and he doesn't bother about it. Did he ever actually tell you that he lived over his shop?"

"Yes," she said.

As we turned the corner, I asked:

"Why did you let Max take you there?"

"He's told you. I saw him in the hall at the Gloucester and I asked him to come with me. I thought we might find some clue as to Eric's friends—a record of someone who might perhaps know where he is—"

"You're afraid he might not be alive, aren't you?"

I felt the impact of my question as we paused to cross the street. She was holding herself quite rigid, her face turned away from me.

"Why—why should I be?"

"Because I told you, it was made quite plain to me over the telephone that someone else might come to harm. Just as an example of what could happen if I didn't hand over the thing with the fancy Chinese name; the 'green fire'."

"Eric must be alive! Francie, he *must!*"

"He is!"

I thought I spoke quietly, but the two words seemed to beat about us in the moment's silence. Then Marcia turned slowly and looked at me, not quite believing that my words were anything but an unsubstantiated statement.

The street was clear, momentarily, of traffic. But we had made no move to cross.

"I wanted to tell you when we were alone,"

142

I said. "But I believe I have spoken to Eric."
I heard her sharp intake of breath as I took
the slip of paper out of my handbag. "A man
stopped me just now and gave me this. For
you."

She took the paper from me as though she
were in a dream. Her hair fell forward in a
bright cloud shadowing her face as she bent
her head to read what was written.

"Is that Eric's writing?" I asked.

She looked up. Her face was very white so
that her lips looked over-reddened.

"Yes. Yes, but Francie, where did you see
him? What did he say?"

"He asked if I were Miss Mannering. Then
he gave me this note to give to you. He
kept looking over his shoulder as he talked
to me."

"He was—scared?"

"He was very, very scared!"

"But what else did he say," she demanded
impatiently. "Something about me—?"

"No. He answered my question as to whether he had telephoned me last night. He said
he hadn't. Then he just thrust the note at me,
told me to give it to you and vanished."

"I don't understand!"

"Nor do I," I said briefly.

"If Eric knows you, then he knows where

I'm living and he could have come to see me at your house."

"Yes."

"Then why didn't he?" she cried. "Francie, why does he come to *you* with a message for me?"

I did not answer because suddenly something became clear to me. He had known someone was watching him, someone who had never heard the name of the girl who was flying from England with the "green fire." He had spoken to me deliberately to point me out. . . . "This is the girl!" . . .

But why? Why involve me?

"Is it far to this place?" Marcia asked, gazing down at the slip of paper. "Shek Ku Bay?"

"I don't know. We'll ask Gerry."

"I'll have to go, of course!"

A man thrust a book with a lurid jacket at me.

"Missie buy book. Velly naughty!"

I elbowed the grubby hand away and we walked on.

As we turned into Tai-yuan Street, I said:

"You'd better be prepared to find Eric wearing Chinese clothes and with his head shaved."

She stared at me, checking her footsteps.

"Oh no! That wouldn't be Eric! It must have been someone he sent. . . ."

"Or it might be his idea of a very complete disguise. A shaved head makes an extraordinary difference to a man."

"You think he's hiding from the law, don't you?"

I shrugged my shoulders.

"Or from someone who hates him and who wants to harm him?" she persisted.

"Whichever way it is, it seems he's in trouble, doesn't it?" I said.

I paused at our gate, pushed it open and let Marcia go through.

Gerry was sitting on the veranda with a drink. He raised a hand in a half salute and as we came up the steps, he rose.

"I can't believe it!" his eyes danced; "no parcels!"

"No parcels!" I agreed. "I haven't stopped to look in a single shop! Marcia, tell Gerry what's happened. I'm going to mix us both something long and cool. We need it."

As I dropped ice into the glasses, I remembered that I had not asked her whether she had found something in the room above Eric's shop that she did not want to tell Max about. That queer excited look I had seen still puzzled me.

When I took the drinks out to the veranda, my brother said:

"I hear Max has wasted no time!"

"Nor has Eric," I said. "Has Marcia told you?"

"Yes. And shown me the note."

I gave Marcia her drink and sat on the veranda steps, wanting a few minutes of hot sun.

"What do you think, Gerry? Should Marcia go to Shek Ku Bay?"

"Not alone," he said. "And not with you! Unfortunately I've got to work this afternoon..."

"But I'll be quite all right," she protested. "I can get a taxi or a bus, or something. And, Gerry, it's obvious, isn't it, that I must see him? Whatever this is all about, I've got to clear Francie...."

I saw her glance move from my eyes to the scar that the sun must be high-lighting. I turned my head a little to hide it. Lucien seemed part of another world.

Gerry rose and went into the house, making no comment. A few moments later, I heard him talking on the telephone.

I sat holding my glass with the pale lime drink up to the light. It sparkled and danced behind the cut crystal. I remembered these glasses so well! They had been my wedding present to my brother and Irene....

Gerry came back saying:

"I've called Max and told him what has happened. He'll come with you, Marcia, to Shek Ku Bay. He says there's a temple there he wants to see."

"That'll be interesting!" I said evenly. "I've always wanted to see a temple."

Gerry turned to me.

"You're not going, Fran!"

I met his sharp gaze steadily.

"Try to stop me!" My voice was light. "I came out here to sight-see, remember!"

"But Fran—"

"Look," I said. "It's Eric who will be there to see Marcia, not the blackmailer to see me!"

Marcia herself said nothing. She was studying her pink nails.

I broke the silence, saying conversationally:

"Max seems to be able to take time off whenever he likes!"

"His job is all high pressure or nothing," Gerry said. "And you know Max! He has always been able to pack twice as much work into a day as anyone else."

It was true, of course. He had learned the art of the conservation of energy. But then he had no emotional problems to sap it; none of the tensions and strains of love. Had he been born with an instinctive guard against it? Or had there been women, kept well in the background; women carefully chosen for their non-possessiveness, their desire, like his, to love and pass on? . . . I did not know. What I *did* know was that if he were like that, it made no difference to my love for him.

I came out of my semi-dream to find that Marcia was not with us and that I was finding the sun too hot. I went to a chair in the shade.

Gerry was lighting a cigarette.

"The wisest thing for Marcia to do would be to go back to England," I said.

"She would probably be followed there."

I slid my feet out of my shoes and kicked them lightly off the chair rest. I said, flexing my toes:

"Why in the world should anyone want to do that?"

"Because of what she would be suspected of still possessing."

"She could have handed it over to Eric before she left."

"They—whoever 'they' are—aren't such fools as not to be watching to see if she makes any contacts, Fran!"

But they weren't! They were watching *me*. Who watched? A coolie passing by on the other side? An English tourist sauntering near me, window-gazing? A Chinese "hong" in a big American car? A pedlar selling tiny, monotonously singing crickets?...

I stirred uneasily. And quite suddenly, another little piece of the puzzle slid into place. I knew *why* I had been implicated.

"Gerry!"

He looked up, questioningly:

"I think I know why I was threatened."

He waited, his eyes very blue in his bronzed face.

I leaned forward and spread my hands. When I was intense about something, I talked partly with my hands, like the French.

"Only Eric knew the identity of the girl who was bringing something valuable out from England. I believe he was somewhere around at the airport when we arrived. He saw Marcia go off with us and he trailed us. Following her to this house and seeing me, gave him an idea."

"To implicate you? And throw suspicion away from Marcia until he could safely contact her?"

"Of course. The blackmailer must be waiting to see if Eric makes a contact with a girl before Wednesday."

"So Farson stopped you very publicly in the street today to give you that note to indicate to whomever watched that you were the girl!"

I nodded.

"Yesterday, too, when I came back here with Max, that same man was leaning up against your wall. He tried to sell me a black fan. . . ."

"Hong Kong is a grossly overcrowded island. Refugees are as thick as bees in a hive. How the devil are we going to find the man who threatened you?"

"At Kam Ho Street on Wednesday night."

"Empty handed?" Gerry demanded. "Without the thing with the fancy name? Oh no, no one's going!"

"Gerry," I said, "if Marcia hasn't got the 'green fire,' then who has?"

"I'm not so stuck on beautiful girls," Gerry said, "that I would besottedly believe one innocent if I thought her guilty! But I'm certain Marcia knows no more than we do. She's puzzled and scared and muddled. . . ."

"There's another point," I said. "As the blackmailer obviously knows Eric, disguise or no disguise, then he must have dressed up like that so that Marcia shouldn't recognise him. After all, she wouldn't look closely at a man in a long blue gown, a darkened skin and a shaved head, if by any mischance she caught sight of him in a crowd. He didn't want her to make any contact with him while someone watched. That's why she is to meet him at Shek Ku Bay. Maybe," I said, "this meeting will clear everything up."

"I wish I could think so!" Gerry said and his expression was troubled.

"By the way, Max is still keen on a hint to the police. I don't much care for the idea."

"Why not?"

Gerry gave me an uneasy grin.

"I'd hate anything to happen to you, Fran! I'd have Lucien and my stepmother to face!"

"Nothing will happen to me," I said. "I'm supposed to have the 'green fire'."

"At any moment they could realise their mistake and I still remember their threat to you that someone could come to harm just as an example to those who won't do as they're told! No, Fran, for the moment we'll keep away from the police!"

I sat huddled in my chair surrounded by comfort and mild luxury. On my finger was Lucien's ring. I had so much...and yet inside me I was shivering because I knew perfectly well that I was in danger. Nor could I help myself, because, for the moment, the source of that danger was unknown. And the precious thing, the "green fire," was as unrevealable as the treasure of Tobermory. . . .

"By the way," Gerry said, "did you ask Marcia to examine her suitcases?"

"Yes. I was there when she did it. There's no lining where anything could be hidden. I even searched my own cases!"

"The idea was too wildly impossible, anyway! And the books?"

"I looked at them myself. An early edition of *Jane Eyre* and a copy of Goethe's *Faust* beautifully bound in vellum. But there's no hiding place, no pages cut out—"

He let the magazine fall to the ground and stretched his arms.

"Did Max say on the telephone whether he had found anything of interest at the Kam Ho Street shop after we left?" I asked.

"He said there wasn't a thing there that could link Farson with anyone, not even a letter or a photograph of Marcia."

"In case the blackmailer saw it!" I said. "Gerry, do you think it is two rival smuggling gangs or—"

"One," Gerry said, "and my guess is that Farson grew too greedy and wanted the lot for himself! But that's only a guess!"

"When I went into Eric's living-room," I said, "Marcia looked oddly excited."

"Why?"

"I don't know and it's no use asking her. If she doesn't tell me voluntarily, then she won't tell me at all."

"Well, let's have lunch and see what this afternoon brings forth!" Gerry eyed the luncheon table set in the courtyard.

I called Marcia and she came at once.

The shade kept the three of us relatively cool—as cool as you could ever be in a humid climate. We ate a delicious fish called *garoupa*, and fruit. We drank thin green tea from glasses the way the Chinese do.

Max was fetching us at four o'clock. Gerry suggested we rest until then. I saw that this was the last thing Marcia wanted to do.

"I suppose," she said doubtfully, "Eric will be there, at that time?"

"If he's anxious to see you, then obviously he'll wait all hours!" Gerry told her. "Anyway, Max won't be free until then."

His manner with her was less gentle than Max's. He did not believe she could be blamed for this chain of events, but his life with Irene had made him on guard against beautiful women.

I heard Marcia close her door quietly as I went upstairs. I slid out of my dress and brushed my hair back, away from my hot forehead and my neck. Then, bare-legged and barefooted, I lay on my bed. From the tall chest, the scent of full blown roses permeated the room—Max's roses. . . .

VIII

Voices roused me. Marcia was talking to Max. I guessed that, too restless to stay in her room, she had gone to sit on the veranda.

I gave a last look at my face in the mirror. I had decided that powder was hopeless in this humid heat, but I used a little to try to cover the fading scar. I drew lipstick strongly across my mouth, and picked up a scent bottle and sprayed myself with Mitsouko. Then I checked the contents of my handbag and went downstairs to join the others.

Max was not there. Marcia told me he had gone to the kitchen for water for the car radiator.

I went to tell Yee Sze that we would be out for an hour or two, and found him polishing glasses and laughing at something Max had said to him. His light-boned Cantonese face had a gentleness and delicacy that always warmed me to him.

Marcia and I walked down to the gate together. I stood looking up at the buildings bordering on the garden while Max returned the water-can to the kitchen. On one side of the wall was a small old-fashioned block of flats. Gerry had told me that it was built on the site of a temple that had been burned down in Victorian times.

On the other side were tall, huddled houses with wooden balconies. There was a Chinese restaurant on the ground floor of the nearest house and the food, Gerry said, was excellent. We would try it some time. Above, lived a fortune-teller and a taxi-driver, with their wives and mothers, their sisters and brothers and aunts and uncles.

As Marcia and I came out of the gate to the car, the restaurant owner beamed at us friendily.

Max introduced us. Shan Wu was fat and bright-eyed. As we talked, we watched him putting three fresh joss-sticks in the small vessel in front of the little shrine at the side of the door. The figure behind the incense-burner was Tso Kwan, the God of the Kitchen.

Shan Wu bowed slightly.

"Missies like Hong Kong? Missies happy?"

We said it was a wonderful place and Mr.

Wu looked as pleased as though he owned it. We nodded good-bye and climbed into the front of the car. Marcia had brought a big cart-wheel sun-hat with her. She tossed it into the back of the car.

Traffic was slow out of the city but presently we reached the green foothills. I could tell that Marcia was tense with excitement. Her hands were locked tightly over her small green handbag. Instead of her gold bracelet she was wearing a wide bangle of thin copper with a pattern engraved on it. She would not wear her charm bracelet again here, I knew. It was far too dangerous. I wondered who, in all Hong Kong, was holding the little medallion and with it, damning evidence against her. But only Max and Gerry and I knew that! The blackmailer believed it was mine. . . .

The afternoon was brilliant and yet without sparkle. The golden atmosphere was heavy-laden; the palms, the frangipanni stood motionless as though the weight of the sun's gilding was too much for them.

Marcia was looking straight ahead as though the beauty of the island meant nothing to her. Max and I talked a little, managed a few forced laughs at old memories.

We were soon within sight of the sea and I watched it in wonder. Turquoise and threaded through with daffodil light, it held the proud-sailed fishing junks in smooth folds of water.

Azaleas blazed in gardens and near the sea we came upon patches of bamboo and wild banana and persimmon.

On the hill to our right, was a squatters' colony. The roughly made huts clung to the hillside, untidily stacked with low, sloping roofs. In them lived the homeless hundreds who had fled from Red China. In winter, I was told, their plight was terrible when the rains poured in torrents down the mountain-side. Too many trees had been cut down to make room for their rough, pathetic homes.

I saw Max keep looking at them and guessed that he was thinking as he used to think in our young days together when we passed a beggar or a legless man. "There but for the grace of God, go I!" Max had compassion.

We had to ask three times before we found Lily Yun's house. It was some way from the beach. Typically Chinese, it was built round a small court and in the neglected garden were a few tired pots of weedy carnations and an untidy stack of bamboo.

"I'd better go in alone," Marcia said.

Max got out and frowned at the house.

"It's not very prepossessing, is it? All right, you go on. I'll be watching."

I got out and stood by his side.

"Cigarette?"

I shook my head. We watched Marcia look for a bell or a knocker. There seemed to be none and she banged on the door in the wall. As she waited, she glanced over her shoulder at us. I think our being there reassured her.

She knocked three times in all. Then Max left my side and went and peered through the grille. They stood for a moment talking and then they walked right around the house, calling, waiting and receiving no answer. Lily Yun was obviously out.

I looked about me for someone to speak to. The place was deserted. Away behind me clung the squatters' huts, the people tiny as dolls on the hillside. Perhaps someone watched us from there. Near at hand, there was no one.

Max came back to the car with Marcia.

"We can't just wait around," he said. "If anyone is keeping a lookout for us they'll know we're here." He nodded towards a pointed roof visible through trees. "There's the temple. We'll take a look at it. If anyone wants to contact us, they can follow us. Then, a little later, we'll come back here again. Maybe we weren't expected just yet."

We got back into the car and I glanced at Marcia. She had hoped for so much as she had knocked on Lily Yun's door. And she had found no one there. I could feel her despair and disappointment as though it were my own.

"Don't worry," I said. "We'll stay around!"

"Eric wouldn't ask me to meet him and then not show up. That is, unless—"

"Unless something had happened to stop his coming?" I asked.

She didn't answer me.

I sat between Marcia and Max and faced the certainty that someone had been around when Eric had stopped me at the corner of Kam Ho Street.

It would be easy to prevent his coming out here. . . . *Or had he really meant to come?* The sudden thought brought a sharp fear. Had he only wanted us out of the way of Gerry's house? Yee Sze was alone there. Anyone could enter, overcome him and search for what they wanted. For the "green fire". . . . Odd how familiarity settled an oddity in one's mind so that it became almost commonplace! I could now use the phrase "green fire" to myself without feeling that I was being a little precious. China was making me accept the poetry of words.

As we drove the few hundred yards to the temple, I was growing more and more certain that we had been sent on this journey for the purpose of getting us away from the house. Yet because it was too late now to go back, I would keep my suspicions to myself until we had had proof that Eric Farson was not here at Shek Ku Bay.

The temple, in its grove of bamboo, was uncared for. The stone steps were worn; the brush-writing on the columns was faded and the guardian lion-dogs chipped and marked with neglect. We walked together towards the courtyard.

By a faded vermilion pillar a little boy sat trying to make sounds come from a piece of bamboo into which he had pierced holes. He glanced up at us from under black eyebrows and, I thought looking into that mischievous dancing gaze, he could have been a baby Pan.

Then he sprang up and ran away and we were alone.

As we entered the temple, I glanced up at the painted eaves. A row of small, grimacing devils leered at us. They were the guardians against the spirits that haunted the roofs.

I looked about me through the motes of golden dust caught in shafts of sunlight.

A woman was kneeling in front of a shrine. I watched her shake the joss-sticks in their cylinders. Some fell out.

I wondered what she was asking the gods for? The birth of a son?...The health of a husband?...Money to buy food or a place to sleep?...The scent of incense rose from the pewter holder. The temple was age-old and decaying, but something was here which moved me. I looked at Max. He was standing a little ahead of me. This could almost have been his place of worship, his religion, he stood so quietly, so detached from us. Presently I turned to say something to Marcia.

She was no longer there!

Immediately my mind alerted. The peace of the temple was gone. So Eric had come for Marcia here! I hadn't heard anyone speak, but perhaps he had crept in and touched her arm and beckoned her outside.

My heart began to thud with a frightened excitement.

The woman at the shrine rose and slipped past us without even looking our way. I glanced across at Max. He had not seemed to see her go. Perhaps he, too, was praying to the old gods....But I had to break through his absorption, to bring him back to us.

I touched his arm.

"Marcia has gone out," I whispered.

He didn't hear me.

"Max!" I said urgently.

He turned his head slowly, smiled at me and touched my hand.

"Do you know," his voice was pitched low, "when I visited my first Eastern temple in Bangkok, I had a sudden thought of you? I seemed to see you standing by my side. Yet I hadn't tried to bring you near me. And now—"

Now we stood together in this age-bound place, closer than we had ever been. And I had to throw the moment away because I was alarmed for a strange girl's safety. . . .

"I . . . I'm going . . . to find Marcia . . ." I said and turned away from him.

I thought he would follow me, but when I was outside on the steps, I realised that I was alone.

I saw the car standing empty. The only movement out here in the sunlight was the shuffling gait of the woman who had prayed at the shrine. She was walking on sandalled feet towards the sea.

"Marcia!" I called.

There was no sound.

I went down the steps and round the side of the temple.

The grove was deserted. A hot breeze suddenly stirred the silver-green leaves of some eucalyptus; bent the fronds of the ferns.

"Marcia!"

I looked round me. I went round the third side of the temple, thought I heard a sound and turned my head.

At the same moment something crashed down on me from behind. I was aware of a terrible splintering, shuddering feeling racking me; my head seemed to burst into flame. Then the shock passed and a great pain clamped down over me, draining me of the power to stand. I stumbled and fell among the ferns. I was not even able to cry out. . . .

In the flash before I lost consciousness, I saw a shadow dart in front of me . . . but it could have been a man, woman or beast. . . . All I wanted with every fighting atom of my being was not to die. . . .

For some time I seemed to swing in a dizzy semi-blinded state. I was aware of voices, of the dry smell of something on which I lay, of a hand touching mine. I even heard a voice. . . . I struggled to open my eyes, to know myself still alive.

"Fran . . ."

Max's voice saying something to me . . . I dragged up my lids and looked from under the shade of Marcia's big sun-hat, which someone had tilted against my head.

They were both there, Marcia and Max. I lay among the green ferns and above me the

164

light wind whispered in the bamboos.

"Don't move yet," Max said, as I put up my hand to feel the back of my head. I drew my hand away. There was no blood on my fingers, but I felt a bump there.

"Someone ... knocked ... me ... out...." I breathed.

"Don't talk either," Marcia said. "We'll get help."

"I don't *want* help!" my voice was faint and tetchy. "I'll be all right in a minute or two."

"There's some boiled water in a Thermos—" Max began.

"Don't give me anything," I said, with my eyes closed.

Then, so gently that it scarcely brushed mine, I felt Max's hand. I half opened my eyes, moved my head slightly and lay against his arm.

Wildly, still half dizzily, swinging back into slow consciousness, I wanted this moment to last for ever. I wanted Marcia to melt into space and leave me here in the shadow of the old temple with Max's arm around me.... I would have had a thousand stunning attacks for a thousand such moments....

It was Marcia who ruined it all.

I heard her say:

"Max, hadn't you better collect Francie's things? I'll hold her."

Her smooth arm slid round me. I opened my eyes. Max was collecting the contents of my handbag which were strewn among the ferns. Lipstick, compact, purse, wallet. I even saw some scattered dollar bills and realised that I had been knocked out in order that someone could search my handbag.

"When you can walk," Marcia was saying, "we must get you to the car and to a doctor. Max said we won't find one here, except perhaps a Chinese one. And they, he says, do odd things for cures, like sticking needles into you."

Again I put my hand to the back of my head and this time I had plenty of strength left in my arm when I put it down.

"I don't need a doctor," I said firmly. "It looks as though I was only meant to be stunned, to give someone time to search my bag." My thick hair, I decided, had saved me anyway from the full force of the blow.

"Even so . . ." Marcia began.

"I'm all *right!*" I insisted. "Just leave me a few minutes longer."

I lay with my eyes closed, and heard the lazy soughing of the sea; I felt the rough fronds of the ferns against my bare arms.

Slowly memory flowed back. I had been in the temple with Max. I remembered the way his hand had reached for mine as though, after all these years of knowing me, it had needed the spell of the old gods to bring us together. . . .

But Marcia had come between us . . . Marcia vanishing in a place where it was dangerous for either of us to be alone so that time must not be wasted in finding her. Or had I imagined more poignancy in those moments in the temple than there really had been?

"Francie—" came Marcia's voice.

"Leave me alone!" I murmured. "Let me think."

She did not ask me what I had to think about, lying there in the thick, warm bed of ferns. She may have thought me still not fully conscious. But I was too conscious, for I realised that nothing had changed between Max and me. I had always been, I *would* always be, Gerry's sister for whom Max felt a very close and real affection sufficient to touch my hand, to tell me of that quite involuntary thought about me in a temple in Bangkok. . . . Only wishful thinking could read love in the light touch of a man's hand. . . .

I moved away from Marcia and opened my eyes.

"I'm all right now." I struggled to get up.

"Here," Max said to her, "take Francie's handbag and get the car door open."

His arm was round me. I leaned against him for a moment.

"I *could* carry you. . . ."

I managed a laugh.

"You'd be very sorry to try!"

He did not argue. He bent and picked me up.

"And don't struggle!" he said.

I had no intention of doing so.

My head was against his shoulder. I put my arms round his neck and moved my face a little so that my cheek touched his.

He set me down very gently by the car.

I refused to sit in the back. Instead I sat between them. The effects of the attack on me were rapidly passing.

"I came out of the temple," I said to Marcia, "to find you. Where did you go?"

"To look for Eric."

"He was there?"

"No," she said. "He . . . didn't come. . . ."

"Someone stopped him," I said, "and followed us here instead."

"And searched your handbag because he believed you were coming here to deliver to Farson what you were supposed to have brought out from England," Max said.

"That doesn't mean..." Marcia stopped. I could feel the shudder that went through her.

"Mean what?" Max asked.

"That they—they have killed Eric...."

"I doubt it! I think they just stopped him coming to Shek Ku."

"... and thought he was meeting *me*," I said and closed my eyes.

Max drove fast and as smoothly as he could and when we reached the house he wanted me to go to bed. I said:

"Have you forgotten I trained for a while as a nurse?"

"No," he smiled.

"Then *I* know when I should go to bed. And it won't be before to-night. I'm all right, Max! I'll say soon enough if I'm not! And now," I added, "shall we have some tea? I always seem to be drinking tea out here!"

"That's what you do in China!" Max told me as Marcia went out to ask Yee Sze to make it for us.

I sat with Max on the veranda, my sore head against a cushion.

"Who," I asked, "is Lily Yun? And where does she come into this?"

"I think Farson just intended to use her house as a meeting place. She is probably a

169

simple woman who knows nothing."

"Max," I turned my head towards him, "they didn't mean to kill me!"

"I'm sure they didn't, but that doesn't mean they won't try to harm you again if it suits their purpose. You must never walk in lonely places alone. And nor must Marcia."

"She didn't mean to, but she brought us a whole heap of trouble!"

"Marcia's a victim, too!" Max reminded me gently. "I wonder if it's wise to let her remain here?"

"But if she went somewhere else," I objected, "she'd be alone."

"I'd undertake to look after her."

It was so quickly, so convincingly said, as though he had thought about it already.

"But you've got your work and your own life! We can't expect to load the responsibility of a stranger upon you!"

He gave me his slow smile.

"She's a stranger to you, too!"

"I know, but it's different—"

He did not ask me how. He said with a light laugh that was intended to be reassuring, "Don't worry, Fran! I don't make heavy weather of things! Nor do I take on anything against my will!"

I stared at the far wall, splashed with sunshine, and made no comment. Max had said nothing that I should mind. He was free to take an interest in any girl, in trouble or out of it.... My unease was purely personal and quite ineffectual.

I heard Marcia's light, quick footstep and reached out to drag round a chair for her.

She had made up her face with faintly sun-tanned powder; her lips were richly, deeply red. The linen dress she had worn had been changed for an orange skirt and a yellow blouse. She looked as vivid as a flamenco dancer. It was like a complete gesture of repudiation of Eric: as though she were advertising the fact once and for all that she was no longer Farson's girl. Even before I looked, I knew she would not be wearing her ring.

Yee Sze was carying a lacquer tray with tea-pot and peony-painted cups and saucers. He also had a letter for me.

"It come today, Missie," he said.

I picked up the envelope. It was addressed in large familiar handwriting and I exclaimed with pleasure:

"It's from my stepmother! Do you mind if I open it now?"

I looked at Max as I spoke. He glanced questioningly at Marcia.

"Shall we let her?" his tone teased.

Marcia was laughing, her eyes, bright as sapphires, looked from one to the other.

"Francie's going to, anyway! Shall I pour out the tea?"

"Please," I said and sat back and slit open the envelope.

My stepmother wrote that she hoped I had had an interesting flight and that Hong Kong was as fascinating as those articles we had read together had made it out to be. She gave me news of Lucien. She had had a word with the psychiatrist who was treating him and he had told her that he was progressing slowly but satisfactorily. He had reported jauntily: "I could almost make a prophecy that we'll have him at the airport to meet Miss Mannering when she returns!" Her last paragraph was short.

"I suppose you have met Max. It's odd, but I always felt it was inevitable that you three should meet again."

I looked across at him. He was having some small quiet joke with Marcia. . . .

IX

The telephone call came early the following morning. Gerry had finished his breakfast; I had just sat down and taken a hot roll from under the damask napkins.

Yee Sze, bowing very slightly, told me that a Miss Lam was asking to speak to me.

Gerry looked up.

"How do you know—?" he began, and then grinned. "Oh, I forgot. You and she got together while your hair was in curlers! And she found you were my sister and decided you were acceptable!"

"You could," I murmured as I left the table, "have put it a little more gallantly!"

I went to the telephone. Tiffany Lam's voice sounded insubstantial and slightly sing-song.

She said, after polite little preliminaries:

"My grandfather is not very well so I am afraid it will not be possible just yet for you to meet him. I am so sorry, you would have liked him. But if you are going to do any shopping this morning and you and the friend staying with you would like to call in and have tea with me, I should be so happy."

"I'd love it," I said, "and I'm sure Marcia would, too."

"I'm so glad." The formality of her manner of speech was very noticeable over the telephone. I felt again she was much more used to speaking Chinese. "I will expect you, if it is convenient, at about eleven o'clock."

I went back to the breakfast table and told Gerry. He said he hoped I would be shown the main rooms of the house because they were full of treasures.

"Mr. Lam Tat Chee is a delightful old man once you can penetrate his ivory tower of insular and rather mannered tradition."

I sat down and poured out coffee for myself.

"I suppose it's all right to go?"

He looked at me sharply.

"Your head troubling you? I told you we should have got a doctor!"

"My head is quite all right," I said, "except that it is very sore. I mean, I suppose it's safe to go out?"

"So long as the two of you stay together, you'll be perfectly all right. No one's going to risk harming you in the centre of Hong

Kong in broad daylight."

"But it's incredible that—that I shouldn't be safe at any time! I mean . . ." I was lost for words.

"That a thing like this should happen to you?" Gerry asked. "You've no idea how many people in the world have said that! The fact remains, drama and melodrama are part of life!"

And I was a victim!

"But please be sensible, Fran! After dark you don't go outside this gate on your own. That understood?"

"I wouldn't even want to," I said bleakly. "Oh, Gerry, and everything was to have been such fun!"

"Don't worry! Once Max and I get our hands on the blackmailer and Farson we'll make up for all this! I'm not letting you go back to England thinking Hong Kong is a vicious place because it isn't."

My handbag lay on the little rattan table. It was the one someone had rifled out at Shek Ku Bay. I said:

"Marcia *can't* have what it is they're looking for, can she?"

"I'm absolutely certain she hasn't!" Gerry said with conviction.

"Then what is the 'green fire' and where is it?"

The marmalade I was spreading was English and tangy and made me think of breakfasts at home. "And," I went on unhappily, "there is still the fact that we know about a crime."

Gerry looked at me in the way he used to do when as a little girl I didn't catch on quickly enough to some wonderful cops-and-robbers game.

"Out here," he said firmly, "if trouble doesn't trouble you, you don't stick your neck out! Opium and white slavery and smuggling . . . *that's* not your affair! You just sit on your veranda, drink green tea and quote Confucius at the moon!"

"I'll enjoy seeing the Lam house," I said, "but I wish the entrance wasn't in that alleyway."

"You're not going to any isolated place. From here to their house you'll have Europeans as well as Chinese around you. You can't come to any harm."

"After hearing the blackmailer's very English voice," I said, "I'm not certain I wouldn't feel safer with the Chinese!"

"I love them!" Gerry said with feeling.

"At any rate, going there will take Marcia's mind off her ordeal to-night."

"I'll have a talk with her later," Gerry said. "She's not going there to-night. Her bravado won't do *you* any good! Only Farson himself can prove to them that Marcia is his girl and not you. And that's what he doesn't want to do!" Gerry rose. "I've got a job of work waiting for me. See you at lunchtime. Be good! Oh, this came from England yesterday." He tossed a five-days-old English newspaper to me.

I sat finishing my breakfast and glancing through the *Morning Standard*. Then I saw why Gerry had it. On a centre page was an article from Max. It was called: "Red China Next Door."

As I read it I thought of all those other articles of Max's from Bangkok, from Damascus, from Delhi. And was there a girl in one of them who mattered more than any other? And would he one day go back and find her? . . . I put down the newspaper with the article only half-read.

I was still sitting there, staring up at—and only half-seeing—an old Chinese woman on one of the balconies over Mr. Wu's shop, hanging her washing with meticulous care on the jutting bamboo pole. She looked so small from this distance and as unreal as the tiny child with the rice bowl who squatted by her side.

"Missie take letters?" Yee Sze was at my elbow. On his red lacquer tray were two letters and a postcard.

The letters were for me from England. I read them with the joy one always feels at receiving some communication from home, however beautiful the place is to which you have gone.

Here in the Chinese garden the sun was already hot on my hair and the street outside busy and full of strange sounds — of sing-song voices, the cry of a street pedlar, the slap-slap of a rickshaw coolie lumbering by. . . .

When Marcia joined me she immediately asked me how I felt.

"Apart from a sore head, fine!" I told her.

"I was too worried to sleep." Her smooth brow was furrowed. "I kept thinking — suppose they had killed you!"

"We're not risking anything like that happening again," I told her briskly. "Neither of us will go around alone from now on, so don't worry!"

She gave me a swift look and her lips parted as though she were about to protest, then her lids fell, veiling her eyes; she ran a finger along the edge of the table.

"That tomato colour suits you, Francie," she said inconsequently.

I glanced down at my bright skirt and wondered what she had been about to say before she changed her mind. She gave the impression of frankness, and yet the secretiveness was there. Perhaps she was still not quite sure of me. Or perhaps she never quite trusted her own sex.

She was just about to sit down when she saw my letters. Lying untidily, as I had tossed them on to the table, letters and envelopes spread out, they looked double their number:

She said:

"What a mail! How nice it must be to get letters from England!"

"When you write to your friends," I said easily, "you'll get some too!"

"*When* I write!" she demanded derisively; "to tell them what? That I was stood-up at the airport? That I haven't yet set eyes on the man I came to marry? One of my girl friends might even try to cash in on it and sell the story to a newspaper for a guinea or two!"

I bit back the sharp comment: "You don't seem to choose your friends any more carefully than you choose a prospective husband!"... If you were as beautiful as Marcia and young and alone, with no one to guide you in your friendships, then you might easily collect the kind of people who would sell your personal story for a few pounds....

I changed the subject.

"We've got an invitation for this morning."

Then I told her about Tiffany Lam. I had forgotten to tell her yesterday how we had met at the hairdresser's—events had moved so swiftly, so violently.

Marcia came out of the sun and sat down again. The bitterness had left her face and she was bright and interested again.

"I'll love to see the inside of a real Chinese house!"

"*This* is a Chinese-type house," I looked around at Mr. Kok's walls, "so it won't be that much different. Only, probably, much more luxurious."

"I'll have to change my shoes. I can't go in these," she glanced down at her fragile green *guipure* lace slippers. Then she lifted her eyes to my face. "They were bought for my honeymoon!"

We had carefully avoided discussing tonight. It was a futile topic between us, anyway, because an impasse had been reached. Yet, I had a lurking fear that Marcia would defy us all and keep the appointment the voice on the telephone had made with me.

I gathered my letters together and passed Marcia the newspaper.

"There's an article by Max on the centre page," I said. "It's good."

She gazed across the garden at the blazing bank of azaleas, shocking-pink and apricot.

"I wonder," she said, "why he has never married?"

Startled, I raised my shoulders.

"Is there a girl?"

"I wouldn't know," I said stiffly. "I haven't seen Max for nearly three years. He could have a dozen girls—"

"When I first saw him, I thought he was the man you were engaged to."

"Oh no!" I said and did not want to explain to her about Lucien.

Marcia looked up at the Peak. I followed her gaze. Streamers of mist stretched across its summit, but where it broke, the trees were green as jade and between them, the new blocks of flats were set in the mountain like pieces of white cornelian.

"He lives up there, doesn't he?" she said.

"He—?"

"Max."

"Yes, he does," I said shortly and rose. I did not want to talk to her about Max, either. I glanced at my watch. "We'll leave at about ten minutes to eleven," I said.

I heard Marcia rustle the pages of the newspaper as I went into the house. She could have thought my leaving her abrupt, but I was not in the mood for all the questions she was prepared to ask me.

I went to my room and tidied up, made my bed out of habit because I always did this at home. Then I left my blue dress out for Lau Fai to wash.

On the tall chest, Max's yellow roses were full-blown. A few petals had dropped. I picked them up and held them for a moment in the palm of my hand: they were as soft and smooth as finely-pressed wax.

I dropped them slowly, reluctantly, into the bamboo basket by the bureau. Then I stood at the window and saw the ferry, tiny as a toy boat, cutting through the strait towards Kowloon, trailing an arrow of foam.

I wondered how long it would be before my stepmother wrote to tell me that Lucien was asking for me. Who would leave Hong Kong first? Max, with orders to cover some story in another part of the Far East? Or I, leaving this fabulous city with a relieved heart, to marry Lucien. . . .

There must be an end to ill-luck, I thought. Old wounds must heal, even those that were self-inflicted. For that was the way I saw my love for Max. He was not to blame. And I had been powerless to help what had happened. I had so honestly fallen in love with Lucien and, had it not been for the car accident and my visit to Hong Kong, my recovery from my first hopeless love would have been complete. I wished fancifully that when I had been in the temple at Shek Ku Bay, I had resorted to a faith in old gods. I would like to have written my name on crimson paper, thrown the clappers to the ground as I had seen the woman at the shrine do, and read my fate in the joss-sticks that fell to the floor from the cylinder.... But I knew my fate! Lucien and the world of the theatre waited for me in England.

A clock downstairs chimed the quarter before eleven. I roused myself, went to the mirror and used powder and lipstick. I put on small swinging gold ear-rings.

My flat-heeled slippers made no sound down the stairs so that when I reached the hall I could hear a soft noise from the guest room. I turned down the passage and paused outside the door.

"Marcia, are you ready?"

There was no answer. I knocked. Nothing happened.

Tentatively I pushed open the door. No one was there but a silky-gauze side curtain shook a little as though someone had just brushed past it.

"Marcia!" I went through the room and out on to the veranda. There was no one there, either.

Harriet Craig was at her easel. But only just! I had a feeling that she had that moment sat down. Marcia was down at the gate. She could not possibly have reached there in the time it took me to open the door and cross the room.

Someone else had been here! Yee Sze? But I could hear him upstairs. Then Harriet Craig? But that was nonsense. What possible interest could she have in Marcia's room? A wind had blown the curtains! But there was no wind. . . .

I told myself firmly that I must not let nerves get the better of me. It would help no one if I began seeing shadows where there were none, hearing voices, rustlings in a room where no one was. . . . I braced myself and began to hum the first tune that came into my head.

Marcia was waiting for me at the gate. She looked back over her shoulder:

"Miss Craig asked me while you were upstairs how long I was staying. Then she asked me if I were just on holiday." She followed me through the gate. "She looked at me oddly, too!"

"I think she's just one of those rather lonely people who are always curious about others because they have such empty lives of their own," I said easily. "I'm sure she didn't mean to be rude."

"Oh no, it wasn't exactly that!" She frowned. "I suppose I'm touchy that people might find out I'd been stood up at the airport." She paused and looked in at a shop which had an amber "Laughing Buddha" in the window. The little god chuckled at us. "Would you mind, by the way, not telling these people we're going to see that I'm out here to get married? I want it to be thought I'm just on a visit, like you."

I understood. This was a matter of pride. I promised to say nothing.

The city swarmed with people. Traders had set their goods outside their open-fronted shops in the side streets. Stalls flourished under tattered awnings, selling bitter cucumber and peppers and piles of orange-peel dipped in sugar. The owner of a street library had stuck the lurid dust covers of his books on an outside wall.

When we were nearing Kam Ho Street, Marcia dragged her feet a little.

"I wish we didn't have to go down that alley!" she said. "Don't you think there's another, a better, entrance to the house!"

I explained that Tiffany Lam would have told us if there were. I said:

"You often find out east that the most beautiful houses are in the centre of the city behind high walls and a small, inconspicuous door. I suppose it's because there's never been any planning about these places."

When we turned down the alley we began to walk faster.

The door of the Lams' house was just a few yards before Eric Farson's shop. As though it were a magnet we glanced towards it. The door was closed and the place looked quiet. I stopped by the door of the house on the opposite side and reaching up, pulled at a bell. I heard its distant clang, as rich and lovely as though it were cast in bronze.

Almost immediately the gate was opened by a Chinese servant. I asked for Miss Lam and he said, with a slight bow, his face impassive, that she was expecting us. We entered upon a small courtyard with flowers in painted tubs with brush writing on them. The mango tree gave shade. An oriole flew from a high branch to a lower and watched us. Before us was a moongate of mellow brick. We were led through this and found ourselves in another, larger courtyard entirely closed by the house.

We walked over paving worked in geometric patterns, between rockeries and latticed panels. Mauve irises and camellias, tiny rare ferns and carnations made aisles of colour between which we walked. I saw an aviary with a large open door. The little birds—crimson and emerald and powder blue—twittered and quarrelled and made love to one another.

Against the far wall of the house was another mango tree and out of its shadow came Tiffany Lam.

Again she wore a *cheongsam,* this one of cream silk with a faint gold thread outlining a pattern of lotus flowers. The dress was tight-fitting, with a high collar and was slit up the sides showing her slender-boned legs in expensive nylons. Her shoes were very high-heeled and her fingers long and red-lacquered.

She welcomed us charmingly and when I had introduced Marcia, we sat at a little corner table in the shade.

Tea scented with jasmine flowers was served us immediately in handleless porcelain cups.

Tiffany and I did most of the talking. Marcia was very quiet. I saw her eyes go continuously to the Kam Ho Street shops, the tops of which we could just see over the graceful curved roof of the house.

I asked innumerable questions about Peking

because I had always longed to see the Forbidden City and feared now that I never
would.

"My name, Tiffany," she explained presently, "is Cornish. Did you know?"

I admitted that I didn't.

Her mother, she told us, had been born in
Penzance. Her First Uncle, she said, had also
married an Englishwoman.

In spite of the slightly formal manner of her
speech—the soft, light voice occasionally
lapsing into the Chinese manner of speaking
English, leaving out verbs—Tiffany Lam was
charming company. I found myself talking of
England, and she listened with an almost
child-like interest.

She had been to Paris but never to London, although her mother used to talk to her about it.

When Tiffany Lam asked Marcia if she was
also on holiday, she said coolly that she was.
Her eyes flicked warningly to my face. She
dipped her fingers into the turquoise-encrusted
bowl Tiffany had handed her, took out a
melon seed and stared down at it, twisting it
in her fingers.

We finished our tea and Tiffany Lam asked
us if we would like to see the room facing us
across the courtyard.

"I am sorry I cannot show you my grandfather's real treasures but only he himself takes people on"—she gave a little hesitant laugh—"a tour of inspection you would call it. You see, he likes to explain everything—all the legends and the history and the Confucian philosophy. He is a scholar as well as a 'hong.' But I can show you this room. And later, when my grandfather is better I hope you will come again."

The room which we entered from the courtyard was large and at first I thought curiously devoid of both furniture and the bric-à-brac I had been expecting. I realised, however, this was the general living-room where the family and their friends sat on the raised cushioned dais. On a very long low table in front of it were fans and a Bonzai in a glazed pot. It was barely two feet high, a pine like Gerry's with slanting trunk and parasol branches.

Tiffany opened the little doors of the red lacquer cabinets. Inside them we saw old carved *fei tsui* jade and porcelain figures; caskets encrusted with turquoise and garnets; pieces of Ming; models of Tang horses.

Our tour of the room was leisurely and as we left it, Tiffany paused and pointed to a hole in the outer wall.

"That," she said, "was made by a Japanese shell in December 1941. I was not here, but my grandfather was."

We crossed the garden to the aviary. In the great cage, tiny birds fluttered and darted—red wings and azure tails; breasts the colour of moonstones; minute perked heads of glossy green or palest blue. . . .

"This is one of the oldest houses on the island," Tiffany explained. "When it was built ninety years ago, the aviary was also started by my great-grandfather."

I did not know the Chinese conventions about morning visits but when we had stayed an hour, I guessed it was time for us to leave.

I thanked our enchanting Eurasian hostess and told her I hoped her grandfather would be better soon. She came with us down the garden to the moongate and as we stepped through it, I glanced back at the house.

The graceful roofs dipped to the old walls, the garden was a living riot of colour unusual, I believed, with the Chinese.

At the window stood a tall old man in a long blue gown. He had a tight-fitting cap on his head and his moustache hung down in two long thin wisps past his chin. He did not move.

I quickly looked away.

I wondered if this girl's grandfather was indeed ill or whether he just did not want to meet us. . . .

X

When Gerry arrived home, he told me that Max was on his way.

"He rang me as I was packing up and told me he was just leaving the newspaper offices." He eyed me. "Did you enjoy your visit to the Lam's house?"

"Very much," I said. "Though we weren't shown all round. I think we're to be asked again when Mr. Lam Tat Chee is better."

"Good. And next time I'll come with you. Talking to a highly intelligent Chinese of the old traditional school is one of the great joys of life—though I'm afraid, like the rickshaws, they're dying out!" He flung himself, with a satisfied sigh, into a chair.

I leaned my arms on the veranda rail and looked down at the irises.

"Gerry, do you trust Harriet Craig?"

"Trust her?" My question surprised him. "I don't know. Why, what do you mean?"

191

I told him about the tiny incident of the noise in Marcia's room. As I had expected, he laughed.

"A momentary freak breeze stirred the curtain," he said, "and with all you've been through since you arrived, I don't wonder your imagination is all over the place! Don't let Harriet Craig worry you. She's just a spinster artist who happens to be more gifted than most. Ah, here's Max!"

I said, "Hallo, Max," and watched him bring up a chair.

It was so like his arrival among us in England—informal, easy, accepted as though he were one of us.

"Marcia went to her room to take an aspirin," I told them. "Her head has been aching all day. She's been gone some time, so I suppose she's lying down." Then I added, tentatively: "About to-night—"

"What about it?" Gerry asked in bland surprise.

"I've a feeling Marcia intends to go to Kam Ho Street," I explained. "She wants to prove to them that I've nothing to do with Eric; to explain—"

"She can explain till the cows come home," Gerry said irritably, "but it won't do any good. She'll only complicate matters and, maybe, run into some sort of danger."

"The Chinese," Max said, apparently with irrelevance, "won't be put off by our manoeuvres—which is how they would see Marcia's coming instead of you. Nothing will fool them, and temporising won't help," he added gravely. "They have infinite patience."

"You think he is Chinese?" I asked.

"Who else," Gerry said, "would use the colorful Chinese phrase 'green fire' instead of the downright English words for what he's talking about?"

"On the other hand," Max continued to stare out over the garden, "he could be using it to confuse us."

We didn't know! That was the point. We didn't know where to look, whom to look for. All we had to go on was a voice on the telephone who had called himself Midnight for no other reason, probably, than that the clock in his room had stopped at that time.

"So we—just do—nothing?" I asked hesitantly.

"I've already said! Exactly nothing. That way, we're forcing him to make another move and that may lead to a mistake. Fran, leave everything to Max and me, there's a good girl! Now, what will you drink?"

"A long iced lime, please," I said, "and I'll call Marcia."

Gerry gave me a long look.

"You're pale!"

"Stop worrying! After-results of stunning aren't nearly so serious as you think!"

"Well," he called back to the clink of glasses, "you're the nurse as well as the patient, so you should know!"

I flicked a scornful look at the doorway and got up to fetch Marcia.

Before I was old enough to take up nursing, I had studied first aid. Practising one evening on Gerry who was supposed to have been the victim of a car crash, I had trussed him up like a turkey ready for the oven. So complicated were my efforts that my stepmother had to be called in to help unbandage him. Gerry had never let me forget it.

The french doors to Marcia's room were just beyond the side window of the living-room.

I called softly, as I came to them:

"Marcia!"

She did not hear me and I moved forward and looked into her room.

She was standing at a little table. Her back was to me and I could not see what she was doing. I called her name again, loudly this time.

She wheeled round. As she did so she took a few steps away from the table and I saw that she had undone the parcel of books again.

"Come . . . in . . ."

Her voice rose queerly, as though she were over-excited.

I pushed back the glass door and entered the room. Both books still lay in their corrugated paper, but one was opened at centre pages. I went over and glanced down at the old-fashioned printing.

"I suppose they're valuable to collectors," I said.

"You'd better . . . have a . . . good look at them!" Her voice still had that high, vibrating quality. I looked at her sharply and then down at the open page. I saw the names "Rochester" and "Jane" but I did not have time to read what they said to one another.

Marcia's arm shot across me and closed the book with a slap.

"Now look!" she almost shouted. *"Look at it!"*

I picked up *Jane Eyre* and my fingers felt a rough edge. I turned the book on end. The spine had been neatly slit right down the back and inside was a tiny polythene pocket separated into minute sections each of which was empty. It was so obviously a hiding-place for something very small and very valuable, that I did not need to put it into words.

I laid the book down and picked up the other. The same cutting operation had been performed on Goethe's *Faust*.

We stood staring at one another. In the shocked silence one thought leapt and beat with wild relief in my mind.

They came and found what they wanted! *I'm safe... I shall never hear from them again....*

Marcia was watching me, arms folded tightly across the green silk of the blouse as though trying to ease the hard beating of her heart.

"But when? Francie, when did they come?" she asked, her eyes on me, fascinated, fearfully excited.

"I don't know!" I seized the butchered books that were my reprieve, "I'm taking these out to Gerry and Max. Come on!"

She followed me out of the room.

I almost ran along the veranda and turning the corner broke into the murmur of the men's voices.

"Look!" I cried and held the books out.

Gerry took them from me.

"Well, blow me down!" he held *Jane Eyre* out to Max. "Pockets in the spines of books. Old books, bound in thick leather. Look how neatly the job is done—"

I watched the two men. Marcia stood against the veranda rail and seemed to look at nothing. The over-excitement had gone out of her. It was as though she had passed the burden of discovery on to the two men and did not care any longer.

"A hiding-place," I said, watching them, "for something tiny and very valuable. It's obvious, isn't it?"

"What?"

"Something green," I said impatiently. "A precious stone—nearly the most precious in the world providing they're flawless."

"Green fire!" Max said holding *Faust,* his fingers on the split spine. "Emeralds!"

"What made you look at the books again?" Gerry asked Marcia.

"I lay down for a while this afternoon because I had a headache. When I got up to do my hair, I happened to go to the chest for something and saw them. It suddenly occurred to me that I hadn't left them there. I'd put them in the cupboard. I thought it was odd, so I undid them."

Max was examining the tiny pockets; setting them against the leather spine.

"They are very carefully made," he said. "Each pocket fits a piece of embossed gold on the spine so that if anyone felt the spine they would think that the slight unevenness and bulge was due to the actual embossing."

"But the question is, when was Marcia's room searched?" I asked puzzled.

Gerry rose.

"I'll find out if Yee Sze left the house at all unattended yesterday or to-day. You and Marcia were out this morning. It could have been then—"

"Lau Fai was here all morning," I told him. "I know because she wanted to wash a dress of mine I'd only worn once."

"But she stays in the outhouse at the back of the kitchen. Marcia's room faces the far side and someone had only to come along the veranda and walk in."

"Which meant," Max's grey eyes were narrowed in thought, "that whoever came here, knew where to look."

I was about to take a long cool drink of lime. My hand, holding the glass, froze. Stiff and appalled I stared at Max and then at Gerry. The full meaning of Max's words jangled in my head, terrifying, taunting. Of course, only Eric would know where to look! And so the danger to one of us was as great as ever....

There was still a chance that we were

wrong. I started to my feet. Gerry had gone to find Yee Sze.

"I've just had a thought," I said shakily to Max. "Perhaps it wasn't Eric! If my room has been searched as well, then we'll know!"

Before he had time to answer I ran through the house and upstairs.

In my bedroom I pulled out drawers, trying to remember how I had left things. Handkerchiefs; an extra box of powder; three tiny handbag-size phials of scent someone had given me as a parting present; aspirin. My chamois leather zipper pouch containing my few pieces of jewellery was also there. I opened it. *Had* I tossed my ear-rings in it like that? Had I pushed my gold petal brooch with the pearl in the centre in the same pocket as my bracelet? Or had someone, searching for emeralds, done that? I dragged open the next drawer. Scarves, my evening handbag, gloves. . . . Below that was the long drawer where I kept underclothes. Had the froth of pink and yellow nylon been riffled? I wanted to think so. Ironically, I wanted desperately to find proof that someone had searched my room so that I would know it had been the blackmailer who had by patient, silent search, found the emeralds. Not Eric who would recognise some of Marcia's things and know where to look. The man called Midnight? But there was no proof. . . .

I left my room and went out on to the landing. Glancing through the tilted venetian blinds, I wondered if someone watched the house, from a window, a littered balcony, even perhaps through binoculars from the tall, new block of flats I could see in the distance. . . . I could imagine unknown eyes . . .

Downstairs I could hear Gerry's voice. He was, of course, worried and anxious and angry. But Gerry was gifted with a happy lack of pessimistic imagination. To him, all things came right in the end. . . . And Max? I stopped thinking and went slowly downstairs again and through the living-room to the veranda.

Max was standing by Marcia's side. They had their backs to me and their elbows rested on the veranda rail. When two people stand together without speaking, their closeness invariably seems to have a deeper significance.

"I've searched my room," I said unnecessarily loudly.

They turned together.

"Do you think it has been disturbed?"

I shook my head.

"Then that means—?" I saw Marcia move a shade closer to Max.

Footsteps sounded and we all three turned to watch Gerry.

"I've talked to Yee Sze. He was out for a while yesterday afternoon and this morning he went to the market. Lau Fai would have heard nothing."

"Gerry," I said. "I've just been to my room. It could have been searched, too. But I don't think so," I added honestly.

Gerry flung himself into the chair.

"We can go round in circles conjecturing! What interests me is this smuggling racket itself," he looked at Max. "I know a great many rich people have fled from Red China and have put their money into small things like precious stones—"

"But why?" Marcia asked. "I thought property was the thing everyone invested in."

"It all depends on your point of view," Max said. "If you're one of those who fear that Hong Kong may be attacked, then it's possible to get away with valuable stones. But you can't put a block of flats on a boat and escape to safety!"

Marcia raised hard, bright eyes.

"When I sent out books Eric asked me to collect for him, was I smuggling out precious stones?"

"My guess is that that's just what you were

doing," Gerry told her. "When you sent the books from England, how did you collect them?"

"Eric would write that a client of his had asked him to find a certain rare book. He had contacted a dealer in London who would deliver the book to me to be sent off."

"Instead of sending it direct? Why?" I asked.

"I suppose," Gerry said, "it was safer for Marcia to post them. It didn't link the man in England with Farson."

"Were they already parcelled up?"

"Yes. I just had to post them, ordinary surface mail and unregistered."

Gerry said drily:

"Because they would be less likely to be suspected that way?"

"They took a great risk," I said. "The parcel could have been stolen."

"No one would bother to steal a couple of books and the risk of a parcel of that size getting lost is negligible." Gerry swirled his drink. Ice tinkled. "Chinese postal sorters and postmen are honest, anyway."

"But this time I had to bring the books out."

He nodded.

"Because the hidden stones were of too great value to risk by any post."

"Absolutely flawless emeralds are rare," I

said slowly, "if that's what they were."

"You're all thinking Farson took them, but I'm sure you're wrong!" Gerry said emphatically. "You know what I believe? That our 'Midnight' friend, Pun Ye, stopped Farson from coming to Shek Ku Bay and came himself and searched your handbag, Fran. Then, finding nothing, he broke in here to-day."

"If you're right," I said on a rising hope, "then—"

"Of course I'm right! And that means there'll be no one waiting at Kam Ho Street to-night. It calls for a celebration, doesn't it?" he grinned at me. "All that is left to be done is for them to fight it out between them, Farson and Pun Ye. We're clear of the whole damn' business! Don't you agree?" He turned to Max.

"Maybe," he said non-committally, as though he did not want to discuss it.

From somewhere in the house a gong struck softly.

"Come on, let's eat," Gerry said.

I looked at Marcia. She was still standing quietly by the rail. I saw Max reach out his hand. I saw her lift her head and smile. How hurt was she? Could I have smiled with that degree of seduction at another man at the very moment when I had learned that I had been used and humiliated by the man supposed to love me? Or was I accusing her of a conscious act which was in reality unconscious? Did I have to mind so much that Marcia's allure was probably essential rather than acquired?

Over a beautiful dinner of duck, with little bowls of fluffy rice we talked of what we would do that night.

Max suggested that we went for a drive and then back to his flat. He said:

"I've got a roof garden I want to show off."

"Oh, Max!" Marcia cried. "How lovely! Has it got a little fountain or, since we're in the East, a lotus pool?"

He laughed.

"It's not in the least elaborate. Just flowers in pots. But I have got a bronze lion-dog and a gilded, but rather chipped *lohan* who has a most beautiful and benign face."

"Has your garden got a wonderful view?"

He looked into Marcia's lifted, eager face.

"Over the sea to the hills of China," he said. "You shall see it for yourself to-night."

I passed a dish of crystallized ginger slices to Gerry. He looked at it longingly and then grinned, laid his hand across his stomach and said:

"The appetite says 'Yes,' but the honourable

paunch says 'No'! Come on, let's go outside and drink tea."

We had barely sat down on the veranda when Yee Sze came out to us. He had an envelope on his lacquer tray. As Gerry made to reach for it, Yee Sze said:

"For Missie, *Taipan,*" and turned to me.

I slit the envelope and pulled out a piece of paper. Something fell with a thud on the floor. A key, large and heavy and black, lay at my feet.

Max bent and picked it up. I turned to the letter. On the flimsy paper was written:

No. 43 Kam Ho Street.

With shaking fingers I held it out. Max was nearest me and took it.

"So now we know," I heard myself say shakenly, "that it was Eric who came for the emeralds. And the man who telephoned is expecting me. . . ."

Gerry said furiously:

"This makes no difference! You can put the key down the drain for all I care! Fran has nothing to do with this and I've no intention of letting her go and explain. . . ."

"But *I* shall!" Marcia's face was almost radiant with her defiance. "Whatever anyone says, I'm going to the shop tonight."

Gerry got up, lit a cigarette, sat down again.

"Look honey," he said with elaborate patience, "I know you think you'll be clearing Fran of any complicity by going. But you won't, you know! They'll only think we sent you to confuse them. You'll stay here! We'll *all* stay here." He looked at Max. "But your roof garden will have to wait till another time."

In the fractional pause, I felt certain that Marcia was relieved that her act of bravado had been vetoed. Then she said with a faint, resigned smile:

"All right Gerry. I'm your guest so, if you say 'No'..."

I watched a bird flying across the garden. It was so unusual to see them down here where there were few trees. Its wings were like pieces of jade against the sky. I wanted to ask what bird it was, but I could not. Instead, I heard myself say in a small, strained voice:

"If no one shows up to-night...what will... they do next?"

"They can't do much," Gerry said easily. "In fact, I think we're being too alarmist. If you two girls don't go out alone during the day-time and keep with Max and myself during the evenings, then..." He spread his hands and gave us a relaxed smile.

I saw Max's swift glance and I guessed he

was thinking that maybe this time Gerry's policy of playing ostrich could be dangerous.

I said cautiously:

"But, Gerry, they've killed once!"

"How do you know it was connected with this? The man could have had a quarrel with Farson."

"Eric didn't . . ." Marcia began and then became silent. She looked down at her ringless left hand and compressed her lips. Nobody asked her what she was going to say. We sat in silence, waiting for our tea. I could hear the clack-clack of the mah-jongg tiles from the Chinese Club in a back room of Mr. Wu's restaurant next door.

Then Yee Sze appeared round the veranda. As he set out the cups and the teapot in its padded basket, Gerry questioned him about the note.

"Coolie deliver, *Taipan!*" he said impassively.

His manner inferred that one coolie was very like another. A refugee, in all probability, from one of the squatters' colonies, or a homeless one grateful for a few cents in payment for the delivery of a letter.

Suddenly Marcia got up in a flurry of movement; her grey skirt swirled round her as she ran from us. Her heels made little metallic sounds on the veranda floor. Gerry shook his head at me as I half rose. He said in a low voice:

"Let her be."

In front of us, as we drank our tea, the camellias were like stars of snowdrift. Had a snapshot been taken of us, we would have seemed to be three people idling in an Eastern garden with not a care in the world... a brother, a sister and a friend....

XI

We had finished our tea and cigarettes. Our conversation had gone round in the same revolving pattern of guesswork. Max sat in the semi-circle between Gerry and me and if I closed my eyes and forgot the thin, sing-song sounds of the evening, of voices and Chinese music, we would be sitting in the garden of our Surrey house talking about Gerry's new car or some friends' forthcoming party. I glanced across at Max wondering if he were remembering those old days. He looked away over my shoulder.

"Do you think Marcia is all right?" he asked.

Quickly, almost too quickly, I got up.

"I'll go and see."

I found her sitting in a chair in her room. For the first moment or two that I hesitated in the doorway, she did not see me. She was so still, so unreal in the dying daylight with her blazing hair and her grey dress, that she might have been painted there.

I called her name and she moved her head slowly towards me.

"May I come in?"

"Of course."

I pushed open the door and entering, leaned against the dressing-table.

"Don't you think," I asked steadily, "that you'd be much happier with us than sitting alone here? Brooding never helped anyone!"

I thought at first she was not going to answer me. She stirred in her chair and put the back of her hand against her forehead.

Then she raised her eyes to my face and even in the dimness of the room, I saw the blaze in them.

"I fell in love with a crook!" the words came harshly from her bitter, curled mouth. "I've been made a fool of!"

I took a few steps towards her. She did not look as though she wanted my arm around her, nor any gentle words. There was a cold anger that, if it required anything from me, it required practical analysis instead of compassion. I tried to think of words.

"There's one thing you will be glad about," I said. "And that is that you found out about Eric before you married him."

"A girl on her own," she said in clear, bitter

tones, as though I had not spoken, "that's what he wanted. There must be no parents, no loving relations to make certain that little Marcia was marrying a good honest man! So many tender things said. 'We're both orphans, aren't we, darling?'" She broke off and turning picked up a packet of cigarettes from the dressing-table. She handed the packet to me. I refused.

"Smoking chokes me!" she said and lighting her cigarette, coughed over it. "The thought of Eric chokes me, too!"

"There still could be some dreadful mistake!"

"Do *you* think so?" Her tone mocked.

"I don't know."

"Oh yes, you do! You know damn' well there's no mistake! When I think of those past few months in England! Walking along Fulham Road to the post office," her voice was low and thin as though she were back in a memory, "taking a rare book to post to Eric in Hong Kong and carrying a letter—'Darling Eric'... 'Dearest Eric...' Dreaming of leaving the job in an insurance office and going East to be married...." She swung round, stubbed out her unsmoked cigarette and laughed. "That was me until yesterday! And now—"

"Now—?" I prompted.

"Nobody's ever going to catch me loving again! Love is weakness; it takes away your will. You stop being self-contained. You want to possess and be possessed. Well, I'll possess! But next time it will be with my head!" She moved over to the wall and flicked out the electric switch. Two rosy lamps lit up the room.

I went to the french doors and pulled the wire screen over them. The first moth, vellum-tinted, fluttered against it.

Marcia walked about the room with quick restless steps.

"I suppose I'll never know what I carried in those books I sent him. A few diamonds, maybe. But when there was a haul of real value, *I* had to be brought out! A messenger of love"—the words snapped furiously from her—"with a fortune in emeralds. . . ."

I said, apropos of nothing:

"Had Eric come to see you at Shek Ku Bay, I wonder how he would have explained it all?"

She wore her copper bangles again to-night, one on each wrist, and they gleamed as she made an impatient movement with her hand.

"He probably wouldn't have bothered. He'd have just made a date to collect the emeralds from me and then given me my return fare! Paid me off. 'Go home, little girl! I'm afraid

I don't want to marry you. Good-bye. And next time you meet up with a crook, make certain you get something more out of it than a ring with a poor-coloured diamond in it!'"

I was letting her talk, letting her work the bitterness out of her. I was also learning about her. I had thought she was strong, stormy and inclined to be hard. Now, I saw all that in action. She would learn *her* way from her mistakes and never make the same one twice. . . .

"Come and have some tea," I said, sounding so like my stepmother's "daily" woman offering her panacea for all trouble, that I could have laughed at myself. Except that the whole affair was too grave.

I heard Marcia say: "All right!" a little ungraciously as I turned toward the veranda door.

In the dressing-table mirror my left cheek with the scar was reflected almost starkly. My mind leapt across continents.

What was Lucien thinking and doing at this moment? I wondered. Would I, one day soon, receive a letter from him full of the old impatience for me? The psychiatrist had promised that, with Lucien's cure, his love for me would return. And here I was in Hong Kong to wait for the summons home . . . and to break the link once more with Max.

"What is it?" I heard Marcia ask sharply. "Why are you looking at me like that?"

I was jerked to the realisation that I had been staring beyond my reflection to hers, just over my shoulder.

"I'm sorry," I turned and smiled at her. "I was miles away. In England, as a matter of fact."

"Doesn't your fiancé mind you being here for so long?" she asked without much interest.

"No," I said briefly, "he doesn't mind. Come on," I touched her arm, "there's no padded teapot known that will keep tea hot indefinitely!"

On the balcony, we sat around and tried to believe we were spending a pleasant hour just chatting and drinking tea. But the conversation was intermittent and uneasy and tension gripped us all.

I fidgeted in my chair, made remarks I had made half a dozen times since I had come to Hong Kong, on the outsize moon, the fascinating huddle of roofs, the waft of incense carried on the still, hot air from Mr. Wu's.

I said:

"I'd like to learn to play mah-jongg," and then I sprang to my feet. "Gerry, can we have some music?"

"If you have the energy to put on the

records," he said. "I haven't!"

I went into the living-room and, kneeling before the radiogram, began looking through the records.

Gerry's taste was catholic. He was prepared to enjoy equally Mozart, Bartok or Johnny Dankworth. I turned over concertos and symphonies, short works by Delius, some musical comedy and came to a Beethoven record that took me back three years.

It was called "For Elissa." I set it on the turntable and to the beautiful, haunting tune stood with my back to the room, listening.

"I remember your stepmother playing that at your twentieth birthday party!"

I looked over my shoulder and saw Max.

"That was just before you left England," I said, my throat tight. "A long time ago!"

"And yet not so long! As I've told you, you haven't changed Francie."

"I hoped I had!"

"Why?"

"I hoped that you would no longer be able to say what you said to me when we said good-bye."

"What *did* I say to you?" he was laughing.

"You said. 'You are . . . so young. . . .'"

My hand gripped the walnut edge of the gramophone and the aquamarine on my finger danced with pale blue light. The diamonds surrounding it streaked purple and crimson and green fire. I dropped my hand quickly.

Max was watching me.

"I hope I can manage to be in London for your wedding. You must let me know the date." The very kindness of his tone hurt.

"We'll probably be married very quietly with no one knowing but those who have to be witnesses," I said untruthfully, knowing how Lucien loved publicity.

"Well, I'll hear through Gerry," Max told me, unperturbed.

We stood in the dim room with the shadow of the veranda keeping off the shafting silver moonlight that was so much more brilliant than in England. The music slowed and quickened, rose and fell with nostalgic passion. "For Elissa"! Who was Elissa for whom Beethoven wrote? Had she loved as I loved Max, without hope? Loving against all modern philosophy which said, in effect: "For God's sake fill your life and forget the man!" That's what I had nearly managed to do! Filling my life with Lucien, certain that in the end I would defeat my own aching memory. . . . And then, with the battle almost won, I had walked straight to the very place where I would meet Max again. . . .

The room had grown darker. A cloud dragged over the moon.

Max moved away from me. I wanted to reach out and bring him back. If he loved me, I thought, he would be so gentle! Not like Lucien who was violent and gay and flamboyant. . . .

The record came to an end. I thought I saw Marcia's shadowy head turn and peer round her chair-back into the room.

I said:

"Max, do you think Marcia will go back to London?"

"I suppose she'll have to, eventually. In the meantime. . . ."

"What?" I asked, my voice quick and a little rough.

"I wouldn't blame Gerry for wanting her out of his house. If he does, I've told him, I'll find her some quiet hotel, or even a kind family to stay with. Cheung Kin and his wife, for instance."

"And who," I asked, "is Cheung Kin?"

"A very cultured and Europeanised Chinese and his Eurasian wife, Lila. They have a charming house on the lower slopes of the Peak."

"If they know about all that's happened," I said drily, "I doubt if anyone, European or

217

Chinese, would fancy the task of taking Marcia in!"

"I think Kin and Lila would do it for me and I'd take responsibility and keep an eye on her."

In a flash I said:

"You're changing, Max! You, take responsibility for someone? You, the one who likes to live free−?" And then I stopped. I could have bitten my tongue out, not so much for the words, but for the bitter ache of my tone.

But Max could not have noticed, for he laughed.

"We all change!" he said.

But I had not! He had said so himself. I was still the young Fran, the girl he had kissed on the cheek and left behind. . . . I picked up the first record my fingers touched. It was a new French song. My fingers shook a little as I set it on the turntable.

"Francie−"

I turned. In the room's dimness I could only see Max standing very close to me, his head bent. I saw a movement of his hand and a swift flame leapt and throbbed in me.

"Yes?" My reply was a mere breath of sound.

At the same moment there was a stir at the veranda door.

"I love this tune," the voice broke the tentative moment into little shattered atoms. Marcia swung with a swirl of grey silk into the room. "Is anyone going to dance with me?"

She walked straight up to Max and even in the darkness I could feel her excitement.

He said, with laughing apology:

"I'm not a good dancer, I'm afraid!"

"Never mind, just move around!" she reached out her arms.

I leant over to the lamp.

"Oh, don't put the light on! The moon's enough!" she said.

I walked out of their slow, rhythmic orbit, telling myself that Max had not been about to say anything very significant to me when Marcia walked in, that she had not broken any delicate thread that would have drawn us closer.

I went out on the veranda and joined Gerry.

"What have you been saying to make Marcia so suddenly gay?" I asked him.

"Nothing, except that I've just been telling her that one day she'll see what a lucky escape she has had! I told her about Irene and that I had learned through her quite a bit about the subtleties of a woman's mind. I told her that if a girl's clever she can get almost any man she chooses. Especially if she's beautiful

219

as well! I'll bet Marcia knew it already, but it probably did her good to hear a man say it!"

Behind me in the dim room, I supposed they were still dancing. I did not want to turn round to see.

"It's you I'm concerned about!" my brother continued. "You're the one who has been dragged into danger. Yet we don't dare go to the police until we can identify the man. It's no use beating the grass if you don't know where the snake is lying."

"That medallion he found on the body," I said. "If it could be proved to be Marcia's and not mine—"

"How can you prove anything," Gerry said practically, "to someone you don't even know?"

"Gerry," I said urgently, "there's *got* to be a climax, hasn't there? I can't go on for weeks like this, never knowing where or when any-one is watching me; not quite knowing who'll get hurt."

"If Farson or Pun Ye don't force a climax, then *I* shall! Irene could put quite the wrong construction on Marcia being here. I'll give her another week and then, if the whole thing hasn't blown sky-wide, I'll go to the police and risk the consequences!"

The voice on the telephone had a macabre and permanent echo in my mind. I had not for one moment relaxed my certainty that it had meant what it said. If Gerry went to the police they would probably prove to their satisfaction that I had nothing to do with the smuggling. But for that freedom from fear someone near me, if not I myself, would get hurt just as an example to the rest of us that no one was playing a child's game of cops and robbers.

I reached towards the blue bowl, picked up a melon seed and cracked it. We had only one weapon—to play for time. . . .

The music stopped and Max came out on to the veranda holding Marcia's hand lightly. She said, pushing her radiant hair back from her forehead and laughing:

"Max underestimates his dancing!"

"You didn't try me too far! I've never got beyond the cha-cha-cha."

"That's all right," she said softly, "I'll settle for that and all the dances that have gone before!" She stood uncertainly on one leg and bent down, "My shoes hurt. They're too new to be dancing in!"

"Take them off," Gerry suggested from the shadowy depths of his chair.

"I'll change them." She slid out of them and carrying them, walked in nyloned feet along the veranda to her room. In her grey dress and her soundless feet, she was like a young ghost in the moonlight. I watched her turn the corner of the veranda.

Max broke the silence.

"I hear you've been to tea with Tiffany Lam."

I said I found her charming but that I wished I could have been shown her grandfather's especial treasures.

"You will be," Max said easily, "Before your stay is over. And that gives me an idea. It's time you tasted Hong Kong gaiety, Fran. I'll give a party tomorrow and we'll ask Tiffany Lam to come along. We'll have dinner on one of the restaurant boats out at Aberdeen."

"Oh, Max, that would be lovely!" Then I added: "Providing we *can* go! There's to-night to be got through."

"Nothing will happen to-night," Gerry said and put his arms behind his head and stared placidly out at his garden. "None of us is stirring from here for Sam Kang Pun Ye—or whatever he likes to call himself. Except, of course, Max when he goes home. But I don't imagine he's in any danger."

"If Miss Lam can come, I'll bring Drew Matheson to make up the numbers," Max said. "He's a newspaper man, too. You know him, Gerry, don't you?"

Gerry chuckled.

"He took thirty dollars off me last week playing poker for charity!"

I had picked up one of the black fans from the table and spread it out.

Marcia was taking a long time changing her shoes.

Restless and on edge, I got up and went down the veranda steps to the garden. I walked for a few minutes among the azaleas and irises, glancing up once or twice at the moon which sprayed a silver background for the old huddled street.

At the side of the house, the casuarina tree stood like a ragged, luminous sunshade. I went close to it and reached up and touched the faintly trembling leaves. As I did so, I looked towards Marcia's room. It was in darkness.

There was some more steps at the far end of the house. I went up them, along the veranda and pushed open the door of the guest room.

The full moonlight showed me that it was empty. I went inside. On the table lay the corrugated cardboard. The books were gone. At the same moment that I noticed this, from somewhere in the house, I heard a quarter to ten strike. It was as though the little clock had eyes and ears. It was telling me where Marcia had gone. . . .

Without knowing what I was doing, I picked up one of the pieces of cardboard and put it down again. My hand, brushing the uneven surface of the little lacquer table, was uncertain, my skin prickled.

I was afraid, for Marcia, for myself. . . I knew that in a wild act of bravado, she had gone to keep the appointment with the man called Midnight at Kam Ho Street.

I turned and ran to find Gerry and Max.

"The utter little fool!" Gerry exploded when I told them she was missing. "But how did she get away without our seeing her? There's only one way out of the garden."

"We weren't exactly facing the gate, were we?" Max said. "If she moved carefully, keeping to the wall . . ."

"She meant to go," I said. "Her shoes didn't hurt her! She was making an excuse to get away from us!"

"She probably thinks she can clear Francie of implication in all this!" Max said quietly.

"I tried to tell her that if she did, she'd never be believed. It would be suspected as being just a way of trying to turn the spotlight off Fran," Gerry snapped. He glanced quickly at his watch. "Come on! Maybe we can get there before he does. I'll bet a bet with you he'll watch to see if she brings anyone with her before he goes in to talk to her." He jumped the veranda steps. "I could wish that girl a thousand miles away. You stay here, Fran."

"Oh no, I won't!" I flew along the passage leading to the kitchen and called to Yee Sze that we were all going out for a while. I said, "And Yee Sze, please lock all the doors while we're gone."

He stood looking at me with faint surprise.

"Yes, missie. If you say—" But I knew he had never been alone in the house with all the doors locked before.

I raced back and joined the men down at the gate.

"You'll only be in the way—" Gerry made a last bid to rid himself of me. But Max laid a hand on my arm.

"There's no time to argue. Let Francie come." For a moment, as I looked up at him, his eyes in the light streaming from Mr. Wu's restaurant smiled straight into mine.

We got into the car and the drive to Kam Ho Street took only a few minutes. When we arrived there, Max said:

"It isn't quite ten o'clock, and my guess is that so far she'll be alone. I think it would be better for only one of us to go to her. You and Francie stay here." He got out of the car, raised a hand in a small half-salute and disappeared down the ink-black alley at the back of the row of shops.

"Suppose we go round to the front," Gerry said. "We can at least keep watch on the place. That padlock you say is on the shop door may mean nothing. Someone could perhaps get in that way."

We left the car in a place where we should not be parking and went down Kam Ho Street until we were level with the bookshop. Then we crossed the road and stood under a light looking up at the unshuttered windows. There was neither light nor movement.

"Hi, Gerry!"

Someone passing, hailed him. He swung round.

"Murrell! Where's your bridge four tonight?"

"I've been to the Fosters' cocktail party and I've only just managed to get away."

"This is my sister, Francie," Gerry turned to me. "I told you she was coming out to stay with me, didn't I? Fran, this is Angus Murrell, one of the lounge lizards from the Peak top."

"I'm no lounge lizard! And if I didn't like

your brother so much I'd bring an action for slander against him!" The tubby young man without much hair gave me a broad grin. I said, "How do you do," smiled, and then, while Gerry and he talked, I turned back and looked up at the window of No. 43.

There was a glow which seemed to come from beyond the room door. I supposed it was a staircase light.

I heard Angus Murrell laugh; heard Gerry say:

"But it's true! He's given up his English doctor and is being treated by a Chinese. He swears he has been cured by dried snake and acupuncture!"

I had only a vague idea that Gerry had told me of the ancient Chinese system of sticking pins into people as a cure for illness. I registered a resolve to ask Gerry more about it sometime. My eyes began to hurt with my concentrated upward staring.... Then someone moved across that distant light. Slender, little more than a shadow. A woman's shadow. And another—a man's. I held my breath. I saw the girl's movement towards him, saw the two of them draw close so that, from this distance, in that dim light, they seemed to be like lovers sculpted in shadow.

Marcia and Eric?

Vaguely I was aware that Gerry and his friend were tossing parting remarks to one another and turned just in time to add my good-bye smile.

Angus Murrell said:

"Bring Francie round to dinner one night. Maeve would love to meet her."

"I will."

"Gerry," I said when we were alone, "watch that window!"

But the sculpted shadows far back in the room were gone.

"I saw her!" I said. "I know it was Marcia! And there was a man with her. Because the room was in darkness, they obviously didn't realise that the landing light would show them up."

"What was the man like?"

"When I saw Eric in the street," I said, "he had a shaven head. I don't think this man—"

"You probably saw Max."

"Oh, *no!*" I said swiftly. *"No!"*

"All right! You don't have to be so violent about it!" his voice was faintly amused. "Let's go back there and see for ourselves."

Max... Max and Marcia... Earlier this evening, I had stood in the living-room with Max listening to an old tune, drawing close to him. And then Marcia had entered and taken him away; danced with him ... had come out on to the veranda with his hands in hers. ... A wild, baseless thought plunged into my mind and would not go. Had Marcia's act of bravado to-night been, after all, to clear me of suspicion? Or had it been to impress Max?

XII

When we reached the corner of the alley, Gerry pushed me back.

"You stay here. Or, better still, go back to the car."

"Don't be silly!" I spoke sharply and reached out and caught his arm as he strode ahead. "Wait for me!"

"Keep out of trouble, Fran!"

"I'm in it!" I said bitterly. "You seem to forget I'm the one they're interested in!"

"All the more reason to stay away!" my brother retorted shortly.

I did not answer him back but as we went down the dark alley I kept very close to his side. The only doorway that was lit was No. 43 and as we reached it I saw that my guess out in Kam Ho Street had been correct. A poor light burned over the stairs. I heard a sound and turned quickly. But it was only the echo of our own footsteps.

The passage door was open and Gerry put an arm round my shoulders. Together we took a few steps into the hall.

I looked up to the top of the landing. At first there was no one there. Then I saw someone come swiftly to the head of the stairs. My heart somersaulted before I realised that it was Max.

Gerry called in a carefully muted voice.

"Are you alone?"

"Marcia is with me," he sounded impatient. "Be a good chap and go back to the car and take Francie with you. If anyone's watching they won't come while a whole army is around. I'm going back to wait with Marcia."

My lips did not move; I made neither sound nor movement but my thoughts spoke to him. 'So it was you in the front room with Marcia! She must have heard you come in and then, in a wild relief at hearing your voice and not a stranger's, run to you. And you took her in your arms to reassure her!'...I faced the poignant, indisputable fact that on such a mixture as compassion and impulse, was love sometimes founded....

"Max is right!" I heard my own small, sick voice say. "Let's go, Gerry."

"But *you'll* still be here—" Gerry argued, frowning at Max. "So I can't see—"

"When I came," Max cut in, his voice rushed and urgent, "no one saw me."

"How do you know that?"

"Because there was no one passing at either end of the alley at the time! Whereas when you and Francie came down, I was at the landing window. There were people around. So will you two please make yourselves scarce? I'm telling you, no one will come while there's a mob of us!"

I turned on my heel while Max was still speaking and walked down the passage towards the door. The bare boards creaked; the place smelt dusty, slightly decayed. Somewhere, I supposed from the next house, I heard the thin rise and fall of minor notes of Chinese music.

Just inside the door lay a piece of paper. It showed very white against the grimy boards and I knew it had not been there when we came in. I stopped quite still and lifted my face. The air was warm and there was no wind that could have blown it there.

"What's that?" My voice was ragged because already I had guessed.

Gerry bent and picked it up and unfolded it. Then he handed it to me.

In English lettering was printed:

Next time, come yourself. And alone, Miss Mannering. We will be in touch with you.

Gerry called up the stairs: "There's no need for you two to wait!"

I stared out into the black alley so that I did not have to watch them come down the stairs together.

I smelt Marcia's scent as she stood reading the note over my shoulder. I heard her quick intake of breath and turned and looked at her. It could have been the ugly naked light that took all the colour from her face.

She said:

"And now they'll make another appointment. And—and if we don't . . ."

"*We?*" Gerry was obviously angry and shaken. "Not '*we*,' my dear, but Fran! *Fran,* because they're being too clever by half! It's my sister they watched come here to-night, not you! And she won't be safe until Pun Ye knows who is Farson's girl. And then—"

"And then—?" Marcia whispered. "*I* won't be safe!"

"Exactly!"

"Let's get out of here!" Max spoke for the first time. He moved to the door, his hand on Marcia's arm.

Gerry took the note from me.

"I'll keep that," he said. "It might be useful!"

As we went down the alley, I thought I saw a movement in the shadows behind one of the back doors. But it could have been our own dark passing reflections in the glass. My knees shook. I had a shuddering, fanciful theory that Pun Ye—the man "Midnight"—was a sorcerer; that he walked with us, invisible ... silent ...

Marcia sat in the back of the car with Max. I sat in front with Gerry. Before he switched on the engine, he said over his shoulder:

"By the way, how did you get out of the garden without being seen?"

"I kept close to the wall," Marcia said. "You were sitting with your backs half towards the gate. There were a few big clouds coming up. I waited till one hid the moon."

"You think of everything, don't you?" Gerry's voice was cold.

"I tried to think of Francie," Marcia replied softly.

Gerry leaned forward and switched on the engine without comment. We were driving along Pedder Street. A large American car drew up alongside us at the traffic lights. There was something so bright about it that I half turned to see who would want to sit in the full glare of the car's interior light. As I did so, I could not help glancing at the back of Gerry's car. Marcia was sitting back in her corner but was leaning slightly against Max's shoulder.

I turned my head quickly and stared ahead of me pretending to be fascinated by the brilliant, neon-lit scene. In the next few whirling seconds I faced the fact that perhaps I had been too proud, too reticent in those old days when Max had been with us. I had never reached out my hand to him, let my hair just brush his face as I danced with him, or leaned lightly against him in a car to let him feel me near him as a woman. . . . Marcia was missing none of the little tricks. Marcia with her coppery flame of hair; her creamy lovely skin; her luscious young body. . . . Well, I was young too and not bad to look at. A man who was rapidly making a name for himself in the theatre had loved me once and would love me again when the psychiatrist had cured him of shock!

XIII

All through the next morning, I waited for the telephone to ring. Once, I even went and lifted the receiver to discover if the line were out of order. It wasn't.

That afternoon we sat in the shade and down in the garden Harriet Craig worked at her painting. I was growing used to seeing her there, yet the faint irritation I felt did not lessen. As usual, when tea-time came, she packed up her things and without looking our way, left.

"I feel mean," I said as Yee Sze brought out tea, "not asking her to join us. But Gerry isn't keen on our getting too friendly—"

"And anyway," Marcia said matter-of-factly, "she doesn't give you much chance to ask her, does she? She keeps to herself and then, like the Arabs, she folds up her paraphernalia and quietly steals away."

Which was exactly what she did, I thought.

As I reached over the table for the teapot, my ring must have glinted in the sunshine, for Marcia glanced at it.

"Are you going to live in England when you're married?"

I said I was and handed her one of the pretty, peony-painted cups. "At least," I added, "we shall make our home in London although as Lucien is an actor, I suppose we shall have periods in New York and on tour."

"An actor?" Her voice warmed. "I love the theatre. Do you think I've ever seen him act?"

"He's Lucien Blake," I said in explanation.

She was so surprised that she stared at me for a silent moment, her mouth a little open, her hand suspended outstretched for her cup. I felt that suddenly with the mention of that name, I had become interesting to her.

"You're engaged to *him?*" she demanded in slow wonder. "I've been here three days and you didn't tell me before?"

"We had other things to think about!" I said briefly.

Her gaze still said: *You and Lucien Blake...?*

"I saw him in *Cat's Eye!* That was his first big part, wasn't it, Francie? The critics raved....I remember, the play haunted me. Then I read he had a car accident. What happened to him? Was he badly injured?"

I told her.

By the way she looked at me I saw that she could not understand why, if Lucien were ill, I was out here on holiday. I could not explain it all to her. For that I would have to go into details about Lucien's character, the way shock had antagonised him towards me, the concentrated psychiatric treatment. And Marcia was not close enough to me for me to tell her all that. . . .

When I had given her the brief facts, I asked her, before she had time for any more questions, about Eric.

She seemed, for the first time, to want to talk about him. I guessed that she had come out of shock into anger.

She had met him on a train, she said, when she had travelled to Cornwall last Christmas to stay with a school friend.

Eric was going to Fowey and during the long journey he told her about his life East, first in Shanghai where he had lived with his father and then in Hong Kong. It had been a very swift mutual attraction and by the end of the journey they had arranged to meet in London after the holidays.

"So," I said, "you didn't know very much a-bout Eric, did you, before you became engaged?"

She said a little mulishly:

"I knew enough! At least I thought I did! Eric talked well. He described a lovely home out here, lots of friends. The bookshop sounded the sort of place where rich people went for rare editions—"

"And you didn't meet any member of his family?"

"I told you, his father was dead. He did not know where his mother was. She completely disappeared when Eric was thirteen."

"Didn't you meet friends of his in London, people who had known him?"

"How could I," she said with a touch of defiance, "when he had spent his life in the East and all his friends were there?"

"I thought perhaps he had come to England to school and had made friends—"

"Eric was on holiday," she said. "We didn't want other people. When we returned to London we had a marvelous time. It didn't matter that neither of us had a host of curious relatives to show each other off to!"

"It might have been better if you had!" I told her shortly.

A kind of on-guard look was in her eyes. She knew quite well that I wanted to say: "You got yourself engaged to a comparative stranger—without knowing his background, his friends, anything? He could have been the biggest crook . . . it seems he is! . . ." And she was daring me to say it!

To disarm her, I smiled straight into those wary eyes.

"The sooner we find Eric the better it'll be for everyone!"

Marcia put down her teacup and got up. She walked to the little tiled plinth and back again. She said shakenly:

"I've done a dreadful thing, involving you! But how could I know what would happen after we . . . we saw that dead man? Francie . . . I couldn't . . . could I?"

"Of course, you couldn't!" I said, trying to sound reassuring. "Sit down and relax."

Sunlight lay brilliantly beyond our patch of shade. Roses, irises, carnations, were like crimson, purple and pink fire, the leaves of the camellias shone and burned dark green . . . 'Green fire' . . . I shivered in the humid air and turned my head towards the gate. I had a queer feeling that any of us sitting on the veranda or here in the courtyard were vulnerable to watching eyes which might peer through the grille of the nail-studded gate.

I thought of the man I was certain was Eric, with the shaven head and the long grey-blue gown. I thought of another man, too, whose face I had never seen but whose voice had menaced me. I who had nothing to do with the 'green fire'! And Marcia, who had everything to do with it, walking free.... Just because an unknown criminal thought he was being smart!

"—if I went away—"

I started and looked up at Marcia who, so restless, was standing again and seeming to be staring straight into the sun.

"I'm sorry," I began, "I only heard half—"

"I was saying that I suppose it wouldn't help if I went away."

"No," I agreed, "I'm afraid it wouldn't! Pun Ye, or whatever he likes to call himself, is too convinced that I'm the one to watch. I'm caught up in this like a fish in a net and there's nothing anyone can do!" I finished my tea and it tasted like liquid straw. I couldn't stop being frightened and as if that were not enough, I had to have my whole self torn apart by Max.... I thought of my grandmother, of her nodding wisdom:

"It never rains but it pours, my dear!"

It was pouring all right, for me!

XIV

I had brought out with me from London a short white dress which the *Vogue* advertisement had described as being "dramatically patterned with huge crimson roses." It had a swathed bodice and a full skirt. It was perfect for an informal evening and to-night we were Max's guests on a restaurant boat out at Aberdeen on the far side of the island.

I had coaxed my hair into little swirls with one sweeping crosswise over the top of my forehead. I was standing back to admire the effect when there was a tap on my door.

I said, without turning my head:

"Come in."

Marcia appeared in the doorway. I saw her reflection over my shoulder in the mirror. She wore a vivid grass-green sheath of a dress. Wickedly simple, it even had tiny pseudo-innocent cape sleeves. At each wrist she wore her wide copper bangles that burned and glowed like her hair.

She looked nothing like the shocked and terrified girl I had first met near Tai-yuan Street. And if she were still suffering from the knowledge that she had been made use of by the man who had professed to love her, she certainly did not show it.

She probably had great emotional recuperative powers, I thought—a tremendous will to triumph over shock.

"That's a lovely dress," I said.

"It is, isn't it?" she walked towards the mirror and looked at herself. She wore the sheerest nylons and bronze slippers. I could see that she would attract men. She had that paradoxical quality that was coolness and flame. It was a birthright. No one in this world could acquire it.

"When I bought it," she was saying, smoothing the dress along her hips, "I was horrified at the price. The assistant told me that it was 'all in the cut.' I said: 'Well, who cares about money when she's buying a trousseau?' Trousseau! That's funny, isn't it?"

I left her at the mirror and went to the window. Over in the north-west the sky was deepening, the apricot-edged clouds casting mauve shadows over the Nine Peaks of Kowloon.

Down in the garden it was very still. Not a

flower, not a camellia leaf stirred. I wondered if anyone peered through the grille in the gate, watching for us, for me. . . . It was queer and fanciful, but in my imagination, so strong as to be nearly real, I could hear singing crickets. . . .

"What's the matter, Francie?" I heard Marcia ask.

"Nothing . . . nothing at all," I said quickly. "Come on, let's go downstairs."

The men were waiting for us on the veranda. Max introduced Drew Matheson. He was a broad-shouldered, ginger-haired young man, who looked as though he would have been more at home striding across the moors of his native Scotland. I was surprised to learn that the "Bonnie, Bonnie Banks" meant very little to him and that he had not been home for years.

We were to fetch Tiffany Lam. Max's big car would take the six of us. Marcia sat between him and Drew. Gerry and I sat behind with room for Tiffany.

She did not keep us waiting when Max called at the house for her. She was wearing a *cheongsam* of peacock blue with a motif of flowers worked on it in silver thread. From one long slender hand she trailed a little Chinese coat of silver and black and green.

We drove up Pokfulum Road and out round the hills. The casuarinas and the camel-foot trees threw patches of shade across the road. We seemed to be driving straight towards the sea and the islands. There was cloud sitting like a top hat over Lantao.

I knew why Max had asked Drew Matheson to make up our numbers. He was very good company and we laughed a lot during the journey across the island to Aberdeen. Absurdity was an infinitely greater panacea for disturbed minds such as ours than intellectual wit.

Drew had been telling us about what he had, at the time, thought to be his great scoop. Years ago, his very first foreign assignment had been in Central Africa. Driving through a jungle village he had come upon some crates hidden in bush. Very young and full of enthusiasm, he thought he was on to some great arms smuggling racket. With the help of his native driver he had dragged one of the crates into the Land Rover and driven to the police. The crate was opened. They contained, he told us sadly, second-hand ear-trumpets for the natives. We scarcely believed his story, but we were laughing as we climbed out of the car at Aberdeen. We wanted so badly to laugh. . . .

Directly we left the car, we were besieged by trousered women touting to row us out to our restaurant boat. Max steered us through the jostling women, towards a sturdy boat-woman in a round straw hat who fought off her rivals and led us to her gay, blue-painted sampan.

Marcia stumbled on the stone landing-steps and laughed. Gerry steadied her. It was now nearly dark. The sunset had been swift and I felt Max's hand guiding me. I said, glancing across at the boats:

"All those lights. How gay! If it weren't for this other business, how happy we could all be!"

"*Be* happy, Fran!" Max said so softly that only I could have heard. "Lose your memory just for to-night!"

On the boat, we sat on wicker settees under a canvas gondola cover and the ferry-woman paddled the sampan out into the harbour.

Max pointed out a boat hung with lanterns. "Look! There's a wedding party," he said.

The noise on it must have been deafening. We could still hear it when we reached the house-boat where we were to dine. The Chinese owner met us and we were taken up the steps past the family's living quarters and through the kitchen.

"If you like," Max said by my side, "you can choose your fish."

He led us to the tanks full of caught fish, lobsters and shrimps and garoupas. We were dining late and I was hungry. Laughing, tension dropping from us now that we were away from the island, we chose our fish. Marcia wanted one of the speckled crabs; I chose garoupa. We leaned over the tanks watching them being netted.

Then we climbed to the restaurant floor and sat at a round table under a gay awning.

Music drifted to us from the boats; streamers fluttered in a light breeze; lights snaked along the water and everywhere there was the hub of laughter.

Half-way through dinner, Max said:

"Look, Francie, the moon has risen."

I turned to look at it, hanging like a witch's ball above the island, pouring down borrowed light and taking some mysterious force from us.

An exhilarating sense of freedom seized me. We were away from the land and from a menacing voice. . . .

Tiffany's eyes met mine on laughter.

"The gayest thing in the world! What is it?"

"To forget yesterday and ignore to-morrow!" Max lifted his glass. "To the everlasting present!" he said and solemnly as though it were a rite, we drank.

I don't know at what stage of that long, animated dinner party I noticed Marcia's excitement. It was neither noisy nor blatant; she wore it like an aura around her and, while Drew was talking, telling us an absurdity with a deadpan face, I glanced at her. I knew without a doubt that the excitement concerned Max. Again and again my eyes were drawn fascinatedly to her. I was witnessing the attempt by a beautiful girl to charm a man... And the irony of it was that there was no conceivable moral reason why she should not....

Later, after we had drunk green tea, Marcia, Tiffany and I wandered off to the stern of the boat. On this particular junk, it was not taken up with family living-space but was for the diners, if they so wished to stretch their legs and stand for a while under the stars.

The space was confined, but at least we were away from the crowded dining part of the deck. Leaning on the gaudy, painted rail, we watched the lights reflected in the black water; listened to laughter, music, the voices of children. Did Chinese children never go to bed, I wondered?

Tiffany was telling us a little about her life in Peking. She would love to show us the

Forbidden City, she said. She talked of the marble boats, dragon gates, golden pillars, and once more I was struck with the names of things—the poetry of words the Chinese love. The Gate of Heavenly Peace...the House of Pure Affection...the Altar of Heaven....

I rested my arms on the rail, listening. Marcia was trying to see herself in her compact mirror.

That was why none of us was quite alert enough to know exactly where the voice came from. Only, in a moment's lull in our talking, it reached us with an uncanny disembodiment. It rose from the darkness, empty, macabre...

It said:

"The waterfront. To-morrow at seven o'clock. A junk opposite shirtmaker Tai Tsang. Bring the 'green fire' and come alone."

Marcia jerked back from the rail so quickly that she dropped her compact. I heard the crack of glass. Tiffany looked round at her puzzled. I stared down into the water because I was quite sure the voice had come from there.

It was Tiffany who bent and picked up the little gilt compact.

"Oh, Marcia, you've broken your mirror!" she held it out.

Marcia made no attempt to take it.

"Who – who – spoke? . . ."

"I don't know," I said. "The voice seemed to come from the water."

"I think it came from below us – one of the family calling to his brother or sister or some-one!" Tiffany laughed. "Someone is going to give a party! With fireworks."

"Fireworks?" I asked quickly.

She nodded.

"I should think that was what they meant by 'green fire,'" she said. "I wonder what it is? A birthday or a wedding? . . ."

I scarcely heard her. I was still peering down into the black water to see if I could detect the slightest shadow of movement. The Chinese, I had heard, were excellent under-water swimmers.

My fingers clung to the rail as though they were glued there. I was even more frightened than I had been that first time when the voice had spoken to me on the telephone. This message to-night meant that we were being watched everywhere. It meant that the pursuit was to be relentless, reaching me when I was no longer on the island. . . .

"Let's go back to our table," I said. Underneath my brisk manner I was trembling.

Tiffany held out Marcia's compact.

"Perhaps you can get another glass fitted. . . ."

"It doesn't matter," Marcia said almost ungraciously and dropped the compact into her bag.

A Chinese family greeted Tiffany as she passed their table. Marcia walked on, dragging at my arm.

"Where did that voice come from, Francie? Do you think he's on this boat?"

"I don't know," I said soberly. "The voice was so curiously pitched in order, I suppose, that it would carry through all the other noises! I think it came from the sea."

"But that means . . ."

"That my next approach is fixed for me!" My voice was ragged.

"They're not very clever, are they?" Marcia said slowly, "or they'd know that Eric has got the emeralds."

I did not answer. I was looking out over the crowded water as we made our way back to our table.

Where was he? Below us in the restaurant-owner's living quarters—a friend of the Chinese family? I doubted it. Then had he dived from one of the sampans around us and swum under water, to hide in the boat's shadow and call up his message? It was so much more deadly than sending us another note or telephoning again; it indicated that, even off the island, I could not escape him. . . .

I wanted more than anything else to get my brother alone and tell him what had happened. But the men were suggesting that, as it was only half-past ten, we should go on to one of the hotels and dance.

On the journey back across the water, I managed to sit next to Gerry on the boat. While I fretted for an opportunity to talk to him quietly, I found myself once more watching Marcia and Max. They sat together and their hands touched. . . . Drew had started an argument on the merits and demerits of living on an island. Under cover of the talk around me, I managed to tell Gerry, briefly, what had happened.

"What am I going to do?" I asked helplessly.

His eyes stared, narrow and speculative, ahead of him. I heard the liquid caress of water, against oar; I saw the brilliant patches of light the restaurant junks made over the sea. . . .

"Gerry—" I urged as he did not answer me.

He turned and looked at me. His good looking, easy-going face surveyed me.

"We're going dancing," he said coolly, "and no one will go near the waterfront to-morrow."

I did not know whether to be relieved or alarmed at his calm dismissal of the order.

Each time we ignored the message of the man who called himself Midnight, the more dangerous the situation might become. Didn't Gerry see? . . . Agitation set my heart racing. What was the use of casually dismissing a danger—it would only increase it. You did not stop a storm by closing your ears to the thunder. . . .

I knew I must talk to Max as soon as possible.

On land again we left our trousered boatwoman and piled in to the car. Back in the city we went to a hotel that had a roof-top dance floor. There was a Filipino band and lights slung in lanterns shaped like dragons. Azaleas in pots were ranged before half-moon mirrors.

Max asked me for the first dance. While we moved round the floor together, I closed my mind to time and events. Childishly, blindly, I gave myself up to the joy of being in Max's arms. But when the music stopped, I seized my opportunity. I held back the hand that was leading me towards our table.

"I must talk to you alone!" I said.

"Then let's go on to the roof garden."

In the half light from the room, the banks of leaves of the camellias looked rich and deep and as steeped in mystery as old Venetian velvet. I smelt the bouquet of jasmine and roses. In the distance, the kerosene flares of the fishing fleet dipped and rose in Deep Water Bay. Below us, in a side street, I heard the staccato shouts of street acrobats performing their lithe monkey feats. Behind us, the Filipino band played a cha-cha-cha.

My fingers curved over the balustrade, my left hand too near Max's. I only had to reach out a matter of inches and I would be touching him. I looked quickly away and, wrapped in the warm night, I told him as I had told Gerry, what had happened on the restaurant boat.

"So someone followed us." He frowned at the darkness. "He had a long journey for his money!"

"It's a fortune," I reminded him grimly, "in little green stones!"

"I suppose he thought you were planning to contact Farson on the boat."

"Max, what do I *do*?" I turned to him, moved a fraction closer. My voice had a child's helplessness.

"*You*, Fran, do nothing!"

"Gerry said that, too," I said unsteadily, "but neither of you listened in to that telephone conversation! He wasn't joking when he threatened. If I don't keep the appointment this time he might get vicious."

"I'll talk to Gerry when we get back to the house to-night. We'll work out something. Some plan that precludes you!" he said kindly but firmly.

"But I can't *be* precluded!" I cried and then, aware of people standing nearby, I dropped my voice. "Suppose I keep that appointment? It's crowded down at the waterfront, isn't it? No one would harm me in daylight."

"Leave it, Fran. Whoever goes, it won't be you!"

"But if someone followed me—you or Gerry—and saw—"

"No!" Max said, and moved a fraction away from me as though the discussion were at end.

I swallowed and managed to control my voice.

"Max, it's horrible—not knowing whom we're looking for! Even if it means I'm risking to look over my shoulder or—or to be alone in the house! You can't fight anything or anyone until you know what, or whom, it is! So for my own sake, somehow, *anyhow!* I've got to know what he looks like! Max, I—" I caught my words back sharply as his fingers came down on my wrist.

"I've told you! Let it be, Fran! I'll talk to Gerry. But *you* must do nothing! We'll all see that no harm comes to you; that you're never alone. . . ."

Words to ease my fear! But only words! How could I be guarded against something unknown, unrecognised? I had managed so far to be calm about it all. Now, talking it out with Max had brought the mounting fear to the surface. It spread like a fog hiding invisible hands, choking me. I leaned against the balustrade as though I could not stand alone.

"He followed me to Aberdeen; he could be here among us! Anywhere." I shot a glance around me, and saw the dim shapes of people. "And any of these—"

"Fran, don't!" his voice was sharp. His fingers gripped mine, hard, crushing my ring into my flesh.

"Doesn't it occur to you that you're the one least likely to be hurt? You're the one who is supposed to be hiding that little fortune in emeralds."

I was irreconcilable.

"Do you think I'm only being scared for myself? Any one of you could be hurt! *You* Max!"

"Oh, Fran!" his laughter was gentle; he took his hand away. "Don't you think Gerry and I are old enough and big enough to take care of ourselves? As for Marcia—well, we've got to protect her, too!"

Like a vivid flashback came the memory of Marcia's hand on the gate of Gerry's house, the gold chain bracelet and the one tiny ring that had held a medallion. . . . The man who called himself Midnight had it but the fact that it could perhaps be proved that it was Marcia's gave me no relief from personal fear. A medallion would be nothing to him whose real name I did not know. He had seen Eric wait for me by Gerry's gate; speak to me . . . *I* was the one. . . .

Somewhere above, a plane circled. The drone of its engine had a faintly uneven sound, like words, two words . . . Green fire. Green fire.

"Max," I said brokenly, "when something like this happens to people, do they—do they break?"

"Some people break easily," he said. "An upset love affair is enough. But *you* won't! You're strong, Francie!"

That word again, used as the psychiatrist in London had used it!

"People say that to you when they expect you to stand up and take every knock that comes!" I said resentfully. "Like those little men hawkers sell on trays at Christmas time that you hit all ways and they never fall over! I'm not strong, Max! Not inside myself where it doesn't show!"

I felt his eyes looking down at me but I did not turn my head.

"I think you're strong in character, Francie."

"Tough? Insensitive? Invulnerable? Self-sufficient?" I demanded. "Is that the sum total of being strong inside? If so, then you don't know me! You never have!" My sudden up-rush of anger eased my fear—like deliberately hurting yourself in one place to stop the hurt in another! "Don't you ever look below the surface of a person?" I demanded. "Don't you ever wonder what's going on behind what people pretend to be?"

"That's what I try to do always." If my outburst surprised him, he did not show it. "If I've ever failed to do that with you, I'm sorry. I thought I knew you very well. But suppose we go a little deeper and admit that no one on this earth ever really knows anyone else?"

"But we can try," I said on the dying flame of my anger.

"What am I supposed to try and do? What, Francie?"

I did not answer. My anger had somehow been part of my fear. I had attacked the one I loved most. But we had gone too far away from the original point. I did not dare go deeply into emotions because Max was perceptive and I would give myself away. Quite suddenly the truth would strike him. He would think: "Oh, God! This girl is in love with me!" And then all my life I would know the humiliation of a secret shared with the one person who should never have known. . . .

I had not answered his question and he was watching me, waiting for it. For my own safety's sake, I had to return to what we had first talked about.

"I'm threatened and I'm scared!"

"Don't you think, ever since this happened, it has been on Gerry's mind and mine?" he asked steadily. "Don't you think we're doing what we think best—and safest—for you?"

"Yes," I said honestly and the word dropped heavily between us.

"We daren't go to the police, Francie. You know that!"

The shining, skin-warm leaves of a camellia brushed my bare arm. Something stirred the bank of azaleas nearby. I started, staring towards them, waiting for a voice. But it was only a light wind playing among them. No one was there, listening, watching. . . .

I saw Max follow my gaze.

"I'll be afraid of my own shadow next!" I said.

Then my trite little phrase made me laugh. I met his eyes.

"That's better!" he said. "Now would you like to dance?"

"I'd rather stay here." I lifted my head to the stars and took a deep breath. My nerves steadied and suddenly I was no longer afraid. Max was by my side and the roses had a silken, Eastern smell.

"Have you ever wanted certain moments to last for ever?"

"Many times," he told me lightly. "You know what the poet says: 'While we have memory, there will be roses in December.'"

"Oh, quotations!" I exclaimed.

He laughed at me.

"It always seems that someone else has put what I want to say so much better than I could ever do."

"That isn't being original!"

"I'm a journalist," he said easily, "not a poet!"

"Besides," I protested, "I don't want the memory of lovely things, I want the things themselves!"

"Then you must learn to perform miracles, Francie!" he said quietly. "Come along, let's go and find the others. And stop worrying about to-morrow. Gerry and I will work something out."

The hand on my arm was steady. I gave one last despairing look at distant Kowloon, flashing and sparkling like a pride of jewels on dark velvet. I dragged a little at his hand in mine. Max felt nothing for me. He did not even understand. He had quoted something about "Roses in December" at me. He thought that behind my fear, which he had tried to allay, I was just a greedy child never wanting to come down to earth.

Oh, Max!...Emotion momentarily unsteadied me. My ankle turned slightly and I stumbled against him.

"Hey!" he held me for a moment. "Did you hurt yourself?"

As I said "No" I looked ahead. There were four people in the wide doorway. Tiffany Lam with Gerry, Marcia with Drew Matheson.

They were coming towards us. Three of them were laughing at something Gerry had said. The fourth, Marcia, looked from me to Max. Then she turned her head away. It was a slight movement that showed her lovely profile outlined against the lights of the room behind her.

I said over-brightly:

"It's quite lovely out there! The view is breath-taking and over the sea—"

"You sound," Gerry cut in, "like a copywriter, thinking up platitudes for a travel brochure!"

"Look for yourself." My voice was still very bright.

Marcia was by Max's side in a few silent steps.

I heard her say:

"Dance with me, Max!"

He looked at me. I said:

"Go along!" and stretched my lips into a smile.

I watched him go, her hand in his, through the door and on the dance floor. I stared at the Filipinos in their dove-grey suits behind the bank of azaleas. Then Marcia, in Max's arms, came between me and the band. I thought: She is the most beautiful girl in the room. Later she, too, might want to talk to Max and be brought out here. He had quoted a line of poetry to me. I wondered what he would quote to her. Or whether her curious witchery would make an original poet of him . . . I hated the thought.

Was Hong Kong ever really silent?

Wrapped in my house coat, I went to the window and pushing open the casements, leant my arms on the sill. I stared down at the lights in Mr. Wu's back room where they played mah-jongg far into the night. Click-clack-clack.... I could actually hear the sounds of the tiles.

I also heard Gerry still talking to Max down below.

Before Marcia and I left them, Gerry had changed his mind about doing nothing. I had listened to him talking out his plan for the waterfront at sunset tomorrow.

Gerry was going to telephone a Hong Kong detective he knew and ask him to come to his office. There he would tell him as much as he thought it safe for him to know at this stage. Gerry himself was going to the waterfront. There, at a distance he would keep watch on the spot opposite Tai Tsang's shirt shop. The detective would be farther away still, watching for Gerry's signal.

The waterfront, he said, was always a place of milling crowds and he knew of a spot where he could safely watch and see who, among the carrier coolies, the sampan women and children, had no definite business with crates or coolies but who waited—wandering perhaps a little backwards and forwards, but always with his eyes turned towards the wooden landing plank opposite Tai Tsang's shop. A man who would be watching for a girl—for me.... He would telephone me, he said, if there were any alterations to his arrangement but in the meantime Marcia and I were to stay home, to remain together. We had said, fervently, that we would.

I leant my forehead against the window frame.

I was tired, frightened but reluctant to go to bed. I don't know which I was most scared of, my thoughts while I remained awake or my dreams if I went to sleep.

Chairs scraped down below and I supposed that Max would be going home. I would wait and see him leave, watch him through the gate. Then I would turn out the light.

I heard their footsteps on the wooden veranda, heard Gerry close the big glass doors and cross the living-room. At the same time Max came in view. I watched him walk half-way down the garden and pause to take a cigarette from his case and light it. I heard Gerry on the stairs, heard him pass my room. Below me, Max pocketed his lighter and I saw him half turn. The next minute Marcia came out of the shadow of the house. She half ran towards him.

Quickly, I drew back; but I could not stop myself watching them. I saw both her hands go out and I knew she said something to him softly. His head was bent. There was no light from the downstairs part of the house, nor even a moon to clarify Max's expression as he stood looking down at Marcia. But there was no need for light. What she said to him I did not know. Nor what he answered—if, indeed he spoke at all.

In a movement so single, so complete that it had a lovely grace of its own, Marcia was in Max's arms. I saw his head bend down, saw her face tilt, her hair flow back. Even the darkness could not quite take away its flame.

Then I could not watch any longer.

I crossed the room, slipped out of my dressing-gown and climbed into bed. There, with the light switched off, lying on my back, I gazed sightlessly up at the ceiling and tried to shut out the images in the garden.

I had no idea how long they were out there together for my room was not over Marcia's and therefore I did not hear her door close. But I lay in that utter loneliness and wondered what art had been left out of my make-up that I could not win as surely, as easily as Marcia, the man I loved. . . .

XV

I dreamed that night I was in a plane that made no landing. I did not know where I was going and it was always dark. Every time I looked at my watch, the tiny hands were tight together, pointing upwards to twelve. Midnight. "Midnight," droned the dream engines...Sam Kang Pun Ye...

I woke with a start.

It was a quarter past eight by the little clock, I was late and I dressed quickly, afraid that Gerry would have left before I got downstairs to breakfast. If I missed him now, I would not see him again until after he had been to the waterfront. He had already told me that he had been summoned to a luncheon party with—as he put it—"a visiting mogul."

I was particularly glad this morning that I had arranged for Marcia to have breakfast in her room since she came to stay here. I wanted to talk to Gerry.

I just caught him before he left. He was late and in a hurry.

He said, all in one breath:

"Hallo, Fran! Sleep well? Yee Sze wanted to bring your breakfast in to you. I said you hated breakfast in bed." Then as he passed me, he gave my shoulder a little shake. "I know what you want to talk about! But there's nothing more to say. I'm doing just as I said last night. If we're careful, we'll catch him to-night. If we fail, there's always another day—"

"And another threat!" I said soberly.

I don't think he heard me. He was half-way down the veranda steps as he spoke. I watched him walk to the gate and wished this was the week-end and he would be with me all day. I didn't want Marcia to myself—not after last night. . . .

The coffee was hot and strong. I ate toast and then peeled an orange. Above me, the Peak was wreathed in silvery mist; Mr. Wu's seventh baby began to cry and, very high above, a great bird flew across the sky. I watched it, wondering if it were an eagle.

I don't know what time it was when Yee Sze came out with a letter for me. My step-mother's handwriting was on the envelope and I guessed, even before I opened it, that she had something to tell me about Lucien. There was no other reason why she should send me two letters in as many days.

"I think you should know," she wrote, "that Lucien has discharged himself from the psychiatrist's care. He has declared that he is cured. The point is, that he is not! But his agent went to visit him and ill-advisedly told him that there was a part for him in a New York play. He should not, of course, have been allowed to see him but was admitted by mistake. The damage was done in five minutes. Lucien decided to discharge himself and fly to New York.

"I went to see him but he refused to talk to me. He just announced, rather theatrically, that the past was dead and that the name Mannering meant nothing to him.

"I thought you should know this, Fran dear, although I am sure Lucien will be writing to you himself. I cannot believe that he means to end his engagement to you."

I stared at the letter. There were other small pieces of news, but I scarcely registered them. My stepmother knew me too well to dissemble or withhold what she believed I should know, and I was grateful for her honesty.

But that Lucien should have said that the name Mannering no longer meant anything to him!...It meant that he still blamed me for all that had happened, that rational thought was as remote as on the day he had railed at me in hospital.

I stared so hard into the sunlight that my eyes, unable to take any more brilliance, became blurred and slightly painful; my vision darkened.

Lucien, his voice high with hysteria, seemed to swim into that darkness laid over the sunlight. Lucien with his lean poet's face; his dark, deep-set eyes; his twisted mouth; shaking and shivering, his handsome features distorted; crying with the unconscious histrionics of great tragedy.

"You've done this to me! My God! All that I've worked for gone, because you swerved that car! Why didn't you think of me, me, *me* rather than that child? You professed to love me—yet when the choice came, it was the child you thought of!" Wild, hating, hysterical words—the last I had heard from Lucien before the psychiatrist had said I must not visit him again for a long time....

And now he was going out into the world of theatre he loved so fanatically, to act and receive acclaim—and to go on hating me....

This was something the psychiatrist, with all his knowledge, had not reckoned upon. Or perhaps he had. Perhaps patients did release themselves and go back to the world only half cured; a twilit world, always a twilit world, where one day some minor catastrophe might hurl them over the razor's edge again, next time into complete insanity. I didn't know. All I was sure of was that my stepmother's postscript about Lucien was meant in kindness to me. "It could be that a great stage success could effect as sure a cure as the psychiatrist." But it wouldn't and she knew it! I could only guess at her distress when she had written that letter to me, for I knew she loved me.

I shook my head a few times to clear it of the blurred darkness and closed my eyes. When I opened them again the sunlight was back.

I knew I must have activity. I got up and went into the house. In a cupboard in the pantry I found scissors and a basket such as we used in our English garden. As I cut flowers for the house, I had a curious sense of unreality, I tried to analyse it. Was it shock? Shock? With the first peach-tinted azalea bloom in my hand I stood up and faced the fact that it was just the opposite. The unreal feeling was my own sense of surprise that I did not feel shock. Perhaps, right from the beginning, I had been a little wiser than the psychiatrist. Perhaps I had known from the first hysterical outburst, that Lucien would never come back to me. Not because of the accident and the failure of doctors to cure him quickly—I guessed the facial scars had healed as mine had done. Nor even because of his psychological state. But because the link that bound us was too tenuous, too dependent on Lucien's pedestal and my adoration at his feet.... Directly he could see compassion for him in my eyes, directly he was in a position where I could treat him as a fallible human being, then the fragile link between us had broken. He was no woman's "man"; he was a star in private as in public life. He could take nothing less because fundamentally he was weak.

And I had known this all the time. Had the psychiatrist known it, too? Had his sending me away been a gamble that failed?

I cut the camellias with short stems and many leaves because they were one of the few flowers which looked best among their own satiny green. Once when I paused, I looked up at the Peak. The mist was clearing. Up there spring would be full of birds' sound—the cuckoo and the oriole, the parakeets and the bulbuls: the air would be cooler and the view would be over the sea and far away, as far as Red China....

I did not realise until I heard Marcia call from the veranda, that I had picked too many flowers. Looking down at my basket as I answered her, I saw that it was full. Reluctantly I returned to the veranda where she stood in her orange skirt.

"Oh!" she said touching the flowers, "how lovely!"

"Strictly speaking," I said, "I shouldn't have been cutting them with the sun on them. But if I plunge them straight into water, they'll be all right."

"Can I help you?"

"No thank you," I said quickly.

She gave me a long, penetrating glance.

"Did you sleep well?"

"If you count a nightmare, no!" I said.

"I didn't either. But that was because I wanted to lie awake. I had too much to think about. You know," she stood by the table playing with the envelope of my letter, "I'm sure Gerry will find that man this evening. After all, to stand waiting at the waterfront—"

"Among a few hundred others also there!" I commented drily.

"Crooks make false moves and get caught in the end! And this man who calls himself Midnight—" she giggled like a child. "Doesn't it sound silly, giving him that fancy name?"

"No," I said shortly, "it doesn't! Not here in China! But go on."

"Well, this man will be arrested and then we'll all be safe."

I rested the basket of flowers on a chair.

"Doesn't it upset you at all that you'll be brought into all this if, and when, they do arrest him?"

"Why should it?" She regarded me steadily out of her dark blue eyes. "I'm not going round crying my eyes out for love of a crook! So I'll tell them my part of the story and I know they'll believe me."

"And when it's all over," I had to ask, "What will you do?"

"Oh, stay in Hong Kong for a while. Until—"

I was certain she wanted me to ask, "Until what?" But I couldn't. I merely said:

"Well, it's a lovely place to spend a holiday in! And you could, perhaps, get a job out here."

"Job? Oh, I'll manage without one for a time. I brought out a little money an aunt left me. It'll tide me over for a few weeks. And after that—"

Again the pause, waiting for me to ask, "After that—what?" And again I did not ask.

I picked up the basket, the scissors and my letter.

"I'm going to tidy my room. After that, perhaps you'd like to go down to the shops."

"Yes," she said quickly. "I want to buy one or two things. A really snazzy swim-suit, for one thing. And some scent. I didn't bring any out with me and you always smell so nice, Francie—"

"Thanks!" I said drily.

I managed to avoid her until we were ready for our shopping.

Marcia was a little more talkative than usual, a little more buoyant. And all the time, while we wandered round the big stores, while Marcia hesitated between a mulberry-and-white swim-suit and an all-yellow—and finally bought both—I waited for her to mention Max. Not once did she do so. I wondered why. Was it reticence? Or was she waiting until after to-night to tell me?

I watched her lips as she talked to the shop assistant. Max had kissed that full mobile mouth; had touched that fine, creamy skin; had looked deep into the gold-lashed eyes. . . . It was all I could do not to shout at her:

Are you in love with Max? Tell me! Tell me!

To stop myself, I turned away. I saw a deep blue beach robe on a stand, and, on an impulse, I said to an assistant watching me:

"I'll have that!"

"Do you often buy things without trying them on?" Marcia asked over my shoulder.

"No, but I'm stock size."

"It's a lovely colour! It'll suit you. You'd better be careful—" She came round and stood in front of me, her voice rippling with laughter. "If you go around looking too glamorous, you'll find yourself in some sort of complication."

"Aren't I already? Aren't we all?"

"I mean an emotional one! Hong Kong seems to me the sort of place where people do things at three times the speed they do in England—things, I mean, like falling in love—"

"I'm already engaged—" I began and the echo of the words hooted in derision at me.

Marcia smiled, softly.

"I'm so glad it isn't to Max!"

Once again she had given me an opening and I would not take it. I busied myself pulling dollar bills out of my wallet. Then I said:

"Let's go and find a place where we can get coffee. And after that I must remember to buy some face tissues."

"And there's my scent. What do you use?"

"Mitsouko," I told her briefly.

"I think," she considered the point, "I shall either buy *Tabac Blond* or *Numéro Cinq.*"

"The store will have testers," I said shortly and took my change and my parcel.

"I can't wait to get down to Repulse Bay and swim and lie in the sun!" she said as we walked out into the street.

But I had never mentioned Repulse Bay—I didn't know it, anyway—and I was quite certain Gerry hadn't talked about it to her either. So this was a date she must have with Max.

I glanced sideways at her and saw the edge of her little smile. Last night they had kissed— and made a date. I thought bitterly; Max might have waited until . . . Until what? They had their lives and they were free to live them as they wished. My ties with Max were secret and my own. I could blame no one, Max least of all, for not knowing of them.

After we had shopped we went back home to lunch. It was a sultry day and as we finished, rain clouds rolled in from the south. It would be a relief to have rain; it would clear the air and freshen the garden. I told Marcia I was going to my room. She said she would sit and read for a while down in the courtyard. "Just in case," she added, laughing, "I can find a breath of air."

I was awake when the rain came. I heard it

beating upon the window with angry hisses and below Yee Sze dragged the chairs indoors from the courtyard to a place of shelter.

The fierce downpour lasted for about a quarter of an hour and then the skies cleared. A short time after the onslaught of heavy drops upon the window ceased, I fell into a hot sleep.

Yee Sze tapping on my door woke me. He asked if he should make tea.

I looked at my watch. It was nearly five o'clock and I had slept long after our usual tea-time. I swung myself off the bed, bathed my face and put on lipstick, did my hair, slipped into my dress.

Marcia was in the courtyard reading one of the paperbacks she had found in the living-room.

She looked up.

"Oh, Francie, I've got a message for you. From Gerry."

"He came home?"

"No, he telephoned about four o'clock. I called to you, but you didn't answer so, as Gerry was in a hurry, he gave me a message for you."

I sat down and waited. Marcia closed her book and laid it on the tile plinth.

"He said that plans to-night are slightly

changed, and he hopes you brought your driving licence out with you."

"I have. But quite by accident!" I said in surprise.

"You're to take the car down to the waterfront and contact him there. He wants those two books. I've wrapped them up all ready—"

Yee Sze came out with the tray. I watched his delicate hands set out the peony-patterned cups. Then I began to pour out.

"Francie," Marcia watched me anxiously. "I hope it's all right! You going there, I mean. You're not, Gerry said, to get out of the car until you've actually seen him. Then go straight to him. If the police get after you for parking in a bad place he'll take care of that."

"But the waterfront is quite a length!" I protested. "Where—?"

"Oh, yes—yes," she drew her brows together in thought. "Gerry said he'll be standing by a place called Yang Hwa's. It's a metal junk shop."

"If Gerry's around, I suppose it'll be all right!" I said uncertainly.

Marcia watched me over the rim of her cup.

"You'll do exactly what he says, won't you?" Her tone was urgent, a little scared. "You won't get out of the car until you actually see him and know you can safely contact him?"

"I don't think I can 'safely' do anything!" I told her. "But I'm not going slap into trouble, if that's what you mean. I've no intention of getting out of the car and going for a pleasant walk along the waterfront just to soak myself in local colour!" There was a sharpness in my voice which I could no more help than I could help the feeling that Marcia should have let me take my own telephone message. It was all very well for Gerry to say he was in a hurry, but I wanted to know more about this altered plan of his. Why want me there when last night both he and Max had been so adamant about my staying home? Why want the books?

I had no doubt about the authenticity of Gerry's message. Marcia had never been down to the waterfront and she would have no idea that there was a metal junk shop there. At the same time, I wanted to talk to my brother. I glanced at my watch. Gerry would not have left the office yet. I would telephone him at once.

I rose and walking into the house, said over my shoulder to Marcia:

"I want to get through to Gerry if I can. I want to know why I'm to go to the water-front."

When I was put through to Gerry's department, his secretary told me that he had already left. He had to make a call at the Mercantile Bank to see an official there and he had said he would not be returning to the office that evening. I told her that I believed he had rung me earlier that afternoon. She, herself, had got through to the house, she said.

I thanked her and returning, found Marcia sitting elbows on her knees, frowning at a far wall.

"It's odd, isn't it, that this man has made a daylight appointment? You'd have thought the night would have been safer for him."

"As his prime wish is for me to hand over the emeralds, the most important thing is to contact me. If he can induce me to meet him more readily in daylight, then it doesn't matter to him! The waterfront is, I believe, just a moving mass of people. Anyone could slip through the crowds without being seen. He's taking no real risk since he's certain I won't contact the police!"

"I suppose not," Marcia's eyes rested on me, wide and distressed. "But Francie, *you* shouldn't be going down there—"

"Since Gerry will be expecting me," I said briskly, "I'll have to go won't I?"

I kept looking at my watch during the next hour. Time seemed interminable. I was on edge with too much to grasp—had I yet understood fully the fact that Lucien was not yet cured? It seemed that I was taking it too calmly—too remotely, even! But when you go in fear of your safety a histrionic love affair falls back into perspective!

Then Marcia and Max. That was nearer! Salt on a reopened wound! . . . But it had happened and there was nothing I could have done to stop it.

Marcia was as restless as I that afternoon. She had walked the length of the garden three times; had gone to put the paper-back novel away.

"I skimmed through it, but it's too highbrow for me," she said in answer to my urging that she should keep it by her until she had finished it.

On her fourth walk down the garden, she stopped suddenly and came back to my chair.

"Suppose I went to the waterfront instead of you?" she began.

"Gerry probably wants me there because I could identify the man by his voice."

"Yes, I see," she brushed her hand lightly over the heads of the carnations.

I didn't blame her for sounding a little too relieved at my not falling in with her suggestion! I told her to fetch the two books she had already parcelled up and went to my room and put on a hat to shade my face. I don't honestly know what security it afforded me, but I was a little beyond clear thinking. I was so taut that my movements were jerky and I found myself holding my breath for long periods as though waiting for something, someone to touch me from behind.

Downstairs I went to the little drawer in the lacquer cabinet where Gerry had told me he kept the spare car keys in case at any time I might want them.

Marcia was waiting for me on the terrace with the two books wrapped up. She walked with me down to the gate.

"Stay in while we're away," I warned, "and don't let Yee Sze go out for any last-minute shopping!"

She promised meekly and stood watching me unlock the car and climb in behind the wheel.

The car was parked so close to the wall that the wing was slightly scraped. I edged out and turned, as Gerry always did, in the entrance to a yard almost opposite to the house. I stalled the engine and in the relative quiet while the car was still, I heard the chant of children's voices practising the four tones of the Mandarin vowel sounds. I decided I must ask Gerry later this evening if there was some sort of little private school there. Later this evening...the full impact of that optimistic thought brought a thin echo of derision. I re-started the engine and with two more turns, had manoeuvred the car along the way I wanted it to go.

I crossed Des Voeux Street and, turning towards the waterfront, found myself caught in a jam of trucks and lorries, private cars and rickshaws. I crawled in the procession, dodged by carriers with their bamboo baskets slung on poles, the loaders and unloaders, the crates—the endless, piling medley of crates! And above, the hot, bright cloudless sky.

I drove once the length of the waterfront, turned inland and came back for a second crawl. I had seen Tai Tsing's shirtmakers shop and metal junk shop was only a little farther on.

I kept a sharp look-out for somewhere to park that would give me a clear view of Yang Hwa's where Gerry would wait and watch. But I despaired of being able to pull up with-out causing a minor accident. Then the man in front of me turned right and I had room to follow and park at the corner of the side street.

All the time I looked for Gerry, thinking hopelessly that it would be impossible for me to spot him in this milling, shouting, vital swarm of carrier-coolies, boatwomen and children clutching rice bowls. Gerry would have to find *me*! Though I doubted now he could do so with the car parked round the corner.

I half-stood up in my seat and then I saw him. He was standing by a pile of round baskets outside what I supposed was the metal-junk workshop; but he wasn't even glancing my way. He was only about a hundred yards from me. By pushing through the crowds I could reach him in less than a minute. I picked up the parcel of books from the seat beside me, climbed out of the car and locked it.

Then I turned. My hat shaded my eyes from the sun but the hot evening glare beat about me. I smelt oil and sea water, squashed oranges that had fallen from a basket and sweating bodies. The noise deafened me. There was also another smell that I could see no reason for, the sandalwood smell of joss-sticks. I edged my way through the crowd. I could no longer see Gerry, now that I was level with everyone else, but I knew the way to go.

Suddenly I felt a jolt from behind. My head was jerked back so that my face was flung up to meet the brassy evening sky. At the same time, the parcel of books I held was snatched from me. I put my hand out and saved myself falling by holding on to the side of a van. Cautiously, I turned my head. No one looked my way; no one was very near. . . . But I knew I was in danger. I did not dare risk trying to reach Gerry. Someone had watched me arrive, followed me and grabbed the books. If the parcel were opened immediately and the theft of the emeralds discovered, I was really in trouble!

There was only one course open to me. I turned and began to fight my way back to the car. I reached it and fumbled in my bag for the keys, wishing desperately that I had not locked the door.

Finally, I found the keys and with shaking hands, fitted one.

"Miss Mannering!"

I did not dare look up. My fingers stiffened round the little key so that I could not turn it.

"You should not cheat, you know!" The voice had its own horrifying gentleness. A hand came down and took the keys from my numbed fingers.

I stood in frozen silence; not even daring to turn my head. Fascinatedly I watched an olive-tinted hand turn the key.

It was too much to dare to hope that I was

being given my freedom after he had found me. Slowly I turned my head, as though impelled by a hypnotic force. The man by my side wore well-cut European clothes, but his face was Oriental. I had never seen him before.

"Will you now give me back the car keys?" My voice sounded clear and almost brave.

The man laughed softly in my face.

"I can't do that, Miss Mannering, you might escape me again!"

"You're dead right. I—" and then I stopped and listened.

From somewhere, just behind me, I heard the singing crickets. The sound was on a thin, monotonous, inhuman wavelength that touched the ears beyond the sing-song cries of the crowd.

The sound jerked the man into action. He swung round to look behind him. Quick as a flash, every part of me leapt into action. I turned to run and cannoned into a couple of carrier coolies with a bamboo pole slung between them.

"Help—me—" I began, my voice high and ragged. They looked at me with less than interest. I swung sideways, trying to get between them and the stream of traffic.

"Gerry!" I shouted. *Gerry!* A car's wing nearly caught me. I tried to catch the door knob as it crawled past, but the driver suddenly accelerated.

Mine was a punny effort to escape, anyway! I waited for the man's voice again. It came, less gently:

"It'll do you no good to try to escape." His fingers were again as strong as a vice on my arm. "Nor to shout for help," he added. "People down here have quite enough to do minding their own business!"

I tried to struggle, but it was useless. He did my walking for me! I just moved, somehow, and as though he had performed some dark magic on me I neither fought nor shouted as he propelled me the few feet back to the Rover. I noticed he had closed the door before he came after me. Now he opened it again. As he did so, one hand and one leg pinned me in a curious immobilising hold that might have been a judo trick.

"Now get in!"

I began to climb in and, in a flash, my hand went to the horn on the steering-wheel. He anticipated my move and wrenched my fingers away.

"Get over!"

"No!" I sat heavily in the driving-seat, my hand still straining to the horn. He was a slight man, and not very tall but he could do what he liked with me. He put a foot into the car and moved me over without effort, at the same time keeping tight hold of my wrists with his left hand.

Gerry's car was very wide so that, to reach for the far door, I would have to lean away from him. That, as he held my wrist, I could not do. I tried to look over my shoulder for Gerry. He must have seen! *Must* have seen? Down a side street in that mob?—

I did not exactly make a decision to play for time; I merely accepted the fact that it was my only chance. I sat quietly, one wrist still imprisoned, and watched him close the car door, turn on the ignition and put the car into gear with his right hand. He was remarkably adept at using it as though he had driven a car, and held someone prisoner at the same time, on other occasions.

He would be watchful of me while we were stationary, but when we moved on again, he would relax. That was when I would wrench my wrist from his grip and jump for it. ... He would not dare come after me in Des Voeux Street or Garden Road.

"Why did you bring two useless books with you?"

"Because," I said desperately, "that's how I found them. Someone knew—what was hidden in them—and—got them first!"

"Miss Mannering—" he paused to manipulate the car, taking his hand from the wheel to change a gear. I wanted to shout at him to stop using my name so often. In the glove compartment of the car there was a small map and a packet of peppermints. If only there had been something hard enough to slash down on the fingers that held my wrist!

"Miss Mannering," he said again, as though he knew his use of my name annoyed me, "I learned a very valuable lesson when I was only four years old. My fingers were deliberately burned to show me that fire was dangerous. *You* should not have played with fire!"

"I told you on the telephone—I gather it *was* you who rang me up and threatened—"

"I telephoned you, yes. But only to ask you to deliver to me what was mine—"

"Smuggled emeralds!"

"Green fire," he corrected.

I watched the car turn the corner of the street. We were in Des Voeux Road and the traffic lights were with us. We crossed the road and cut up a turning before Pedder

Street. There were no traffic lights here. After that, I did not know Hong Kong well enough to recognise where we were.

"I told you on the telephone that I know nothing about your emeralds! I don't even know the man Farson!"

"It is not intelligent to lie!" he said, "I saw him greet you by your gate; I saw you with the books coming from the alley behind Kam Ho Street. I saw our—er—friend speak to you again the next morning. He made an appointment with you in Shek Ku Bay, only I could not allow him to keep it—"

"You miss nothing, do you?" I said with false bravado. "You attacked me! You searched my handbag! Well, now you must know that I don't have the emeralds!"

"Your brother and your friends came along too soon, Miss Mannering!" he said. "I really did not expect you to keep the emeralds in so obvious a place as your handbag! This time—" he left the sentence unsaid.

This time *I* would be searched. It would be unspeakably horrible. And when he could not find the emeralds, he might try to torture me into telling—telling what I did not know!

We were turning a corner and he slowed down. I flung myself sideways, but I was not quick enough. His fingers dragged me back into a sitting position close, much too close to him . . .

"Why don't you find out from Eric Farson where the emeralds are?" I demanded.

"You imagine that he hasn't been—asked?" The pause before the last word was horribly significant.

"And he didn't tell you!"

"He couldn't—because he doesn't know where they are!"

"And you believed him!"

"Miss Mannering, you're not being very intelligent if you think I could be bothered with you if I thought for one moment that Farson had what I want!"

My flesh felt clammy, my heart alternately beat with hammer-thuds and subsided into scarcely beating at all. . . .

I said in a last effort of shaken despair;

"If you'll let me go I give you my word I'll do all I can to find what you want. I don't know where the emeralds are—I never did know. All I was shown was the slit up the spine of those books—what have you done with them by the way?"

"I threw them," he said, "straight into a basket of fish." He took a long, rasping breath and bent my arm. "If you struggle again, I shall have to hurt you. Do you understand?"

I stared out through the windscreen. We had come to one of the squatters' colonies on a hill outside the city. He drove a little way past it and then turned up a track. There he stopped the car.

Again, in a single movement I flung myself away from him.

I might have known it was useless. With the car no longer in motion he had two hands now with which to drag me back. He pulled me after him out of the car and in my resistence I bruised my arm against the steering wheel. As I half stumbled against him, I felt something harder than human bone press my side. I might have known, too, that he carried a weapon—

There were people on the hillside, but we were shielded from them by trees. As though he knew what I was preparing to do, he said: "Calling for help will do no good! You hear the noise they make up there? Radios blaring, children— One cry is like another. Whatever it is, they will not interfere, not up here, Miss Mannering."

I was unprepared for his sudden thrust towards a door. As he spoke, we had unexpectedly come upon a hut behind some bushes.

He twisted a rough latch and pushed me inside.

As the door closed, I flung myself against it. His arm shot out and I fell back with a sob that was half-fury, half-fear.

"Do sit down, Miss Mannering," he said and I began to hate my name!

Because I had not the strength to stand any longer, I sat down on a low plank bed that had a slightly ragged, but perfectly clean, rug upon it.

On the other side of the room was a bench. A man's clothes were folded neatly on a shelf. On the second shelf were cooking utensils. There was, however, no window. No escape but the door . . . and the hut was roughly but sturdily built. A woman could not break that door down.

There comes a moment of utter defeat when you can take no more fear and when you know it is useless to try to fight. The only thing then left is to talk; to play for time—for what that was worth since no one would yet miss me!

Perhaps, I thought, I could break this man's conviction that I was the one he wanted. I would ask questions, and maybe he would see, in my ignorance, my innocence.

"Eric Farson stopped me twice," I said. "You saw that! The first time he tried to sell me a fan; the second, he gave me a note for—

for a friend. Each time, while he talked, I heard the sound of singing crickets. You have a pedlar around to watch Eric, don't you?"

"There are many pedlars and hawkers in Hong Kong."

"But this one is special, isn't he?"

"You ask too many questions!"

"Then," I said, *"I'll* tell *you* something, Mr. — Mr. —"

"Call me Sam Kang Pun Ye —"

"Which I've learnt means 'midnight.' That's fancy! I'd rather have your real name."

He laughed, watching me, wary of my sudden attempt at coolness.

"Well, what are you going to tell me?"

I said:

"Just that my brother will report to the police that his care is missing and I with it, and they'll trace it here."

He put his hand in his pocket and drew out a cigarette case. He opened it and handed it to me. It was, I saw, a most beautiful thing of carved jade and it held small cigarettes such as a woman might smoke.

I shook my head.

"No thank you."

They could be drugged, I thought, and watched him take one and light it from a gold lighter.

There was one question I had to ask, though I dreaded the reply. My lips stiff, my throat seemingly constricted, I asked:

"What—are you—going to do—with me?"

"Either you have the emeralds on you. Or, if you haven't then, as I told you on the telephone that first night, Miss Mannering, I have to make an example. Someone, I'm afraid, has to be hurt to teach the rest what happens to them if they don't give up what is not theirs."

"The—rest?"

"Whoever else knows about it. Your brother, perhaps; your newspaper friend; Miss Gallard. . . ."

So he knew us all!

"My brother is in Government Service. If you think—"

"The price is high enough to tempt even a Government servant to theft," he said.

"My brother would never—"

Again he cut me short. But this time his voice was soft.

"Have you ever dreamed of such beauty as flawless emeralds? They are like purest fire—'green fire'—"

"You can stop being poetical," I said, "I haven't set eyes on them!"

My shoulder hurt where I had bruised it

against the steering-wheel; my wrist burned where it had been gripped during that journey.

If I were very quiet, I would be able to hear someone come by the hut. Then I would shout—hard and long!

I saw the man look at his wrist-watch.

"I shall leave you here for a while. And when I return you will tell me where the 'green fire' is. If you do not"—he lifted his slight shoulders—"then it will be a pity."

I was frantic for him to leave me. Left alone, I might think out a way of escape. Let him go quickly—

He laid his cigarette case on the table.

"You may want to smoke."

He walked to the door, opened it and went out into the evening of golden light and singing birds. I did not hear a key turn in a lock and I waited, scarcely daring to breathe. I heard him start up Gerry's car, heard it back and drive away. Of course, I thought, he was going to dump it somewhere miles from this spot so that it could not be traced back to the hut and me. . . .

As soon as the sound died away, I started to the door. I pulled the latch but it would not open.

Did it lock? And if so, how? It was so dark in here with the door closed that I could scarcely see. I remembered however that I had seen a candle in a saucer on the shelf. In my handbag I had some matches. I groped for them, found the candle and lit it and set it down on the table. In its light, the lovely cigarette case was a soft melting green, the carving was many-handed Shiva. But it was not for me to go dreaming over some lovely object. I had to find my way out of this place.

I went to the door again. In the dim candle-light I pushed and pulled. I tried my full weight against it. It shivered but did not give. I prowled round the tiny space of the hut. There was not a chink in the wooden shack that could help me tear my way out. I was a prisoner until the man chose to return.

I sat down again on the low plank bed and put my hands to my head.

By this time Gerry would surely have realised that his plan had failed and gone home to find out why I hadn't met him at the waterfront.

And Marcia? And Max? I did not want to think of them now!

A wild thought came to me as I watched the candle's steady flame, that I could burn the hut down. But I would be trapped that way. Like someone drowning, everything about these three fantastic days reeled through my brain from the moment when I had taken pity on a lonely and beautiful girl at Kai Tak Airport.... What was the whole thing after all, but a search for a glittering green fortune and a question of crooks' honour? For I was certain now that they had been a kind of criminal syndicate and Eric had cheated. . . .

XVI

I sat, my ears strained for a sound. Once I thought I heard someone treading the rough ground, cracking twigs under their feet and I called out. I called twice and banged on the hut wall. But no one came. It must have been a wild thing, even a bird, an oriole in a near-by tree branch.

And all the time I was falling deeper into that place, beyond terror, where nature becomes merciful, numbs the senses and dulls the sharp edges of the imagination. I stood staring at the candle. When it had gutted out, what would happen to me? I leaned my head back against the wall of the hut. And suddenly I was certain there was a sound outside.

The man, my very deadly enemy, coming back? Or a stranger passing by? I took a chance and called out:

"Hallo out there! Get this door open! *Hallo!*"
They might not understand a word I said,

but they would surely recognise the urgency of my voice.

Someone was at the door, I held my breath. Then there was a clatter as though a chain had dropped.

I shot to the candle and blew it out, edging in the darkness, towards the door.

It swung wide and through it came an old man. He had a pole and on it a dozen or more tiny cages. From them came a drowsy, monotonous sound. The little singing crickets were settling themselves in their toy prisons for the night.

The old man stared at me and said something in Cantonese which might have been an oath. Whatever it was, he was obviously not pleased to see me though I think he recognised me. He had small watery eyes which gazed at me balefully. He kicked the door back and rested his pole against the bench. He said nothing, but his gesture with the door was plain. I was to get out.

In a flash I shot past him and was stumbling over the uneven ground, running towards the road.

I guessed the old man had not bargained for his hut to be used as a prison for me. I reached the road and immediately drew back. At any moment my assailant might return, on foot or in his own car. I must keep hidden as nearly as I could, at least until I reached the city. I walked the way the car had come, diving behind trees, wading through knee-deep fern. The sky was an angry crimson and gold and there was a scent of honeysuckle. Insects skimmed about my head and un-trimmed bamboo scratched my legs. I saw cars pass; I went swiftly past the squatters' colony of rough huts. But I was in no state for the long walk home.

I decided to go down to the road and watch for a car going towards the city. If there were two people inside, and one preferably a woman, I would ask for a lift. I did not dare stop one with a single man passenger in case, when it came to a halt, I should see the face I dreaded smiling in triumph at me.

It was rapidly growing dark. I must have lost count of time in the hut. I knew I was going in the right direction because the lights of the city, like a pilgrim's dream, lay ahead of me. But still so far away . . . so far. . . .

A car came along the road, driven so cautiously that for a moment my heart turned over, fearful that it was my enemy searching for me. Then I saw that two people sat in it. One was a woman with a wide-brimmed hat, and they must be elderly tourists, driving cautiously in a strange country. I shot out of my hiding-place and ran into the middle of the road. That way, they had either to stop or run over me. I braced myself ready to jump for safety if they feared this was some kind of hold-up, and accelerated; but to my relief they slowed down, the near-side window opened and a startled face with protuberant blue eyes looked at me.

"Have you been in an accident?"

"No. Yes, I mean!" My voice rushed on: "I wonder if you could be very kind and give me a lift into the city?" I must have sounded distressed and quite harmless for immediately the woman opened the car door.

"Of course. Get in."

She moved over and murmuring "Thank you" I sat next to her on the wide front seat.

"Where do you want to go?" The man was not nearly so keen on having me as a passenger. He gave me a suspicious oblique scrutiny.

"My brother lives in a house on Tai-yuan Street," I explained, "but if you could drop me anywhere near where you're going, I'll find my way home. I'm Francie Mannering, by the way, and my brother works at Government House. I—I thought you ought to know—" I added lamely.

I sensed a relaxing of their tension.

"What's happened to you Miss—er—Mannering?" the man asked. He had a faint British north-country accent.

"Someone stole my brother's car—and me in it," I told them. "Then left me—" It was, after all, the truth. And enough for them to know.

"We'd better drop you at the police station then," the man said. "I don't know where it is. Do you?"

"No, and I'd rather see my brother first. He'll be anxious about me. You see, I'm a stranger here—I'm on holiday."

"So are we," said the woman brightly. London was full of friendly, faintly cockney voices like hers.

"You've had a horrible experience!" The man's voice was kinder.

"Are you hurt?" His wife touched my arm and I winced.

"Bruised, that's all!"

"The East is barbarous—"

I said, "There are criminals everywhere!"

"That's so! We've had our house outside Manchester burgled twice and the first time our Danish maid was threatened." He was a nervous driver. He braked almost at the sight of another car. I wondered why this odd little couple had come to Hong Kong.

When we arrived at the town centre, they

insisted on my directing them to Tai-yuan Street. When we reached the corner I saw their surprise and their quick, furtive dismay. Was I, after all, who I said I was?

"I live just down there where you see that wall—" I explained. "It encloses my brother's house and garden, so I'll get out here—"

"Well, if you're sure you'll be all right!"

"Perfectly," I said and thanked them again, my smile as wide with relief as gratitude.

I actually ran down the street, pushed open the gate and to my utter relief, saw that everything seemed normal here. There was a newspaper and drinks on the rattan table on the veranda and a cigarette lying in the ash-tray, still burning. When I reached the living-room I stopped dead. A strange man stood there. He was not very tall and he had ginger hair. Instinctively I backed and at the same moment I heard Gerry's voice on the telephone saying:

"Thank you! No, there's no message."

The next minute he came into the room and saw me and his eyes snapped at me in anger.

"Where in the name of goodness do you think you've been? Here was I—" he broke off, looked at me more closely and said sharply: "Fran, what's happened?"

I sat down, saying weakly:

"I got caught by—by the man—you went

304

down—to meet." Now that I was safe reaction set in. I closed my eyes to stop the room going round.

"What you want," said my brother, "is a drink!"

I began to protest that I wanted nothing more than to sit in a chair and try to pull myself together, but when Gerry put a small pony glass of brandy into my shaking hand, I sipped it gratefully.

"It's a sacrilege to put good brandy into a glass like that, but never mind! Now, what happened, Fran?"

Over the crystal rim I looked questioningly at the ginger-haired man.

"This is Inspector Davis," Gerry said. "And you've guessed," he turned to the red-haired man, "that this is my sister. Now, let's hear what you've got to say."

He was still, I could tell, faintly angry with me.

I told them everything, every detail I could remember. They sat listening without interruption. When I had finished my story, Gerry said quietly:

"I gave Marcia no message for you, Fran!"

My hand jerked so that the brandy in my glass nearly spilled over.

"But, Gerry, I know you did! I spoke

later to your secretary–"

"I rang to ask if Max happened to be with you. I'd tried to get him at his office and he wasn't there. I wanted to ask him to come down to the waterfront too. You were asleep, Marcia said, and so I gave her the message for Max should he turn up here. I also wanted him to bring the books–"

"Marcia gave me the message as though it was I who was to go down."

Gerry looked at the detective and I read their thoughts.

"Gerry," I urged, "call her and find out why she sent me!"

"I can't. She isn't here."

"So–someone came for her, too!"

"No," Gerry said. "She went voluntarily. And she's gone for good, bag and baggage! She left this." Gerry picked up a piece of note-paper from the table and held it out to me. The writing was large and scrawling as though she had been in a hurry.

Thank you so much for all your kind-ness. I can't tell you how dreadful I feel at the trouble I've caused. Please believe me! I had no idea what I was plunging us all into. Now I'm going right away so that you can forget me.

And forgive.

MARCIA.

"Charming, isn't it?" Gerry asked, watching me.

"And you don't know where she's gone?"

"No!"

I tossed the note back on to the table.

"But you can find out, can't you?" I said to the inspector. "She's a British subject."

"She can go and jump in the sea for all I care!" Gerry said furiously.

"We don't even know the name of the man you want. He calls himself Sam Kang Pun Ye—" I said to the inspector.

"Which means exactly nothing!" he said. "He could just as easily called himself Mr. Daylight! They have a penchant for fancy names!"

"I dread to think what will happen when he finds me gone—"

"Miss Mannering, I want an exact description of him, of the hut, and any other little detail that you can think of which will give us a lead." He tore a small page out of his notebook and gave it to me with his pen.

"Will you draw a map as nearly as you can of the place where you were held?"

I did so. I drew the main road, the two

bends before we reached the squatters' colony. Some way beyond that I drew double lines to indicate the cutting up which I was taken, and the hut standing alone.

The inspector studied it.

"Now will you try to describe in detail what the man with the fancy name looked like?"

I did my best. I even told of the jade cigarette case he carried.

"I don't believe the pedlar was in the plot at all!" I said. "I think he was just being paid some small sum to keep watch on Eric and to report when he contacted me and if I gave him anything—the emeralds, in fact. While I was at the waterfront I heard the singing crickets again and I think it was a warning sign that my brother was around. The man had to think quickly, so he used your car, Gerry, to take me to the hut. He probably thought the old man would be out for ages and he'd be safe to search me there. But he had to get rid of the car first."

"The pedlar couldn't have got from the waterfront to the hut in the time," the inspector said, "if it's where I think it is. So it wasn't the hired man you heard at the waterfront but another pedlar—a perfectly innocent one probably going to his slum home behind Connaught Street." The inspector moved across the room.

Suddenly I remembered that I had left my handbag behind in the hut and that my hat must have fallen off during my struggles in the car.

I said:

"If you find a handbag in the hut, Inspector, it's probably mine. Thank heaven I left my wallet at home, here!"

"Your handbag," Gerry said, "is the least of our problems, Fran!"

At the veranda door, Inspector Davis turned.

"If we can't find the hut, I may have to ask you to come along to help us, Miss Mannering."

"Of course," I managed a smile. But I prayed that he wouldn't need me. I had had enough for one day!

When Gerry and I were alone, he gave full range to his white-hot rage against Marcia. I did all I could to stop him so that I could think. I had a strong feeling that Marcia had not sent me down to the waterfront with any desire to injure me and I wanted to try and work out her reason. But Gerry was so voluble that in my overwrought state he only added to my confusion, and I could not clear my mind for a single quiet thought of my own.

It was a sound outside the house that checked his really eloquent language. We both heard it at the same time. Someone was walking up the path. We listened to the tread on the veranda steps and turning, simultaneously, saw Max.

"And where the devil," Gerry blew out at him, "have you been?"

He looked utterly taken aback, then his eyes went cold.

"I've been with Marcia. Have you any objection?"

"After all we'd said last night about the girls keeping together to-day, yes, I have!"

"But Francie was with you—" Max began.

"How do you know that?"

"You sent for her. If you want my opinion I think you were doing a risky thing—risky to her, but it was your affair."

"And where is Marcia?" They faced one another, these two friends, like antagonists.

"At the hotel," Max said. "Where she asked me to take her. She had an idea she'd complicated your lives enough—"

"She's damn' well right, she has!" Gerry exploded.

I pushed myself out of my chair with unsteady hands. If they were going to quarrel over Marcia, I could not stay.

"I'm going to wash and change. I can't sit around like this."

As I crossed the room, Max saw my dishev-elled state for the first time. "Francie, what has happened?" His voice sharpened.

"You tell him." I looked at Gerry and pulled the door to behind me.

I felt unutterably weary as I climbed the stairs to my room. I washed my face, changed my dress and torn nylons, repaired two broken fingernails and used my brightest lipstick. Then, when I was tidy and clean again, I sat down on the bed. I could still feel the touch of fingers on my bruised wrist, still re-experi-ence the terror of that voice that held all the menace in the world behind its cat-like soft-ness. What would have happened to me if the old pedlar had not come back? What . . . ? And then I pulled myself up. Nerves were only torn unnecessarily by imagining things which had never happened.

I dragged myself off the bed and went to the mirror. Nothing had changed outwardly save for my livid wrist. The bruises on my shoul-der were hidden by the short sleeve of my green-patterned dress. I turned and went downstairs again. There was a deep silence about the house. I found Gerry still in the living-room.

Max was not there.

"Where is he?" I asked.

"Gone to fetch Marcia. She owes us just a little more than a 'thank you' letter!"

"Oh, Gerry, let it be!" I cried. "Let her go—"

"That's just what I don't intend to do! I want her here to explain why she sent you down to the waterfront. For God's sake! She could have cost you your life!"

"But she didn't," I said, "and she never intended me to be harmed."

Gerry gave me an uncomprehending stare.

"Can you read her mind?"

I shook my head.

"I've a shrewd idea, though, that she sent me away because she wanted to be alone with Max. She was tired of me always tagging along. I believe she intended to call him once I'd gone. And she didn't think for one moment that I would be harmed. I was to contact you down at the waterfront. I would be quite safe."

"Marcia—and Max?" he stared at me. "Don't be a little idiot! Why, they scarcely know one another!"

It was no use trying to explain. Gerry had a temporarily jaundiced view of women, particularly beautiful ones. He would not believe that something had sprung up, quick as a flame, between them. But I understood. It was the way things happened...between Lucien and me, for instance. I remembered then that I had not told Gerry yet what was in my stepmother's letter that morning.

But this was not the moment.

"I wish you hadn't sent for Marcia!" I said feelingly. "I wish you'd let things be!"

"She could have cost you your life!" he said again. His fair hair was rumpled. Gerry always looked very young when he was angry.

"But she didn't *mean* it!"

We'd said all this; floundering, we were gong round in circles. . . .

Then, short and sharp and imperative, the telephone rang.

"If that's the police, would you be prepared to go with them to find the hut?"

"I'd rather go to bed and sleep for forty-eight hours," I said wearily, "but if they want me to help, I shall have to go, shan't I?"

Gerry had lifted the receiver. I heard the one-sided conversation.

"Then we'll let her go. . . . It's nothing to do . . ." he paused and listened. "Always suppose we find them there! . . . Oh, all right, I'll come along. No"—he shot a glance back into the room at me—"I think Fran's had enough for one night—" He waited, listened, then said: "Very well, if we must, we'll be there!"

"And what," I asked as Gerry came back

into the room, "was that about?"

"When Max got to the Gloucester there was a note for him. Marcia has gone to Kam Ho Street. We don't know why, but I said I'd take you along—"

"I've no intention of being left here on my own," I said firmly, "not to-night!"

"—because you are the only one of us who can identify both the blackmailer and Farson," Gerry went on.

"And the police? Are you sending for them? For Inspector Davis?"

"I didn't wait to ask Max what he'd done about that!" Gerry said.

If Max had even thought of it! I ran by Gerry's side to the car.

If Max had thought of anything but going after Marcia. . . .

XVII

As we came along the alley I saw the door to Mr. Lam Tat Chee's house was open and a faint light streamed out.

A small shadow hovered near the wall. As we drew level, we saw that it was Tiffany.

"Oh, it's you Francie—and Gerry!" she cried in relief. "I heard someone call out. It came from—from there—" she nodded towards the open door of No. 43. "It—it was a girl's voice—and she sounded very frightened."

Gerry went into the house, calling. "Is anyone here?"

There was a pause. We closed in behind him, listening.

"*Hallo—*" A faint voice answered him from somewhere at the top of the stairs.

"Marcia! Are you alone?"

"Yes. I thought—oh, Gerry, I'm glad you're here!"

"Come along down!"

"I want you to come up," she cried. "Please—come—"

Gerry said:

"There's a light in the shop, too. I'm going to investigate." He turned to us. "You go on up, Fran, and get Marcia down quickly. Don't wait for arguments or protests. Drag her down if she won't come otherwise!"

"It's her fiancé's shop," I said as we ran, one behind the other, up the dim narrow stairs and into Eric's living-room. Marcia was pressed against the wall and she had lied to us. She was not alone.

There was a man in a corner by the window. I thought by the way he crouched there, his eyes half-closed, that he was injured. He wore Oriental clothes and his head was shaven.

"It *is* Eric!" I whispered.

Marcia did not answer me. I saw her gaze go past me and I swung round. Tiffany stood behind me leaning against the closed door and she was no longer a friend. In her hand was a small revolver. She held it very steadily and her charming face wore a faint smile.

I wasted no time on exclamations of surprise.

"Gerry is downstairs," I said, "and a toy gun won't frighten him!"

"Always supposing he has time to be frightened!"

I heard in the moment's stunned silence, a furious hammering and shouting downstairs. For a frozen moment I stared at the lovely, delicate-boned girl in the black *cheongsam*. We had, as Tiffany Lam had said, walked neatly into a trap. Gerry had expected to see Max in the lighted shop. In a cold fear, I wondered who had closed the door on him. I could hear the blasts of expletives mingled with the noisy radio music from next door and the clang and whirr of machinery somewhere down the street. There were two of them, then. One had lured Gerry to the shop and locked him in; the other held us at the point of a gun.

I swung round and looked at Marcia. Her face was ashen, her eyes focused with horror upon Tiffany. I tried to force her to look at me so that I could give her a message. I wanted her to attract Tiffany Lam's attention so that I could spring at her and make her drop the gun. But Marcia seemed paralysed. And the man on the floor was obviously of no use to us. He had not been shot at so I guessed he had been terrorised by threats. He had a coward's wide, evasive eyes.

There was a sound on the stairs.

"*Gerry,*" I shouted.

Tiffany moved away from the door, but the little gun did not waver an inch from its focus on the region of my heart.

"Gerry—" my voice trailed off.

I might have known! The man who came swiftly through the door wore a well-cut London suit. But his face was Oriental. I knew that cold, unamused smile. I wondered whether he would offer me a cigarette from a carved jade case.... I had escaped this man once to-night. I wasn't going to escape again....

I wanted to speak, to mock or defy: but my throat had dried up. The fear I had felt in the hut was nothing to my terror now.

There was a horrible hush about the house. Gerry's voice no longer mingled with Radio Hong Kong. I guessed the man had silenced him before he turned his attention to Marcia and me.

I felt a whirling faintness. For a second or two I knew he was speaking to me but I could not grasp what he said. Then I took a grip on myself.

"...because one of you," the man was saying, "has the 'green fire'!"

I looked down at his hands. He had no weapon, but then with his judo tricks, he had no need of one—not when he was dealing with ordinary people like myself and Marcia and Gerry....

I crossed my arms tightly in front of me to try to stop the panic-beating of my heart. I said to Tiffany Lam:

"So you got to know me deliberately!"

"With a fortune in emeralds," she said, "would you expect me not to keep a close watch on you?"

"You and—" I looked at the man.

"Peter is my cousin," she said. "Peter Lam."

"What have you done with my brother?"

"He is safe," said Peter Lam, "and shut up. If he gives no trouble, perhaps I shall not have to harm him. But only...perhaps! Because, you see, I think you will both give trouble. I must apologise for not believing you, Miss Mannering. I know now that it was your friend and not you who came with the emeralds." He looked past us at the man on the floor. "You, Miss Mannering, were his false trail. But you understand, don't you, that I can't let you go—not now that you can identify us to the police."

I put my hand to my forehead and found it wet.

Max will be here any minute, I thought. He'll get the police...Just hang on, keep them talking. They think they've got all night....

I turned and looked back at the man on the floor. His head had slid gently to the ground as though he were unconscious.

I said, desperately playing for time:

"You could, of course, tell me what all this is about. I think I have a right to know."

"You have no right to know anything, Miss Mannering," said the man. "You should have kept out of this affair. This is nothing to do with anyone except we four—" He identified them with a slight nod of his head, Marcia, Eric and then Tiffany. I had never seen such a steady and beautiful hand as hers....

"You're wrong about it all!" Marcia spoke for the first time. "I knew nothing! I just brought out books as I was asked to do. All I was told was that they were rare first editions. Eric will tell you...."

"Farson can tell us nothing we want to hear," said the man.

While they talked I wished desperately that we could have air in the room. It was stifling—stuffy and rank-smelling.

I wondered if the old piles of books gave it that smell. Or the rotted orange on the table....

I drew a long breath to try and identify it. And then I knew!

It was heavy and oily. Someone had spilled

petrol. I looked about me in alarm. Had Eric stored tins somewhere and had Gerry, somewhere below, kicked one over in his attempt to get out?

"My cousin," the man was saying, "is going to search you both." He indicated a screen. "Because one of you must be carrying the emeralds. If you aren't, then we search your brother's house, Miss Mannering. To-night."

The police, I thought, were looking for him. They would come, they *must* come, before it was too late! That smell ... That seeping, sickly petrol smell. ...

Play for time ... say anything to make them talk! Max will come soon ... and the police ...

"It was you, who followed us to Shek Ku Bay," I said.

"Of course," said Peter Lam. "I did not know then that you had been telling the truth all along, Miss Mannering."

I wished again that he would stop the constant use of my name! It was an uncanny trick that identified me with him.

"Who was the man—you killed? The man I saw—lying in the passage—?"

"He was Farson's assistant. But I did not kill him. Farson did that!" He nodded towards the man on the floor. "He was killed because he found out what some of the books carried, and he was blackmailing."

I heard Marcia give a little cry.

Tiffany had been standing like a small, perfect statue. Her black *cheongsam* glimmered with silver thread in the poor light of the room; her small head with its raven's-wing hair was turned towards her cousin.

"We're wasting time, Peter!"

He smiled at her. "I talk too much! Very well, you search them—"

I backed sharply. Behind me, Marcia said:

"You can search us, but it'll do you no good. We haven't got your emeralds."

"But we must make certain!"

"I think you're too late—"

She had quicker ears than I. Only after she had spoken did I hear a sound below. Men's footsteps. I heard Gerry shout and a tremendous relief passed over me. He was alive! A door crashed as though it had been burst open.

The footsteps sounded on the stairs.

Peter Lam wheeled round. Only Tiffany remained calm. She handed him her gun and moved to a small side table. I saw her fingers close over something small as the door burst open.

Max was there. And Gerry. I didn't dare move, but I said quickly:

"They've got a gun. Be careful!"

Something in Tiffany's furtive movement drew my gaze back to her. The thing she held was a small box.

I saw the match in her fingers.

As I cried out, the smell of petrol seemed stronger than ever. It wasn't down below, it was here in this room. When they had searched us, they had meant to keep us prisoners in a burning room because, free, we could identify them.... But their plans had gone wrong.

"Look out!" I screamed.

Gerry shot forward. The match struck, glowed, dropped.

In that wild moment, I saw Eric move. He shot out of his pretended unconsciousness, snatched a book from the table and hurled it at the light. The room went dark except for the flames which sprang from a corner.

In the flickering red glow, I felt hands drag me to the door. I heard Tiffany's high, excited laugh. Dazed and choking, I was half-pushed, half-carried down the stairs.

Then I heard Marcia cry sharply:

"My hand! Oh, my hand!"

It was impossible in that struggling huddle of bodies, lit dimly by the flames behind us, fogged by smoke, to find her. I guessed that it was Peter Lam who had turned off the landing light to give Tiffany and himself a chance to escape in the chaos and darkness.

It should not have been so difficult, even in darkness, to get down those stairs and out of the burning house! And then I realised, that we were being deliberately impeded.

Someone gripped me and I fell against the banisters.

"The emeralds...Come on...Give them up!" The voice hissed in my ear.

"If you think—I have them then you're mad!" I gasped.

Peter Lam's face was thrust against mine. I struggled against the steel grip holding me back, but this small dark man had the strength of a lion.

"Gerry! Max!" I cried out.

Suddenly the hands let me go. There was a shout of pain and gentler hands caught me and carried me down the last few stairs.

When we reached the passage and the fresh air came to meet me, I saw who had hit out at the hands holding me back, desperate even in that panic moment, for the emeralds. It was Gerry.

"Where's Max?" I cried on a high, wild note. I fought my brother's detaining arm. "I've got to find him!"

"Don't be a little fool!"

"Max!" I cried again, impotently, as Gerry thrust me out of the door.

Still half-blinded by smoke, my eyes stinging, I stumbled into a group of uniformed men.

"Careful, missie—" A Chinese policeman steadied me.

Torches lit us. Gerry was by my side and Marcia was there and the Lams, all of us, mixed up somehow with the police. All except Max. . . .

I tried to elbow my way through the police. In my terror, I imagined Max knocked out by Peter Lam, lying unconscious in the flames.

As I pushed through the crowd that had collected from the neighbouring houses, I saw Peter Lam held by a policeman. His eyes watched me. He had accused me once more of having the emeralds. I wondered whether, in that shabby back room, Tiffany had already searched Marcia. And then I lost all interest in them. I had managed to reach the door of the burning house. I tried to elbow a policeman's arm out of the way. I had to find Max. I dodged out. He had a rug over his head and he reeled a little in the doorway and flung the rug away.

"I stopped—to dial—'Fire.'"

"Oh, Max!" I sobbed. But no one heard me.

The narrow alley was a mêlée of moving bodies in the darkness, of shouts and flailing arms. Acrid smoke poured down on us and the crackle of flames eating up Eric's cheapjack furniture grew louder.

And then somehow, strangely, out of the chaos, I saw some sort of order. The police had taken control and we were being escorted down the alley. At the same time, I heard the fire engines stop in the street at the other side of the building.

Inquisitive, gesticulating Chinese surrounded us and out of the noise, I heard Gerry's voice say to me:

"We have to go down to police headquarters, Fran."

"Haven't we had enough for one night?"

"It won't take long, missie," said the policeman on my left.

Either Inspector Davis had caught up with the Lams, tracing them to Kam Ho Street, or Max had brought the police with him. I did not, at that time, know. But at the end of the alley two police cars waited. The Lams and Eric were driven swiftly away and as we crossed to Gerry's car, the crowd closed in on us.

Gerry spoke to them sharply in Cantonese

and pushed me into the car. At the same time, Max opened the rear door for Marcia.

I sat staring ahead of me at the vivid neon signs — candy-pink and daffodil-yellow... Hong Kong by night....

By my side, Gerry turned on the ignition and the car purred softly to life. The crowd surged forward—those who had not gone to watch the firemen—and grinned and peered at us. The Rover moved forward, honking, and the crowd fell back.

It was almost over. Just a few police inquiries and then I would no longer go in fear....

The car turned into Pedder Street. I heard Max say something to Marcia. I could not hear what it was, but Marcia's reply was as clear-cut as a knife-thrust into me.

"Oh, Max—darling!..."

I heard no more. I could take no more! I burst into tears....

XVIII

The police held Eric and Tiffany and Peter Lam. The rest of us were allowed to go home. I had taken a look at Marcia's hand which had had Max's big handkerchief tied round it. The wound had bled profusely and looked clean but I had given it a temporary dressing from the first-aid box Gerry carried in his car.

As we climbed back into the Rover, he said:

"We'd better drop Marcia at the hospital and let them take a look at her hand. Max, perhaps you could stay with her and then take her back to her hotel."

"The hospitals are probably over-crowded here," I said quickly. "Marcia can come back with us and I'll dress it properly for her."

"There's no need for anyone to bother," her voice came from the back of the car. "If you'll take me to the hotel—"

"You're coming home with us!" I spoke so firmly that I hoped no one would overrule me.

I knew Gerry wanted to be rid of her; but I *had* to talk to her. I wanted to know why she had gone to Kam Ho Street to-night, and I wanted to be reassured that she had not intended to harm me when she sent me to the waterfront. For some odd, unexplained reason I did not want to go through the rest of my life believing that the girl Max loved had deliberately tried to endanger my life. . . .

We were very quiet on our way back to Tai-yuan Street. I had passed through the stage of exhaustion following upon fear and I was not even tired any longer. From some unknown source I had found a new energy. My brain was alive with questions.

What would they do to the Lams? Deport them? Imprison them? I thought of Tiffany, her silk clothes, her French scent, her perfectly-kept nails which had probably never been broken by hard work in her life. I wondered how her grandfather would take the news. Or had Tiffany and Peter's half-Western blood alienated him from their birth? Had he given her a home out of duty rather than love and now would he return completely to his house of treasures, his jade and ivory . . . ?

Questions . . . Questions . . . And one remaining, fascinatedly unanswered. Where were the emeralds?

At the house, Yee Sze was waiting for us. I wondered how much he knew of the tension there. Perhaps some underground grape-vine system among the Chinese had told him more than we guessed he knew.

But when he came into the room in answer to Gerry's call, he gave no hint that anything was unusual.

Marcia and I asked for tea. Max and Gerry had whisky.

While I dressed Marcia's hand, I asked her how she had hurt it. She did not know, she said. In the dimness as we had rushed down the stairs, she had caught it on something jagged—a nail or a piece of wood.

When we returned to the living-room, Max had downed his drink and announced that he was going back to the shop to see if they had managed to check the spread of the fire.

"I won't be long," he said. "Then I'll come back for Marcia."

"Yes, you'd better!" Gerry said shortly.

A small silence hung between us until Max's footsteps had died away. Then Gerry turned and gave Marcia a cold stare.

"Well? Why did you do it? Why did you send Fran to the waterfront?"

Colour flooded her face which had been grey with fatigue.

"It—it seemed the only thing to do. Max wasn't here and you wanted the books. I thought I was doing right."

Gerry made a swift, repudiating gesture with his hand.

"Don't give me that!"

"But it's true—" she began. And then she stopped and bit her lip.

"You can't lie yourself out of *that* one!" Gerry's voice was ice-cold.

I watched her closely and knew that I had been right in my guess. She was too scared to go out alone and meet Max and if he came here, I would be around, so she sent me away. Her offer to go down to the waterfront in my place had been meaningless. She knew I would not let her go.

Gerry walked across the room, adjusted the screen at the veranda door and said, with his back to us:

"Let's have it, Marcia! Why did you send Fran down to the waterfront?"

"I—I've told you—" but her voice weakened and wavered.

If I didn't interfere at once, she would be under Gerry's angry, merciless fire and she might tell the truth. I could not bear that, not to-night! For my own sake, Max's name must not be brought into the conversation—

not here, not now. . . . Later, when I was less vulnerable. . . .

"Forget it!" I said sharply. "It's over and done with. There's something *I* want to know. That morning I came into Eric's shop and found you there with Max, you looked excited, as though you'd discovered something. Had you?"

She frowned, apparently trying to recall it. Then she shook her head.

"There was nothing to discover!" She smiled a little. "And now it's all over and the police have finished with us—"

"On the contrary," Gerry joined in, "they'll want you for a whole lot more questioning!"

Marcia sat very still, her eyes cast down. The curved, dark gold lashes on her cheek had an almost childish sweetness.

"They can question me at the hotel." She lifted her cup and finished her tea. Then she rose. Her eyes were very bright, very alert. "I've no intention of running away, if that's what you think. I've no reason to. But I want to get to bed. I want to sleep—"

I sat curled up in a big chair and thought that she was suddenly in a very great hurry. She was not even intending to wait for Max to take her home. Why? What had I said to alarm her?

I started up and stood between Marcia and the door.

"You *did* find something at the shop, didn't you? Why are you afraid to tell us?"

"Oh, not more questioning!" she cried. "Really, Francie, you've been wonderful and I'll be indebted to you all my life for the way you've tried to help. But that doesn't make you witness for my prosecution!"

"Let her go," Gerry said, suddenly.

"When she has answered my question."

I was aware that Gerry was looking at me in a puzzled way, but I did not take my eyes off Marcia. I quite expected her to push me aside and walk out of the room. But something in my expression must have held her prisoner.

For nearly half a minute no one spoke. I did not dare let the strength of my gaze waver. She thought I knew something and she was frightened. I saw her shoulders sag a little and the fire go out of her eyes as though my strength had defeated her.

"What—can I—tell you?"

"Nothing! It's Gerry who must know." I was bluffing and my heart pounded. "And if you don't tell him, *I* will!"

"—tell him—?"

I out-stared her and I won.

"I found a book with a slit spine"—she whispered on a breath—"but how did you know? When—?"

"Go on," I cut in, pretending no surprise.

"It was among the pile on the floor." She swallowed with difficulty.

I looked across at Gerry. His eyes were like blue glass watching her.

"So," I said, "you knew where to look in the books you had brought with you!" I waited and she nodded. "And no one entered your room and touched those books." I went on. "You did it—and found the emeralds."

She was wearing her grey dress and her face was ashen so that her only colour was the coppery hair and the reddened mouth.

It had been a shot in the dark and it had worked. I wondered in the moment of silence, why. Perhaps the events of the night had weakened her resistance against us, or maybe the intervention of the police terrified her.

"I found the emeralds," she agreed and her voice was so quiet that I had to strain to hear. "I had just taken them out of those polythene bags when you came along the veranda calling me, Francie."

"Dear God, so all this time—!"

"Yes, Gerry, all this time I had them!"

"Where?" I whispered.

She looked at each of us in turn.

"I'd been used, cheated and humiliated. Eric had pretended to be in love with me so that he could arrange for me to bring out his—his damned emeralds! His loot!" She snapped the word. "I'd been turned into a criminal, so, like any criminal, I had a right to payment for my services." She looked at me. "When did you know I had them?"

Before I could reply, Gerry took a few steps towards her, his face dark with fury.

"You were so keen on payment, that you didn't bother to think what you were doing to my sister, did you?"

"I said—I was so very—sorry—"

"Like hell you were! With thousands of pounds' worth of emeralds hidden away! Now—*give!*" He thrust his hand, palm upward, at her.

She backed away.

"It doesn't matter whether you do or not," he went on as she stared at him, beautiful and stubborn. "The police will get them from you in a far less comfortable way! In a cell, sweetie!"

I saw a shudder run through her. Her great eyes rested, mesmerised, upon Gerry.

"Why did you go to Kam Ho Street to-night?" I asked.

"Eric rang me at the hotel. He had been watching the house and saw me leave. He—he thought I still had the emeralds and—"

"And you had! You have!"

She ignored Gerry's clipped comment.

"I wanted to meet Eric just once. I wanted to go to him empty-handed; to watch his face when I said: 'I've had an interesting plane flight, I've seen Hong Kong, all at your expense. And now you can sing for your emeralds!'"

"He could have attacked you."

She shook her head.

"I'd left that note at the hotel for Max. He'd come and find me, I knew. And Eric is a coward. You saw the way he behaved in front of the Lams, pretending he was unconscious until he saw his chance to douse the light and make his escape."

"Suppose we stop talking," Gerry said in a tight, hard voice. "What have you done with the emeralds?"

"They could," said she flippantly, "be at the bottom of the sea!" It was a last fling of bravado.

"Fran," Gerry said. "Ring the police. Get Inspector Davis."

I moved. But Marcia was quicker. She lifted a foot and shook off one of her shoes. Then she sent the other skidding over the polished floor.

I darted for them. Something had slipped down from the toe of one. It was a tiny piece of plastic material. I opened it and spread it on the table.

Five green stones, glittering, flawless, clear as water, lay there. The "green fire". . . .

Gerry had picked up the other shoe. In the toe was another minute plastic bag and in that were four more emeralds, each wrapped separately.

"You utter little fool!" Gerry said hoarsely.

Marcia moved swiftly, picked up her shoes and, carrying them in her hand, walked out of the room.

There was nothing we could do to hold her. But I ran out on to the veranda and called her. She was already half-way down the garden and she did not look round.

"Wait!" I called. "Let someone take you home. It's nearly midnight. Marcia, don't go back alone!"

The shadowy figure did not falter. I heard the gate open and close.

"She'll come to no harm," Gerry said from behind me.

I leaned against the veranda rail. It was a warm night but I was shivering from spent emotion.

Ever since Marcia had split the spines of those tooled-leather editions of *Jane Eyre* and *Faust,* the emeralds had gone with her—a fortune tucked in the toes of her slender, high-heeled shoes. . . .

Gerry came out on to the veranda, asking:

"How in the world did you guess she had them?"

"I didn't. I was bluffing. Like you, I thought Eric had them." I turned and faced him. "I don't know why she fell for such a trick."

"She was over-tired and I think the fact that the police now had the case in hand scared her. She was a novice at theft!"

I yawned and shivered.

"Go to bed, Fran. There's nothing more to be said or done to-night."

No, there was nothing more. Except to discover Max's reaction to what had happened. But even that, I told myself, I knew! He would go to her to-night and she would tell him everything. And this time, she would not lose!

I was undressed when I heard Max's voice talking to Gerry in the room below. I fought against going downstairs, but in the end I slid into a dressing-gown, tied the silk sash and combed my hair. Exhausted as I was, I still minded what I looked like in front of Max.

They had moved on to the veranda. I went across the living-room and stood at the glass door.

"Hallo, Max. I had to know whether they managed to stop the fire spreading," I said lamely.

"It was confined to Farson's place. Those buildings in Kam Ho Street aren't like the Chinese slums where a fire would raze a street before it could be put out."

"Gerry had told you?"

"About Marcia? Yes. At least she gave them up!"

"She didn't have much alternative after I'd said the police would be questioning her again." Gerry lit a cigarette.

"I think it's pretty obvious that had she intended to keep the emeralds," Max said, "she would have got away. She could have flown back to England while the Lams were still watching Francie. But she didn't. She stayed—"

(Of course she did! She wanted you, too, Max! She was greedy! She gambled on too much. . . .)

I knew I could not stay down here, could not sit and listen to Max's quiet defence. I rose from my chair, saying to him:

"See you to-morrow."

He looked at me in surprise.

"Of course, you don't know, do you? I only

told Gerry over the telephone this morning and I suppose there's been no chance to tell you. I'm leaving tomorrow for Bangkok. That's my sort of job these days, Francie! Sudden hails and sudden farewells!"

I stood quite still by the table. The emeralds were gone—I suppose Gerry had put them in a place of safety until the inspector, or someone, would collect them. I actually managed a smile as I looked at Max and he would never, never know the superhuman effort of it!

"Aren't you lucky, travelling for free!"

His eyes rested on me kindly. He looked tired and I thought how wonderful it would be to rest with him in the warm Hong Kong night, quietly, not talking, knowing that we loved one another and that we had all our lives together. . . .

"I looked in at the office," he was saying, "and rang the police from there. There's no reason why they should want me any more, but if they do they know where to find me in Bangkok."

"Does Marcia know that you're going away?" I didn't look at him as I asked.

"I told her this afternoon. I'll be keeping in touch with her. And I'm taking the emeralds to the police headquarters on my way back tonight."

"*You've* got them!" I looked at Gerry in surprise.

"I'll be going that way so I can drop them in and explain," Max said.

"What will they do to her?"

"She should have handed them in at once, of course. But she didn't steal them!"

Didn't she? Didn't she gamble on no one ever knowing she had them? Would she ever have told us where they were had she not been over-tired, frightened by police questions and then incriminated by my bluffing? Then again, *could* I be certain she meant to keep them? It could be that even if there had not been that scene here earlier to-night, she would have handed the emeralds to the police. . . .

Gerry broke the silence.

"Are you all right Fran? You look very white!"

"I haven't exactly had a pleasant evening, have I? I'm all right, only tired." I moved to the door to stop any formality of shaking hands. Smiling across at Max, I said: "Then we say good-bye, don't we?"

I was not prepared for his swift movement to my side.

"Good-bye, Francie. And I hope you'll be very happy."

Our hands touched. Quickly I drew away. I whispered: "Thank you," as I went through the door.

I was glad he did not know that there was little chance of Lucien and I ever marrying now. Pride was a foolish thing but at the moment it was all I had. . . .

I went back to my room realising that some time soon I must tell Gerry, too, about my stepmother's letter. But not yet. I could not face his sympathy, until both Marcia and Max had gone and the pain and the brief sweetness as well as the terror of these last few days was dimming in my mind. . . .

XIX

I would have given much to have stayed in bed the following morning. When I woke at seven, sleep had not refreshed me. But I could not rest. I had to see Gerry and find out from him if Inspector Davis had done with me or whether there would be more questions.

Gerry looked surprised to see me so early. Yee Sze was just bringing coffee to the table when I arrived in the courtyard.

The sun was already warm on the chairs, and the tiles and the needles of the Bonzai were trapped in golden light so that from a distance the tiny tree looked as though it had burst into bloom.

Gerry assured me that from now on he could take care of all the questions.

"You can settle down to enjoy yourself," he said. "We'll start getting around, meeting people, going bathing. We might even get some sailing."

"What will happen to Marcia?" I asked.

"I don't know and I don't care! She'll probably be put on the first plane back to England. And there she can stay so far as I'm concerned!"

I sat back in my chair and thought of the emeralds as I had seen them lying on the table in the living-room—nine flawless pieces of stone—green as young spring grass, glittering like the eyes of animals ... "Green fire"....

"By the way, I had a letter from home yesterday," Gerry said.

"Yes?" I waited.

Ever since he was a little boy, whenever Gerry was embarrassed, he would frown deeply. He was frowning now.

"There was something about Lucien in it, wasn't there?" I asked, helping him out.

He nodded. I lifted my coffee-cup and was surprised to find how steady my hand was.

"Do I have to drag it out of you?" I began impatiently. Then, meeting my brother's distressed eyes, I said: "Perhaps I can tell you what's in that letter. I had one, too! Lucien has discharged himself from the hospital! I was going to tell you when I had the chance, only so much else has been happening!"

Gerry sat twisting his fingers round the handle of his cup. I knew he was still afraid

I would make some kind of tearful scene.

"Those rolls look delicious," I said. "Eat them!"

He did not seem to hear me. His eyes flashed to my face and away.

"I suppose things are better coming straight—"

"Much better," I said quietly.

He looked at me, his eyes distressed.

"Lucien has issued a statement to the Press that the engagement is 'off.' Mother's letter asked me to break it to you. If you want my opinion, Lucien is a louse and you're well rid of him—"

He was talking to cover his embarrassment. But I stopped listening. I had been prepared for anything Lucien might do, and yet I felt shock—not so much at the news but at the fact that Lucien could not have brought himself to tell me first. I was no longer engaged to Lucien Blake—but I had to learn of it through a report in a newspaper....

I was very near to hating men. Lucien—and Max...

"You're all right, Fran, aren't you?"

I came out of the terrible empty place to find Gerry's eyes watching me anxiously. I smiled across the little table.

"I'm quite all right. And none of it is really

unexpected. In spite of all the psychiatrist said, I think I always had the feeling that something like this would happen. Don't worry! I'm not going to moon through my stay with you! I'm going to enjoy myself."

I watched the relief spread like a light over his easy-going face.

"It's a pity Max has had to go away," he said. "It really would have been like old times with the three of us—"

"If Max had stayed, you'd have had to put up with Marcia, too," I said. "And you wouldn't have liked that!"

He pushed his plate away and passed his cup across to me for more coffee.

"I'm not quite with you."

I took a grip on myself.

"Wasn't it obvious to you that they were in love?" My voice sounded harsh.

Gerry stared at me as though he thought I had gone a little mad.

"Here, take your cup!" I said impatiently.

He set it down very carefully, then he let out a long breath.

"Dear heaven! The way you women manufacture affairs!"

"I'm not making anything up. And stop being patronising!" Then, forcing myself to speak calmly, I went on: "I've seen them together, Gerry, when they haven't known I was around. I—I wasn't spying on them. I just—happened—to see—"

"All right! So maybe you've seen them kissing. Well? Do you translate a kiss into an avowal of love?"

I wished desperately that I had not started this conversation. But now I was too deeply into it to withdraw.

"With some men," I said, "I wouldn't think anything of it. But with Max it's different. Max wouldn't—"

"Wouldn't what?"

"Play at love," I said helplessly.

"For Pete's sake," Gerry exploded, "he's a man not a saint! He's high, wide and free! If he likes to kiss a girl, why the devil shouldn't he? I'll make a bet that Marcia did all the running. She's that sort!" His eyes narrowed. "Anyway, why are you minding so much?"

"I'm not!" I said defiantly. "I'm just telling you what's happened."

"If Max has really fallen for that beautiful—er—witch, then he has my sympathy! I'll make a bet with you that she only got herself engaged to Farson because he painted a glowing picture of life out here and it sounded preferable to her job as a secretary in an insurance office. Then, disillusioned, she set about straight away to net some other poor fish. Her heart wasn't broken over Farson; I've lived with her sort! Irene—" he reached over and flipped up the lid of the cigarette box. "Oh, what the hell...?"

I watched him light his cigarette.

He was right, of course. Hadn't I seen for myself the way Marcia had worked on Max? Hadn't I been envious of her art? A subtle touch of the hand; a look; copper-gold hair just brushing his cheek; a soft breath of helplessness. "Oh, Max!" A young girl, beautiful and betrayed, turning to him. . . . What chance had he?

It was mid-morning when I knew I had to see Marcia again. I wanted the process of clarification to be completed. Deep inside me, I knew the answer to the question I would put. I would ask: "Are you in love with Max?" She would either think my question impertinent, which I doubted, or give me a soft, triumphant "Yes."

It would be over then! The last question asked and answered; the misty, doubtful places of the mind swept clean and an immense nothingness in its place. I would know the worst and the spiritual surgery would be terrible, but it would be clean-cut.

I was in the living-room when I saw Harriet

Craig come up the path. It surprised me to see her because it was the afternoon sunlight, in all its vital brilliance, that she liked to paint. But instead of making for the shed where she kept her easel, she came straight up the veranda steps. I saw she had a painting under her arm.

"I thought you would like to see the finished painting of the house," she said, and held it out to me.

Like the street scene Gerry had shown me on my first day, it was strong and vibrant. She had caught so beautifully the winged sweep of the roofs, the bluish shade of the veranda, the young green of the casuarina and the mushroom tint of the dry earth in the iris beds at the foot of the steps. The windows, too, of tall clear glass, reflected colour. I peered more closely and saw, at the guest-room window, the vague shape of someone standing there. Copper and deep blue—copper-gold hair and a blue dress! . . . I gave a little gasp.

"You've painted Marcia there!"

Her white-hooded eyes met mine. I supposed the twist of her lips was meant to be a smile.

"I thought they would like that—your brother and Miss Gallard, I mean. In future years when they look at the picture—"

"In future years," I cut in sharply, "they won't even know one another, Miss Craig!"

She shook her head at me as though I were some blind, recalcitrant child.

"It really is rather silly to pretend, isn't it?"

"Pretend—what?"

She took the painting from me and propped it up on the Chinese rosewood table, against the wall.

"It was clever of your brother, wasn't it, to bring you out as a kind of chaperone? Everyone knows who Marcia Gallard is—"

"Everyone—except me! Please—tell me—" My voice sounded like ice.

But Harriet Craig was not intimidated.

"Irene always knew there was someone else."

Her words so struck at me that for a moment I stared at her in dumb surprise.

Her eyes were wide open now and she was trembling with excitement. She was enjoying her outrageous accusation.

"Your brother wanted her to leave him so that he could divorce her for desertion," she said in an unnaturally loud voice. "He wanted to marry again, but he was not prepared to take the blame, was he? I suppose, with you staying here, he thought it safe to bring the girl to live with him!"

So now I knew! This thin, bitter woman

had been spying on Gerry, egged on by Irene! Anger boiled up in me.

"So that's why you went to Marcia's room one morning! I nearly caught you, didn't I? You hoped you'd find some proof of their supposed affair to take back to Irene—a photograph, perhaps, or some letters. But you found exactly nothing—or did I disturb you before you'd looked thoroughly? Too bad, Miss Craig!"

"I think," she said coldly, "you could see Irene's side of it before you start being righteously angry!"

"I know Irene's side, thanks! She made my brother's life a misery with her jealousies and her nagging! And you can go back and tell her that there is nothing between Gerry and Marcia—in fact, he doesn't even like her very much and she's no longer staying here. *I* brought her to the house because she was quite alone in Hong Kong."

"You say—she's gone? *Left?*"

"Left!" I said shortly.

I waited, expecting her to go. Instead, she went over and picked up the painting and stared at it for a long time in silence.

"I think," she said in a subdued voice, "I should do something about that window before Mr. Mannering sees the painting."

"I certainly should!"

351

She turned and looked at me and said in a rough, embarrassed voice: "I was sorry for Irene. That's why I said I'd help her any way I could—"

"Help her to get evidence for a divorce from my brother! Only it didn't work, did it?" I said calmly. "I think it would have been more honest if you had watched my brother without pretending to be interested in painting his house and garden!"

"But I *am* interested! Painting is my life."

"Then I should keep it that way, Miss Craig," I said as matter-of-factly as I could. "It's a lovely hobby. Don't let playing private investigator interfere with it!"

"I'm sorry. I really did think—I could help—"

"Let's forget it, shall we?" I said quietly. "And now, I have to go out. Good morning, Miss Craig."

She turned on her heel and walked out of the room, taking the painting with her. She was half-way down the veranda steps when I called to her.

"Bring it back without the face at the window."

She turned and for a moment our gaze held. Then she smiled faintly. "I'll do that. And I hope Mr. Mannering will like it."

"He'll like it very much," I said.

I stood watching her go, her body at that odd angle as though, like a blade of grass, she were bent in the middle.

I wouldn't tell Gerry what she had said. At least, not for a long time. My anger had subsided and I felt an odd kind of pity for her. She was plain and perhaps lonely and unloved. Irene had charmed her into doing what she had. Pretty and plaintive and putting on her "I have been betrayed" act, she had found someone to watch Gerry. Only Harriet Craig had made a great mistake.

And now that was over and I was back with the more personal thing I had to do. When I thought that Harriet was well ahead of me down the street, I let myself out of the gate.

Tai-yuan Street had never seemed more busy, more cluttered with people. I walked the length of it and presently came to the big shopping area. The store windows glittered. Chinese silks and Paris scents; jade and ivory, soapstone and amber.... Above me the sky was a deep blue.

I felt curiously calm. It was almost as though I were anxious to know the worst—to receive it and crawl away somewhere by myself. Up to the Peak top, perhaps, among the oleanders and the frangipani, the orioles' and the bulbuls' song, to bleed a little in spirit before I faced Gerry again at lunchtime.

I walked over to the desk at the Gloucester and inquired for Miss Gallard. Now the moment of meeting her had arrived, my calm, miraculously, did not leave me.

The clerk left me to make inquiries. Then he came back.

"She is not staying here any longer," he said. "She left a message for a lady who might call. A Miss Mannering."

"I am Miss Mannering."

"I was to tell you that she is staying somewhere quietly for the next day or two and then she is leaving for Bangkok."

Without seeing her, without speaking to her, I had my answer!

I thanked the clerk and went out into the hot, humid street. My throat was parched and my feet ached. I would have given anything to have stayed in the Gloucester and had coffee. But I did not want people around me. Nor, now the moment had come, did I want to go to the Peak top. Rickshaws were dying out in Hong Kong, but I found one and told the coolie to take me to Tai-yuan Street. When we got there, I overtipped him and pushed open the gate. It fell to with a crash of wood and iron behind me. I could scarcely wait to get to my room, to lie on my bed on the counter-pane with the raised white dragons embroidered on it and face the fact that once more, I had to remake my life.

Someone moved from the shadow of the veranda. My heart lurched. I saw Max's hand lifted in a small salute.

I walked up the veranda steps heavily. I did not want Max to talk to me about Marcia. Looking up, I met his kind, grey gaze.

"Shouldn't you be on the plane for Bangkok?"

"I postponed leaving for a few days."

Pleasure and pain twisted inside me. I sat down in a chair and said, weakly:

"Why don't you pour yourself out a drink?"

"For the simple reason that I don't want one, thank you." His eyes were amused. "I came to talk to you."

"About Marcia!" My voice was flat, drained of feeling. I felt like a statue sitting there, my hands folded, my eyes relentlessly on Max, waiting for what I knew he had to tell me.

I watched him pick up Gerry's black fan from the table, spread it out and fold it back again.

"I know," I said at last, unable to bear the long silence. "I know all about you and

Marcia. She's going to Bangkok with you, isn't she?"

He looked up sharply.

"What gave you that idea?"

"Max," I said and gripped my hands in my lap, "you don't have to pretend. I—I know!"

"So you keep saying, Fran, but I'd like to be told what you know!"

I got up and went to the veranda edge and looked out over the brilliant garden. I couldn't say it, not in the actual words! Instead, with my back to him, I put it in an oblique way:

"If I loved someone, I wouldn't pretend!"

"Nor would I!" he paused. Then he said in a changed voice: "If you're inferring that I love Marcia, then you're quite wrong. I don't!"

The veranda rail held me upright. I could not turn round and look at him. I stared at the parched, brilliant garden until my eyes hurt.

"Marcia is in love with *you!*" I said, tormenting myself.

"Where in the world did you get that idea from?" he demanded.

"I'm not blind," my voice was rough-edged. I had to drag the truth from him for my own sake. "And now she's going to Bangkok with you."

There was a short silence. I had found something he could not deny, I thought desperately. I closed my eyes and heard the voices of children beyond the gate.

"Always supposing Marcia is able to leave Hong Kong before this case against the Lams and Farson is over," Max spoke carefully, quietly from somewhere near me, "she is perfectly free to go to Bangkok. In fact I believe I once told her what a lovely city I found it. All right, so she goes to Bangkok! But she isn't going with me.

"And if she was, would you mind?"

Colour flooded my face because the question took me so much by surprise.

"I – I felt that there was such an – an attraction between you," I said defensively.

I saw him smile, his eyes silver-grey, warm, kind.

"There was!" And then he laughed outright. "I'm human, Fran, and I'm as susceptible to a beautiful girl as most men. We needed each other, just for a little while. But it was all very innocent. All Marcia wanted was admiration to boost her morale after Farson's treatment of her – and who are we to blame her for that? All *I wanted* was to ease my own fury with myself."

" – Fury – ?"

"Because when I left England nearly three years ago, I was every kind of a fool! I had one dream, to wander round the world and be free. The dream stayed with me all this time. Then—you came to Hong Kong and I met you again and I knew—"

"—knew what?"

"That I'd been every kind of a fool!" he said, again almost impatiently. "I'd grown up in those years, I'd learned what real values were. But I was too late. You were engaged to Lucien Blake."

"But I'm not!" The three words came like a small, wild cry. I had no control over them.

"So Gerry told me last night. That's why I'm here to-day. Only once in my life have I ever said 'I love you' to a woman—"

I felt him take my hands, drawing me away from the veranda rail.

"And that," he continued softly, "is now, Fran!"

He can't have expected that I would go straight into his arms ... straight from a broken love affair with Lucien. ... But then, he didn't know! It was something I had to explain, later. But not now—not here in Gerry's Chinese garden with the azaleas full out and a pale, beautiful butterfly on the irises at my feet; with someone playing thin reed music and the sun like liquid gold around us. For one full, glorious moment

I was aware of everything at once.

I reached towards him without taking my eyes from his own silver-grey gaze.

"Max!" I said and lifted my face so that he could kiss me.